The King's Investigator

Part II

The King's Investigator Part II

(Dragging It Out A Bit)

being unnecessary

Chronicles of Brother Hermitage

by

Howard of Warwick

From the Scriptorium of
The Funny Book Company

The Funny Book Company

Published by The Funny Book Company
Dalton House, 60 Windsor Ave, London SW19 2RR
www.funnybookcompany.com

Cover design by Double Dagger.

ISBN 978-1-913383-15-2

Scriptorial appreciation is due to:
Mary
Susan Fanning
Karen Nevard-Downs
Lydia Reed
Claire Ward

Howard of Warwick's Middle Ages crisis: History-ish.
The Domesday Book (No, Not That One.)
The Domesday Book (Still Not That One.)
The Magna Carta (Or Is It?)

Explore the whole sorry business and join the mailing list
at
Howardofwarwick.com

Another funny book from The Funny Book Company
Greedy *by Ainsworth Pennington*

The King's Investigator Part II

Foreword: Previously in The King's Investigator

Once upon a time, King William of England, Duke of Normandy had his very own investigator.

Brother Hermitage - funny name for a monk - would hurry to wherever a murder had occurred, give it his earnest attention and somehow work out who did what.

Frequently, this hurrying was at the direct behest of the king in person; a behest that was traditionally accompanied by threats of death and burning to the ground if he didn't get on with it.

Hermitage, who would rather be in a small room investigating the lexicography of the post-Exodus prophets, did his best to avoid his duties but hiding and pretending not to be in were to no avail.

He even noticed that murders had started hurrying to wherever he happened to be at the time, a worrying development; but then Hermitage worried about most things most of the time, so developments were grist to his mill.

How he arrived in this situation has already taken 19 books to explain, so it's hardly going to be covered in a simple foreword. Suffice to say that he was desperate to escape his burden.

His close companions and friends, both of them, were also dragged into this mire. Wat, reformed weaver of imaginative tapestry for the very broad-minded, and Cwen, a talented weaver with her own shady past and a strong line in anger, brought vital talents to the field of investigation, talents that Hermitage sadly lacked: the ability to suspect that some people might be lying and a bit of common sense.

Hermitage's hopes were raised when, after yet another

murder, a monk appeared who actually wanted his job.

Without giving anything away, while at the same time encouraging purchase of The King's Investigator Part I, Hermitage's dearest wish was granted; he was no longer the King's Investigator.

Being king of one of the most important realms of the period, as well as duke of part of another one, William could not be without his own investigator, so he appointed a replacement.

Which is where it all started to go wrong; as usual.

Now read The King's Investigator Part II.

(Caution; contains spoilers. Quite a lot of them.)

Caput I: The King's Investigator

'Make way. Make way there. Make way for King William's own investigator.' The calm and confident tones of Nicodemus, newly appointed King's Investigator, slithered their way down the corridor and into the ears of any who might be listening.

'There's no one there.' Prior Athan's voice, as rough and forthright as his appearance, did its best to destroy the moment. He helpfully pointed in the direction of the completely empty space ahead of them. 'And we're in King William's Tower of London with all the other Normans. I don't think anyone's going to take any notice of what you say.'

Nicodemus granted him a condescending glance. 'People in my position don't worry about things like that. Someone could be about to step out of a door and now knows not to.' He gave a slow and sad shake of the head that Athan would never be able to grasp the niceties of elevated status.

The shake was accompanied by a slightly cautious frown, as Athan was known to respond to condescension by punching it in the head.

'King's Investigator, pah!' Athan spat. 'The last one who had the job was an idiot. Perhaps it goes with the role.'

'Brother Hermitage is irrelevant.'

'You're right there.'

'King William has now appointed me.'

'Only because Hermitage said so and you happened to be in the room at the time. The king hasn't actually told you to investigate anything.'

'Which is extremely useful. It will give me time to establish the office of the Investigator.'

'Establish the office?' Athan spoke as if he had just learned some foreign words and, while having no idea what they meant, thought they were probably rude. 'If you're going to come over all courtly, I might just leave you to it.'

Nicodemus gave no reply to that, no reply which made his preference on the question quite clear.

'And without me around, goodness knows which of these Normans will stick a knife in you thinking that you're some uppity Saxon who's got above himself.'

Nicodemus grimaced slightly at that very practical thought.

'On your own in this place?' Athan smiled in that horrible way he had. 'You wouldn't survive a week.'

Nicodemus reflected on his position and on Athan's particular talents. 'I suppose that sometimes aggression is the better part of valour.'

They had left the king's presence with gracious bows[1] The audience had been perfect. Not only the king himself but Le Pedvin, William's right-hand man - when a right hand was needed to kill someone - and Ranulph de Sauveloy, himself an appalling fellow but in a more administrative manner. But he was very well thought of by William, which was all that mattered.

The question of what happened after they left the presence hadn't really concerned them at the time. Not being in the presence of King William and his closest was generally for , where the denouement of the latest investigation had turned out very well indeed, as far as Nicodemus was concerned.the best where Saxons were concerned.

'Where exactly are we going?' Athan asked with disarming

---

[1] *The King's Investigator*; probably best to read it first.

simplicity.

'To the investigator's chambers.'

'And where are they?'

Nicodemus hesitated for just a moment. 'I'm sure they'll be around here somewhere.'

'You think Brother Hermitage had his own chambers here?' Athan looked around the timber walls. 'I can't see him taking chambers even if they were offered. You know what a timid fool he is. He'd stay as far away from the king as possible.'

'And that was his mistake. I can take the duties of the King's Investigator to new heights.'

'Oh Lord,' Athan muttered.

'The king will come to depend on me for his, erm..,'

'Investigations?'

'Just so.'

'About which you know nothing.'

'You forget that it was I who created the role of King's Investigator in the first place.'[2]

'Only as part of yet another scheme that went horribly wrong.'

'Anyway,' Nicodemus went on confidently. 'I won't be doing the actual investigation.'

'Really?' Athan sounded intrigued. 'Are you thinking of mentioning this to the king at all?'

'I will have people for that sort of thing. I am the King's Investigator. I'm in charge. It's my job to tell other people what to do. And then castigate them when they get it wrong.'

'People, eh? I expect they're queueing up in your chamber. We'll be able to talk to them once we find it.'

---

[2] The first place being *The Heretics of De'Ath*; it seems so long ago now.

'I don't think you realise what an opportunity this is.' Nicodemus's impatience, normally so well controlled, was starting to show.

'I've been on the receiving end of too many of your opportunities. If I hadn't taken the first one, I'd still be a real prior in a proper monastery.'

'De'Ath's Dingle?' Nicodemus sounded horrified.

'Well, nearly proper monastery. I wouldn't be wandering homeless, my life's new purpose being to make sure no one finishes you off in the dark.'

'I am the King's Investigator.'

'You keep saying that and I don't notice anything changing.'

'It doesn't matter what you think of it,' Nicodemus wearily explained. 'It is an appointment from the king. Directly from William himself. I'm alongside earls and barons and the like.'

'I'm not sure William sees it like that.'

'It also doesn't matter what he sees.' Nicodemus stopped walking and turned to look Athan in the eye. Then he looked left and right to make sure no one was in earshot; also, looking Athan directly in the eye was not very pleasant.

'I was the bishop's man in Lincoln, was I not?'

'You were.'

'Appointed by the bishop.'

'I imagine that's a requirement.'

'Yes, I expect you would. But of course, the bishop himself never went to Lincoln; too far away from the important job of keeping himself in favour in court.'

'So?' Athan clearly couldn't see where this was going.

'So, if I tell people I am the bishop's duly appointed amanuensis, who's to argue?'

Now Athan got it and gaped slightly. 'You weren't

appointed by the bishop at all?'

'He just never got round to it.' Nicodemus shrugged.

'Never got round to it because he didn't know anything about it at all?'

'I suppose that's a possibility. He was all the way off in Dorchester.'

'Good God.'

'Language!'

Athan shook his head with a wry expression on his face; he almost looked impressed.

'It was easy to announce something and simply look confident. You'd be surprised how gullible people are. Now I have a real appointment from a real king. In front of witnesses.'

Athan nodded silently.

'I've made a good living abusing positions I mostly didn't have. Now I've actually got one, the possibilities are endless.'

Athan gently moved his head from side to side. 'You're revolting.'

'Thank you. Now, if the King's Investigator tells some humble Norman or Saxon to do something, what are they going to do? Go to the king and check that it's all right or do what they're told?'

'Particularly if the investigator sounds confident enough.'

'Now you're getting it.'

Athan developed a small frown. 'Hermitage had to actually investigate real murders and then tell William what he'd found.'

'As you so nicely put it, Hermitage was an idiot. If he'd for one moment seen the advantages of his position, he could have organised things and lived a comfortable life.'

'I don't think you know Hermitage very well.'

'He had those other two hanging on,' Nicodemus made it half a question.

'Wat the Weaver,' Athan spat the name onto the floor. 'And the girl.'

'Ah, Cwen, yes. If our young Brother had the slightest bit of sense, he'd have sent them off to do the murders, while he did the reporting.'

'Slightest bit of sense, eh? You really don't know Hermitage.'

'The point is that a better man is in place now. A man who knows how to work a job to that most important priority, his own self-interest.'

If there was any conflict in Athan, any turmoil between ignoring this naked avarice and his religious duty to address it, it didn't show.

'But there is a most urgent task ahead of us,' Nicodemus went on. 'The very first step that must be taken.'

'And that is?'

'We have to tell everyone that I've been appointed. It's no good having a fine position if no one knows about it.'

'And how do we go about that?' Athan asked, not sounding hopeful. 'I don't think the Normans will like Saxons making announcements.'

'Oh, nothing so blatant. It's good that the king and Le Pedvin and de Sauveloy know, but they're way above us in the hierarchy.'

'I'm glad you think someone is,' Athan grumbled.

'They won't bother spreading the word. It would be like asking you to remember the names of the novices. We need someone much more humble. And preferably an awful gossip.'

'You have someone in mind?'

'They'll turn up. They always do.'

Nicodemus resumed his stroll along the corridor, but at least his announcements had stopped now.

It wasn't many more paces before they simply came to the end. This particular route didn't go anywhere, other than to the chambers that led off it.

'Perfect,' Nicodemus smiled.

'Really?' Athan couldn't see what was so good about a pointless passage.

'No passers-by,' Nicodemus explained.

'Isn't that bad? If you want people to know all about you?'

'Oh, it's far better if they know all about you but not where you are. That way you don't get nuisances popping in asking you to do things.'

'Like your job.'

'Exactly.'

'And nuisances like the king.'

'I couldn't have put it better. The office of the King's Investigator needs to be in the tower. It would not look good if I were away from His Majesty.'

'But would be very poor if His Majesty actually knew where you were.'

'I can see that you're going to fit right in.' Nicodemus smiled in the face of Athan's contempt for all of this.

'Of course, if you prefer, we can turn down the appointment and go back to whatever it was we were doing before?' he offered Athan. 'What was it? Just surviving, yes, that was it.'

'All right,' Athan surrendered. 'Just don't be too unbearable about it. Well, any more unbearable.'

Nicodemus granted Athan a slight incline of the head. 'This will do.' He nodded towards a door.

Athan considered it. 'And if it's Le Pedvin's private chamber?'

'I doubt it, down here, but if it is, we say we're lost.'

'If it is, we might be.'

Nicodemus appeared unconcerned about what was behind the door and pushed it open without knocking.

'Ah, there you are,' he said as he strode into the space as if he owned it.

The figure sitting behind the table looked up in surprise. He clearly didn't expect to be disturbed in whatever it was he did in here.

He was a young fellow, clearly Saxon judging by the state of his clothes and the haggard look about his face. The table in front of him was covered in a profusion of parchment, all of it scattered as if it were trying to escape his clutches.

'What do you want?' he bleated, his voice expecting the worst.

'I am Nicodemus, the King's Investigator.'

'Oh God,' the bleating descended into a pained wailing. 'What have I done now?'

'What have you done?' Nicodemus asked, taking the authoritative high ground with ease; and without any authority.

'Look,' the young fellow gestured towards the table of parchment. 'I'm getting through them, but some of them are in Norman and it takes me time to read.'

'Hm.' Nicodemus considered the table and frowned as if this were the very purpose of his visit.

'People will get paid, I promise.'

'Paid?' Nicodemus barely controlled the excited squeak in his voice.'

'You're Saxon, you understand.'

'What do I understand?'

'Just because I was organising the supplies for the old fortress, William made me carry on. Except he doesn't pay, of course.'

'You organise supplies?' Anyone with the barest scintilla of sensitivity would have been able to see Nicodemus's mind dribbling with excitement. The young fellow was too distracted. 'What is your name?'

'Aelfnod.'

'I'd change that if I were you,' Athan suggested.

Aelfnod raised an eyebrow.

'Not very Norman,' Athan explained.

Aelfnod shrugged that he knew this. 'Bit late now.'

'And you pay for the supplies as well.' Nicodemus was anxious to get back to important matters.

'Yes, except my instructions are that the Norman suppliers get paid first and the Saxons preferably not at all.'

'Ranulph de Sauveloy?' Nicodemus enquired.

Aelfnod's shiver at the name was all that was needed.

'This is excellent.' Nicodemus rubbed his hands. 'The perfect spot for the office of the King's Investigator.'

Aelfnod looked lost.

'I have just been appointed by the king and I need somewhere to work.'

'Work?' Athan made the question sound like a cough.

Nicodemus ignored him. 'This will do nicely. And it will be convenient having you close at hand so that you can cover our remuneration.'

'Do what?'

'From the Latin, remuneratio, recompense.'

Aelfnod still seemed puzzled.

'You can pay us,' Athan said blankly.

'Oh, right. Did the king say how much?'

'He left that to our discretion.' It was obvious that Nicodemus was barely resisting the temptation to rub his hands in glee.

'I suppose I can add you to the records,' Aelfnod started looking for a particular piece of parchment.

'Oh, this needs much more discretion than that.' Nicodemus moved closer to the table as if sharing a great confidence with Aelfnod. He even looked back to the door to make sure no one was there. 'You see, the job of the investigator is very confidential, hence the appointment directly by the king.'

Aelfnod nodded but found voice to a question. 'And what is an investigator, exactly.'

'What is it?'

'That's it. You said you were the King's Investigator. Well, being the king's anything usually means trouble, but I have no idea what an investigator does.'

'Ah. It comes from the Latin, vestigo, vestigare, to track.'

Aelfnod frowned. 'Why does a tracker need a room to work from? Shouldn't you be out, you know, tracking things?'

'In this case, the tracking is very particular.' Nicodemus leaned even closer and gave his words a horrible significance. 'The King's Investigator tracks..,' he drew breath, 'murderers.'

Aelfnod swallowed.

'You can see why the king would want that sort of thing kept very private.'

Aelfnod agreed with a grimace. Then his brow lifted. 'Are you going to investigate the Normans? They've murdered most people.'

'Hardly,' Nicodemus scoffed. 'The king of the Normans is not likely to want that done.'

'I suppose not.'

'Malf was the most recent.' Nicodemus said.

'Oh, right. Yes, we heard about him. Hard to miss a Norman being killed outside the king's door.'

'There you are then. Of course, it doesn't do any harm to tell people I've been appointed King's Investigator,' Nicodemus said casually. 'That's quite reasonable. But once an investigation is underway it needs to be kept quiet.' He even tapped the side of his nose to emphasise the secrecy.

Aelfnod now seemed to be in awe of all this and slowly nodded.

'Good.' Nicodemus clapped his hands. 'Well, now we've found a suitable work chamber, we can look for some housing appropriate to our position. We'll take a few coins to set things up.' He held out his hand, simply expecting it to be filled.

Aelfnod hesitated for a moment but then reached below the table and emerged with a small purse. He seemed on the brink of a decision about this tale he had been told, but the purse was out of his hands and had vanished into Nicodemus's robe before he had a chance to say a word.

Nicodemus and Athan turned back towards the door and the smug satisfaction now settled itself comfortably on the King's Investigator's face.

As they approached the door, a shadow fell across it. Nicodemus was about to dismiss this interloper from his presence when something caused him to pause.

'Ah, there you are,' Le Pedvin said as he blocked their exit. 'Hiding down here so no one knows where to find you, eh?'

Nicodemus did extremely well to look shocked at the very

idea.

'I know where everyone is,' Le Pedvin said with calm but terrifying menace. 'Congratulations on your appointment, by the way.'

Nicodemus acknowledged this with a nervous bow.

'And now, King's Investigator, I've got a job for you.'

'A job? How marvellous. Only too keen to begin.'

'Yes, you are.' Le Pedvin put a horrible hand on Nicodemus's shoulder and started to lead him away, Athan dragging on behind. As they left, Le Pedvin turned back over his shoulder. 'And Aelfnod,' he said, 'I do hope you haven't given these two any money.'

Aelfnod's smile in no way reflected his state of mind.

As they left the chamber, there was an indiscernible noise and where Nicodemus's foot had trod, there now sat a small purse.

Aelfnod leapt forward, snatched it up and firmly shut the door.

Caput II: The King's Investigation

[3]Le Pedvin directed them towards more inhabited parts of the tower but had at least taken his cadaverous hand from Nicodemus's shoulder, which was a relief. Although the thing had all the substance of a shrivelled claw, it somehow carried an awful weight. Nicodemus suspected it was the spirits of the people it had killed who were now jumping up and down on it.

Athan's grumbling progress behind was no comfort. The clear translation of the various noises was that he should have known this would all go wrong; and here it was, going wrong. And it was all Nicodemus's fault, obviously.

'Come,' Le Pedvin said as he turned and pushed open a door.

Inside was his personal chamber, so much was obvious from the most cursory glance.

There was a cot.

Nicodemus supposed that was all you needed really, but the place was still on the sparse side, even for a man of war. He quickly swung his eyes around the room looking for any other sign of human occupation. Human comfort was completely out of the question, but a bit of food and drink would have been encouraging.

Le Pedvin shut the door behind them, which revealed the other occupants of the room: all the weapons.

Of course, they would be behind the door. Where else? There was no point having a sword at the back of the room when the people you needed to kill would be coming in the

---

[3] If you haven't yet read *The King's Investigator* Part I, this chapter is going to ruin it.

15

front.

There was a sword at the back of the room as well, Nicodemus now noticed. It was lying by the cot, probably just in case it was needed in the night.

The gathering by the door looked like a collection of carpenter's tools. There were different implements for every conceivable function. Slicing, shaving, piercing, removing, making holes and making them a bit bigger; all were represented. Which one to choose though, that would be the problem? How did Le Pedvin know what he wanted to do to people when he went out in the morning? He couldn't carry them all, surely?

Maybe they were for visitors.

Nicodemus was a visitor. He stood up straight and looked obsequious.

'Peter,' Le Pedvin said without further explanation.

Nicodemus nodded. 'The fellow who killed Malf and then disappeared?'[4]

'And the one I sent my useless son, John, to find,' Le Pedvin agreed. 'The clue as to whether he succeeded is found in the word, useless.'

'I see.'

'Excellent. Off you go then.'

Even Nicodemus's devious mind, which usually tried to stay two steps ahead, stumbled over the instruction. 'Find Peter,' he eventually came out with.

'I think that's what I said,' Le Pedvin complained.

It didn't do to have Le Pedvin complain about anything, not with all his friends by the door, just waiting to join the conversation.

---

[4] It is now too late to read *The King's Investigator* Part I - you were warned

'Of course,' Nicodemus bowed.

'And bring him back alive,' Le Pedvin added. He clearly thought that any instruction to go and get someone meant go and kill them.

'Naturally.'

Le Pedvin frowned at that response. 'I want him here as a hold over de Sauveloy. There's no point parading a corpse in front of the king to show what an idiot de Sauveloy was for keeping a killer as his assistant.'

'Absolutely.' Nicodemus was running out of sycophantic agreement.

'Well,' Le Pedvin mused momentarily. 'You can parade a corpse in front of the king, obviously. Goes down very well. But you can't keep doing it, can you?'

'I imagine not.' Talk of parading corpses was doing nothing for Nicodemus's calm. And he could feel Athan's smile behind him.

'A week or two at most.' Le Pedvin appeared to be absorbed in happy recollection.

'Find Peter,' Nicodemus tried to get back to the task, mainly in the hope that he could leave the room next.

'And anyone who's helped him.'

Nicodemus nodded at the unhelpful addition.

'Did your son learn anything useful?' Nicodemus chanced.

'He's never managed that before, but you can always ask.'

Nicodemus bowed once more and started to move slowly back towards the door, hoping that he wouldn't bump into anything sharp.

'Oh,' Le Pedvin added as an afterthought. 'There's a bit of a tradition where this investigation business is concerned.'

'Really, my lord?' Nicodemus didn't like the sound of this.

'Yes. The threat of death.'

17

'Threat of death?' Nicodemus thought that the whole room must have heard him swallow.

'You get a threat of death as encouragement.'

'Ah, thank you, my lord,' Nicodemus managed.

'You're welcome. And bring him back to me,' Le Pedvin gave his final order. 'For God's sake don't let de Sauveloy get wind of this.'

'No, my lord.' Nicodemus increased his pace and gathered Athan as he retreated to the door, which he quickly opened and made good his escape.

'Oh, Lord,' Nicodemus sighed as he leant back against the closed door.

'Not going according to plan?' Athan enquired brightly. 'Why am I not surprised?'

All Nicodemus could do was point a finger at Athan as if it were backed up by a withering diatribe that he hadn't quite thought of yet.

'Find Le Pedvin's son,' Nicodemus said as he strode away.

'Not going back to the King's Investigator's chambers, then? To see the helpful Aelfnod again? The one who now knows our true status in this place?'

'You heard our instructions,' Nicodemus snapped. It was not like him to snap at all. Calm, control and confidence were his only weapons. He couldn't allow himself to be disarmed by some raving Norman who kept a sword by his bed and probably one in his bed as well. He glanced back at Le Pedvin's door and gave it a serious sneer.

'I heard your instructions,' Athan corrected.

'Oh, you were there as well.' Nicodemus continued speaking as he walked. 'In fact, I think that you're probably the best person to go looking for Peter. I can't imagine he's that keen on coming back and will need some persuasion.'

'I can leave that to you. You are the high and mighty King's Investigator, after all.'

'I am,' Nicodemus agreed. 'And if Le Pedvin hears that the angry-looking monk who follows me around is not following the King's Investigator's instructions? I imagine he has the very tool for a job like that propped up by the door.'

'He probably has a bigger and sharper one for King's Investigators who don't deliver.'

'Then we're both in trouble, aren't we?'

Athan simply grumbled at that.

'There's nothing better to bring people together for a common task,' Nicodemus mused. 'Mutual distrust.'

'Any idea where this son is then?' Athan asked. 'Or are you just wandering the corridors at random? Again?'

'Some guard will know. Why is there never one around when you want one?'

Le Pedvin's chamber, being not too far away from the king's, was at least in the main body of the tower, and so they found their way to the entrance with little difficulty.

Two Norman guards stood there, one on either side, but their attention was focussed outwards, alert for some threat against the person of the king.

After the conquest, the coronation, and the subjugation of most of the south of England, those who posed a threat to William were keeping a very safe distance.

Barons in the north and the west, even enemies at home in Normandy, had quickly realised that the north or the west or Normandy were much healthier locations than anywhere near the king.

Even so, these Norman guards looked to be more conscientious than most. Probably because they knew Le Pedvin might sneak up behind them at any moment.

Nicodemus strode out between them and then turned as if just remembering something.

'We seek Lord Le Pedvin's son. Have you seen him?'

The guards considered Nicodemus and Athan as if disappointed by the things that were getting in the tower these days.

'Clear off,' one of the guards said.

'Spike him,' the other suggested.

Nicodemus sighed his disappointment. He had got this down to such an art that even Norman guards, who seemed perfectly willing to do him harm, paused. Something in their minds told them that they'd done something wrong, they just didn't know what it was yet.

'I am Nicodemus. King William has this day appointed me King's Investigator. I have just been in discussion with Lord Le Pedvin about a most urgent matter and agreed that I would find his son for him. And you want to spike me?'

Now the guards knew what they'd done wrong and it had Le Pedvin in it.

'We saw him down by the gatehouse,' the spike-suggesting guard offered.

'That's better.' Nicodemus made a great play of studying their faces, it being his clear intention to remember them for his next discussion with Le Pedvin.

He then turned and walked down the steps from the tower itself and off towards the gate for the whole compound.

Athan followed, shaking his head at the encounter. If it had been him, he'd have clapped the guards round the head. He couldn't be doing with all this talk.

Thoughts of clapping people round the head brought him round to considering their position, their task and a possibility that might be offering itself.

'What do we do when we find this John?' he asked as he caught up with Nicodemus.

'With any luck, we ask him where Peter went, he tells us and we send some guards to go and fetch him.'

Athan coughed. 'Hardly likely. If it's known where he is, John would have brought him back already.'

'Not if he's as useless as his father suggests.'

They were approaching the gatehouse now and some waved signal must have been given by the guards at the tower as all the Normans milling about were most respectful. They weren't threatened or even approached. In fact, the signal must have said this pair had something to do with Le Pedvin and so were best left alone completely.

'A further thought occurs to me,' Athan said.

Nicodemus stopped walking and turned an intrigued eyebrow towards Athan. 'A thought? To you? Do tell.'

Athan scowled at the insult but ignored it, for now.

'Le Pedvin said he wanted Peter and anyone who had helped him.'

'I do remember that, yes.'

'But it is only Peter he wants alive.'

'I worry about where you're going with this.'

Athan sounded in speculative mood, which was not like him at all. 'If we were to find someone who had aided Peter in his escape, Le Pedvin would probably be quite grateful to hear that they'd been dealt with.'

'Who do you have in mind?'

Athan took a breath. 'Hermitage.'

'Brother Hermitage?'

'I don't know of another one.'

'Correct me if I'm wrong,' Nicodemus said, the contempt for an idiot clear in his voice, 'but Brother Hermitage was with us in the room when Peter disappeared.'

'Doesn't mean he wasn't involved. Doesn't mean he hasn't helped the man after the event. He's like that,' Athan sneered, 'helpful.'

'Anything's possible, I suppose.'

'So, we could deal with Brother Hermitage and find Peter at the same time.'

Nicodemus seemed to think that this was over complicating things unnecessarily.

'Hermitage could be long gone,' Nicodemus dismissed this distraction from their task. 'If he's got any sense, he'd have run for the hills as soon as the king said he didn't need to be Investigator anymore.'

'There you go again,' Athan was critical. 'Assuming that Hermitage has any sense.'

Nicodemus shrugged.

'And that disgusting weaver,' Athan went on. 'He's probably loitering around trying to get some business for his filthy tapestries.'

'It's too much of a distraction,' Nicodemus concluded. 'Le Pedvin has told us to find Peter and so that's what we have to do.'

'Which we will.'

'Dragging Hermitage into things will only add difficulty. And in any case, he probably didn't have anything to do with Peter at all.'

'Who cares about that?' Athan asked. 'You're the expert at abusing your position. What's so troublesome about this?'

Nicodemus seemed to accept that blaming people for things that weren't their fault would not be a problem in principle. 'Why bother?' he asked.

'Why bother?' Athan was outraged but managed to keep

his voice down. 'Why bother dealing with Brother Hermitage? Are you serious? The Brother Hermitage who ruined the whole De'Ath's Dingle business?[5] The same who dropped us right into Le Pedvin's lap in the first place. And that took some getting out of.[6] Never mind all that business in the marshes[7] and the latest shambles.[8]'

'Hm,' Nicodemus pondered.

Athan pressed his advantage. 'Here you are, the King's Investigator, just settling into your new-found status. An important mission from Lord Le Pedvin, no less, and the one monk who ruins everything you touch is still out there somewhere. He's just waiting to step in and take it all away.'

'But he's an idiot,' Nicodemus protested.

'I'm not saying he does it on purpose, I'm just saying that it happens all around him. He can't help himself. I tell you, with Brother Hermitage still alive and kicking, the chances are that he's going to kick you. You know I'm right.

'And now you're in a position to do something about it. You're the King's Investigator, not him. If you order him dealt with, he will be.'

'By you?'

'Probably not,' Athan sounded disappointed. 'If it's going to be done, it had better be a Norman hand. I'm sure you could persuade someone. It'll be a chance to extract your revenge.'

'What?' Nicodemus was confused suddenly.

'Extract your revenge on Hermitage.'

---

[5] *The Heretics of De'Ath*
[6] *A Murder for Brother Hermitage*
[7] *The Case of the Clerical Cadaver*
[8] *The King's Investigator Part I* - you can see why Athan's not that keen on Hermitage.

Nicodemus shook his head. 'It's exact. You exact your revenge, not extract it, for goodness' sake.'

'You get your revenge your way, I prefer mine extracted,' Athan smiled nastily.

'Perhaps we could just have him locked up.'

'He'd escape. Or the prison would fall down, or they'd lock up the wrong monk. No, it's got to be something more permanent.'

Nicodemus gave this further thought. 'As a prior, are you really supposed to be encouraging the murder of monks?'

'Depends on the monk,' Athan said nonchalantly as if this wouldn't be his first.

Nicodemus was non-committal. 'We'll see how it goes.'

Athan grumbled.

'I'm not promising, but I'm not saying no, either. The first and only thing we have to do is find Peter. Our lives depend on that. If we can attend to Brother Hermitage at the same time, without any risk to ourselves...,' he left the thought in the air.

'I'm sure we'll manage,' Athan bared his teeth as if preparing to bite someone. 'Let's find this John. If he doesn't know where Peter is, he may be able to tell us where we can put our hands on Hermitage. And then we can strangle him with them.'

Caput III: Instructions Issued

'Brother Hermitage, eh?' The old man sat in his large and comfortable chair and considered the report he had just received. He pulled his fine robes around his shoulder as if the message had put a chill into the air.

'That's right, master,' the messenger replied. 'Funny name for a monk, but that was what I was told.'

'They are all funny people,' was the simple summary. 'He uncovered the details and brought the affair to an end?'

'That is so.'

The actual language of this conversation was arcane and unintelligible to most. The men spoke it quickly and with ease, as they did every day, but it provided a mostly impenetrable shield to the casual eavesdropper.

'That is unfortunate,' the master considered the information.

The messenger could only nod his agreement.

'What was this monk doing interfering in the first place?'

'I understand that he was the King's Investigator.'

'Investigator, eh? Vestigo, vestigare, to track. And he tracked events to this conclusion.'

No reply was necessary.

'This is most disappointing. I must summon the others to discuss the next steps. What has happened to our man? Is that known?'

'It is. He made good his escape and brought me this word. He has one of our number with him, they should be safe.'

'Ah, some good news in all of this. He was not taken by the enemy then.' The old man reached around the side of his chair and lifted a small drum beater that hung there. He used this to strike a gong that stood to his right.

The sound filled the extravagant tent that they occupied and echoed off into the distance. The master waited until this had died away before striking the gong a second time.

The young messenger raised his eyebrows at what was clearly an unprecedented action.

'Urgent matters,' the master explained.

Before the sound of the second gong had faded, two more old men appeared from the back of the room. They were similarly dressed to their summoner, and while they were too old to actually hurry anywhere, their steps were as rapid as prudence allowed.

'What's amiss?' One of them called.

The old master simply gestured that they should take the chairs that sat either side of his and listen to the tale of the messenger.

With quite a bit of puffing and panting, the men made their way up three low steps and collapsed into their seats.

When one had recovered from the exertion, he made his familiar complaint. 'We should put these chairs at the bottom of the steps.'

The old master sighed. 'You know very well that when you can no longer make it to the chair, your time in it is over. That has ever been our rule.'

'Stupid rule,' the other muttered under his breath.

'Shut up, you old fool,' the third put in.

'Don't you tell me to shut up, you young upstart.'

'Masters, masters,' the old man urged. 'Urgent matters are before us, now is not the time for argument.'

The other two grumbled quietly but were now prepared to listen.

The messenger bowed to them and repeated his brief

report. 'Our man, Peter, had successfully infiltrated the enemy and was in position. He had completed the first act and was getting close to their leadership.

'The Norman king, William, then summoned his investigator, a monk called Brother Hermitage. Yes, funny name for a monk,' he said before the old men could comment.

'This Brother Hermitage uncovered Peter's position and he had to flee.'

'The monk?' one old man asked.

'No, Peter,' the messenger explained with some impatience.

The man nodded as if he agreed that fleeing was probably wise in the circumstances. 'Was the monk a Norman?'

'No, a Saxon.'

'Then why would he put Peter in this position?'

'Two reasons, I think. The first was that Peter was attempting to establish himself as King's Investigator, for the position and influence, you understand, and the monk was probably jealous.'

The old fellow who had asked the question accepted this. 'And second?'

'It seems that King William threatens everyone with death if they don't do what they're told.'

All three men scoffed at such crude and unimaginative leadership.

'The monk most likely feared for his life.' The messenger shrugged that this seemed to be a bit of a pathetic excuse, but then that was probably monks for you.

'When did all this happen?' The third man asked.

'Only very recently. I was waiting nearby, as instructed, and as soon as Peter brought me word, I made haste here.'

'I told you we had come too close,' the one who had had

trouble with the steps now complained. 'They'll find us.'

'At least the three of us could run away,' his companion chortled. 'We'll leave you as a sacrifice.'

The master waved this interruption to silence. 'Peter is safe?'

'He is secreted not far from the Norman tower.'

'Then he is still ours to instruct.'

The messenger hesitated a moment, words on the tip of his tongue that might be best kept there.

'You have more?' The master asked.

'Not directly related to our actions, but there were others with the monk.'

'Others?'

'Weavers.'

'Weavers?' The troublesome old one asked. 'What have weavers got to do with anything?'

'They appear to be companions of the monk.'

The old fellow simply shook his head that he now failed to understand the modern world at all.

'Weavers, you say?' the master sounded more interested.

'Wat the Weaver,' the messenger announced.

'Wat the Weaver, indeed? We have heard of him and know some of his works.'

The other old men gave vent to dirty cackles.

'And a young woman, named Cwen.'

'Peter told you all this?'

'He did. And we waited in sight of the place long enough to see the three of them leave.'

'They are gone?'

'They headed into the Saxon village that has sprung up by the walls. We didn't see them after that. Peter remained and I made haste to get here.'

The master considered all of this and beckoned to his fellows. 'We will consider,' he announced.

The messenger took a step away while the old men put their heads together. In fact, the oldest of the three, who could barely get out of his chair unaided, was joined by the others.

The consideration seemed to quickly move through debate and into dispute. Differing views were voiced with commitment and passion and dismissed with what started out as reason but soon became contempt.

If they had bothered to look at their messenger, they would have seen him roll his eyes at this. He even took to shaking his head and muttering his own one-sided debate. This was carried out in a low voice as he knew all three of the old men were conveniently deaf. He even did quite a good impression of three old men who can't agree on anything.

'It's always the same,' the messenger grumbled. 'Sit there pontificating on all manner of issues great and small, but ask you to actually deal with a problem staring you in the face and you haven't got a clue.'

'Did you say something?' the old master asked.

'No, no master. I await your instructions.'

'Hm.'

'Instructions as to what I should do next. Where I should go. Who I should talk to. What I should tell them. That sort of thing.'

The master returned to his debate.

'You know,' the messenger added to himself. 'Something actually useful that might work? Hopeless optimist that I am.' He puffed his cheeks out and gazed around the tent, fully expecting his wait to be a long one.

Frequently, when he got home and explained how hard his

day's messaging had been, his wife suggested that he should listen carefully to what he was told, and then ignore it completely and do what he thought best. In fact, the two of them had five times as many good ideas in a day as their three leaders had had in their overly long lives.

'You'd think one of them would have the decency to die soon,' she suggested.

'But what'll happen then? A slightly less old man will step up to take his place. And you know they're queueing up.'

'But all they want to do is have the seat. They don't actually want to do anything with it. Of what use to people is a leader whose overriding and greatest ambition for them is simply that he should be their leader? Once they've taken the seat, that's it. They don't think they have to do anything else; apart from accept our adoration.'

The messenger whole-heartedly agreed, but he was only a messenger. What could he do?

'Change the message,' his wife suggested.

'You know that expression, "don't shoot the messenger"? It's not just an expression.'

'We have reached a conclusion.'

The messenger was brought out of his reverie by this somewhat startling development; startling because it had happened so quickly.

'We have developed a scheme of infinite cunning,' the old master announced.

'Infinite, eh?' the messenger tried to sound impressed but didn't get his hopes up.

'This is what we want you to do.' The old man beckoned the messenger to draw near so that the infinite cunning could be imparted in confidence.

. . .

Message received and understood, the messenger's first instinct was to pop home, have a chat with the wife and decide what he really ought to do. If the instruction he had been given constituted infinite cunning, he'd hate to see what a half-baked plan from three old idiots would look like.

He couldn't help but think that the time for change was drawing nearer and nearer. Real change, not the replacement of one old idiot with a new one.

But change was always so messy and dangerous. And the messengers of change tended not to fare very well.

No, he would do as he was instructed and then moan about it afterwards; as usual.

Perhaps, in the swirl and chaos of recent developments, some change for the better would come. Probably not, but you could only hope.

All he had to do now was find Peter again. He hoped that the man hadn't moved from his hiding place. Then he hoped that when he delivered his message, Peter wouldn't look at him and say something like, "are you serious", or "you jest, surely?"

He would have his, "look, I'm only the messenger," speech ready. If Peter wanted to defy his instructions, that was up to him.

The messenger often wished that he was a more courageous messenger, but you had to be practical at the end of the day. Particularly if you liked seeing the end of the day; and the one after that.

Courageous messengers went down in history and were spoken of in legend, mainly because they didn't live very long. This messenger preferred the idea of going down in history as one of the world's oldest messengers.

His journey back towards the Normans was speedy and straightforward. The river provided a much safer and faster route than traipsing the Norman-strewn paths and roads.

The tide was on the turn and so the waters were kind as he paddled his simple boat in the lee of the north shore, the south being solidly Norman territory now.

He felt some sympathy for the old master who had complained that they had come too close to the enemy. Being off in the far west was much more comfortable, although he knew the invaders were bound to get there sooner or later.

And when they did arrive, who would be expected to bring word of attack? Messengers. Typical.

Recognising a particular willow that hung out almost parallel to the water, the messenger swung his craft around and manoeuvred it neatly into a tiny hidden harbour of tree trunk and riverbank.

Securing the vessel with a rope, he clambered forward and out onto solid ground. Although the journey had been short, he was always grateful to get off the water. Tales were told around here of bizarre river creatures like sirens, only uglier. Creatures who climbed aboard your boat and simply talked at you until you jumped over the side and drowned. Being a messenger, he believed most of the tales he was told.

He found familiar landmarks and followed an animal trail that led from the water's edge.

On a couple of occasions, he stopped still in response to some unexpected noise, but this was basic messenger training. It didn't stop him thinking he should have stayed at home and stuck to domestic business; deliveries and collections mainly. There was no danger in that. Well, only when people complained that he had brought the wrong thing or that it was a month late.

He had been flattered by the attention of the old men who said that they needed him for this important mission. It was his wife who had pointed out that they were taking him as messenger because they really weren't bothered whether he made it back or not. By that time, it was too late.

'Peter,' he called out softly once he was sure that he was near the hiding place.

'The masters send me,' he gave the right sequence of words.

There was a rustling and movement in one of the bushes nearby and Peter's head appeared. It looked left and right and then spotted the messenger.

With a further check that they were not being observed, he gestured that the messenger could join him in his bush.

Once under the cover of the bush, in what was actually quite a comfortable retreat, the two men relaxed.

'Where is the other?' the messenger asked.

'He scouts about,' Peter assured him. 'To make sure we are not discovered.'

Despite this precaution, Peter had the look of a man who was hiding in a bush from people who wanted to kill him. But that was his job. Infiltrating the enemy took great courage, and the messenger simply assumed that Peter had it.

'What news?' Peter asked.

The messenger took a breath. 'The masters have an instruction.'

'Excellent. I shall return to them immediately.' Peter made to move. 'You brought the boat?'

'I did,' the messenger acknowledged, 'but..,'

'But what?'

The messenger always hated delivering messages that it was obvious people didn't want.

'The instruction requires an action before your return.'

'And what might that be?' Peter sounded as if he'd had enough instructions from the masters and that he had done his bit.

The messenger gave the instruction.

Peter simply looked at him. 'You are joking?' he said.

Caput IV: Brother Hermitage

Brother Hermitage. Brother Hermitage. Brother Hermitage.

Brother Hermitage had woken the following morning, but now opened his eyes and looked at the roof of the hut in which he had spent the night.

He thought it was one of the most wonderful hut roofs he had ever encountered.

'Brother Hermitage,' he muttered to himself contentedly. 'Just, Brother Hermitage. Not Brother Hermitage the anything. Certainly not Brother Hermitage the king's anything. Most assuredly not Brother Hermitage, the King's Investigator.'

He even smiled and took pleasure from the moment. He knew that he shouldn't, and it would be tempting fate, but he couldn't help himself. He didn't believe in fate anyway. This was the will of God. He had done his duty and was now relieved of it.

The weight of his role had been lifted from him yesterday, but he could still feel it floating away into the sky and taking his worries with it.

He was sure some more worries would float down to replace them, that was just the way he was. Still, they would be nothing like the worries of having King William and the awful Le Pedvin breathing down his neck. Investigate this, investigate that, deal with a murder, solve several, and do it all by tonight or we'll kill you. Those were real worries. But he didn't have them anymore. They belonged to Nicodemus.

He felt slightly guilty at passing his troublesome life on to Nicodemus; he'd feel guilty passing it on to anyone. But the previous night, as they considered the recent collection of truly bizarre events, Wat and Cwen had persuaded him that Nicodemus was the best place for the king's troubles to rest.

The man loved that sort of thing. Being a functionary of someone more important than he was seemed to give him enormous satisfaction. And who more important than the king?

As for the murders, well, they were sure that Nicodemus would have a way of passing on the actual work to someone else. That also seemed to give him enormous satisfaction.

If there were any more murders, of course.

Hermitage assured them that there would be. He had become convinced that murders followed the King's Investigator round like some troublesome dog. When the first one turned up, Nicodemus might feel aggrieved towards Hermitage.

Wat and Cwen comforted him that Nicodemus would be revelling in his moment and would be completely unbearable about it. He certainly wouldn't let a little thing like a murder get in the way of him being more important than he was yesterday.

They also tried to tell him not to care less about Nicodemus anyway. After all, the man had been a trouble to Hermitage in almost everything he did. If this role turned out not to be what was expected, it would serve him right.

But there was also Athan to consider. The prior seemed to have nothing but ill-feeling towards Hermitage. And now he thought about it, the most likely outcome was that Nicodemus would get Athan to do the investigations. Who else did he have?

Then, when things went awry, Athan would feel aggrieved towards Hermitage; after which he would come and do something about it.

Wat and Cwen promised him that they would be long gone by then. They would spend one night in the village by the tower and then head back to Derby.

As he retired for the night, he told his latest concern to leave him alone. The king had taken his burden away and idle speculation on his part was not going to disturb this night.

Nonetheless, as he closed his eyes, he couldn't help but wonder whether the murders were not following the King's Investigator at all, they were following him.

He was still young and tried to look forward to a long life without any murders to prove that argument wrong.

Now, as he considered the delightful hut in which he rested, the one with all the holes and the rather peculiar smell, he took quiet satisfaction from the fact that he had gone through an entire night without a single murder. And the king himself was just over the other side of the fortress wall. If ever there was an opportunity for a passing murder to stop by and introduce itself, this was it.

He even counted to three, just to give the day a chance to go wrong before he moved.

With no urgent cry, no shout of his name, no gurgle of the victim to disturb him, he rolled over and stood. He then ducked as he realised he was taller than his hut, and stooped out of the door opening to consider the world before him.

It looked exactly the same as it had the previous day, but there was no one waiting for him, demanding to know what he had done about whatever it was he was supposed to be doing.

There were Normans, but they were starting the business of the day; opening the gates of the tower and getting the bridge repair crew to work on the span over the moat, which had mysteriously suffered further damage overnight from the swirling English waters.

Saxons started to emerge from their crude dwellings, only to be shouted at by the Normans for not doing something or other, and not doing it quickly enough.

Life really did appear to be back to normal.

The shouts and complaints of another day brought Wat blearily from his hut. He raised a hand of acknowledgement to Hermitage and then yawned loudly, stretching his arms out above his head.

Hermitage took in the sights and sounds of this Tower of London, William's new redoubt and scourge of the Saxons, and breathed a sigh of relief that it was nothing to do with him.

He even gave a morning wave to More the Boatman, who was starting his day's business by ferrying Normans across the moat, thereby avoiding the bridge, which he swore was not safe.

Wat wandered over.

'Well, Hermitage. Ready to say goodbye to all of this?'

'And never see it again,' Hermitage replied.

'Dudda asked if we wanted to stay in the village for the noon meal,' Wat said.

'That was kind of him. Although I'm not sure they can really spare the food.'

'And I thought you'd be anxious to be on the road as soon as light allowed. We could be close to St Albans by nightfall if we get a step on.'

'That would be wonderful.'

'I'll give Cwen a kick. She's usually the one shouting at us to get up and not laze about in bed all day.'

It was true that Cwen seemed to have an innate ability to wake just before dawn. Just sufficiently before dawn that she could be up and about and scowling at people as they dragged themselves into the day.

Wat returned in a moment. 'Not there. Probably popped down to the river.'

Hermitage nodded. He'd need to pop down to the river himself before they set off.

They spent the time gathering their simple belongings together so that they would be ready when Cwen returned. Wat's pack was anything but simple, but it was always ready for a speedy departure.

Hermitage didn't have a pack or any possessions at all to speak of. His small devotional volume was always to hand, so he didn't even need to go and get it.

'What is she doing?' Wat complained. 'Do you think she's having some trouble?'

Hermitage didn't care to speculate about what trouble Cwen might be having. And from his understanding of his friend, he knew there was no way he was going to ask, let alone offer to help.

They waited a few more moments.

'Oh, for goodness' sake,' Wat complained. 'Come on, Hermitage.' He strode off down the path towards the river and the undergrowth that provided the privy for the not insignificant Saxon village.

'Cwen!' Wat called. 'What are you up to?'

That wasn't the question Hermitage would have asked.

'Are you all right?' he enquired gently.

'What do you want?' A gruff male voice enquired.

'We're looking for Cwen,' Wat shouted back.

'What's a Cwen?'

'You'd know if you had one. There are no young women in there with you?'

'Certainly not. What sort of bush do you think this is?'

'Where's she gone?' Wat asked, a frown on his face.

'Perhaps we missed her on her way back?'

'There's only one path.'

Hermitage didn't have an answer to that.

'The sun's been up for half an hour now and she hasn't shouted at anyone. Perhaps she's sick?' Wat seemed genuinely concerned.

'She wasn't in her hut,' Hermitage pointed out.

'No, but if she got sick in the night she might have wandered off.'

Hermitage could tell that this was not the moment to speculate about what sort of sickness she might have that made her wander about.

'Check the hut again,' Wat said.

'You already looked.'

'I know. But I was expecting to find her sitting on her cot. She could be on the floor.'

If his own hut was anything to judge by, Cwen's would not be so spacious that you'd miss someone lying on the floor. In fact, you'd have to be pretty flexible to be able to lie on the floor at all, most of it being taken up by the cot.

He told himself to stop being so particular. They were looking for Cwen, that was quite straightforward.

Back in her hut, there really was no sign of her. She was not on the cot, under it, or hiding by the back wall, as Wat explored them all.

'Where can she be? It's not like her to go anywhere quietly.'

They stood outside the hut, scanning the surroundings for any clue as to where Cwen might be.

'We could ask More,' Hermitage suggested, nodding towards the boatman who was just returning from his latest crossing.

'What good will that do?'

'He might have seen her. He's probably been up most of the night interfering with the bridge.'

'And you expect a sensible reply?' Wat sounded hopeless but they walked over to the boatman anyway.

'More!' Hermitage called. 'Have you seen Cwen?'

'Eh?' More called up from the shore of the moat.

'Have you seen Cwen?' Hermitage enunciated the words carefully.

'Oh yis,' More nodded happily.

'There you are,' Hermitage comforted Wat. 'Where is she?' he called.

Without any further custom at the moment, More secured his boat to the shore and wandered up the bank towards them.

'Where's who?' More asked, grinning at them in the way that he grinned at virtually everything that went on around him, whether it warranted a grin or not.

'Cwen,' Hermitage repeated before Wat could shout the name. 'You said you'd seen her.'

'That's right,' More nodded merrily and displayed his single tooth to show how happy he was. 'Small girl,' he said. 'A bit fierce.'

'Yes. That's her.'

'I ferried her across the river, you know.'

'This morning?' Wat demanded.

'No, no, yesterday.'

'We know you ferried her yesterday,' Wat ground his teeth. 'We were there. Remember? Have you seen her today?'

'You didn't ask if I'd seen her today,' More complained.

'Well, we are asking. Have you seen her today?' Wat was obviously resisting the urge to grab More and shake him about a bit. He clearly knew that this would do nothing to get the information they needed, and would necessitate actually touching More, which was not really wise.

'Erm.' More pointed his beard towards the sky as he pondered this difficult question. 'No,' he concluded.

'Argh.' Wat walked round in a small circle.

'I might have heard her, though.'

'Heard her? What do you mean, heard her?'

'You know, sounds and the like.'

Wat clenched his fists. 'Hermitage, you talk to him.'

'What did you hear?' Hermitage asked the boatman.

'Disturbances.'

'Disturbances?'

'In the night. In the village,' More nodded to confirm the disturbances.

'What kind of disturbances? Animals, people?'

'People. Moving about, they were.'

'Where exactly? Can you point to the spot?'

'It was dark,' More explained.

'So you couldn't hear properly,' Wat complained to himself.

'Over there.' More pointed towards the centre of the village, where the three of them had slept. 'And then over there.' More moved his arm to the left. Down towards the river. 'Then there was the sound of a boat.'

'You heard that all right then?' Wat checked.

'Oh, I can tell the sound of a boat,' More said proudly. 'Quite a small one. Old, I'd say, single oar, three people. Be a bit risky on the river with three people in that thing.'

Wat and Hermitage were considering the boatman with some awe.

'Made of wood though,' More went on. 'Not skin. A single rope to tie her up. Two of the people had boots on and one not.'

'Didn't get their names, did you?' Wat asked.

'Don't be silly,' More replied. 'Who's going to shout out their names when they're sneaking about on a boat at night?'

'You knew they were sneaking?'

'Oh yis. Sounded like a proper sneak to me.'

'And you should know.'

'Hee, hee,' More cackled and nodded his agreement.

'What could this have to do with Cwen?' Hermitage asked.

Wat was fretful. 'If she heard people sneaking about in the middle of the night she'd go and tell them to stop.'

'Which they might not be happy about.'

'Quite. We need to see if there's any sign of these sneakers in the night.' Wat strode away back towards the village.

'Thank you, More, you've been most helpful.' Hermitage said over his shoulder as he too walked away. He skipped in alarm as he saw that More was right behind him.

'I'll help,' More nodded.

'I'm sure they didn't leave the boat behind.' Hermitage felt bad about questioning More's motives.

'Oh, they didn't. I heard it go. West, it was.'

'Then?'

'I like to be helpful.'

Hermitage thought it more likely that nosiness was at root but didn't feel that he could tell More to clear off. He couldn't tell anyone to clear off.

Wat's steps were fast as he entered the village once more and scanned the ground for any indication of people moving about in the night. The dawn would have seen everyone up, so any signs from the night before would be trampled away.

'Nothing,' he complained. He moved away from the central space between the huts and went round the back of the ones they had been sleeping in. 'Here!' he cried.

Hermitage and More hurried to his call.

There were definite signs of disturbance. The undergrowth was flattened, and recently as it was still green and healthy.

'That's what I heard,' More reported, pointing at the plants.

'It leads off towards the river,' Wat pointed at a clear trail of destruction.

'Looks like someone didn't want to go,' More said unhelpfully.

'They've taken Cwen!' Wat was distraught and angry at the same time. 'Who were they?' he demanded of More.

'I don't know,' the boatman squeaked.

'You probably know all the people who sneak around in boats at night.'

'I do,' More agreed. 'And it wasn't any of them. It was strangers.' He said the word, strangers as if they were the close kin of dragons.

'Quick,' Wat instructed. 'Down to the river.'

'They'll be gone now,' More said, but he said it quietly to Hermitage.

Wat had run ahead, throwing the undergrowth aside in his haste, but his voice wailed back to them, and probably to every other ear for a mile up and down the river. 'No!' he howled. 'Oh, God no. Cwen!'

Caput V: The Body Turns Up

Hermitage and More hurried as fast they could to find Wat, but his cries of anguish were an easy beacon.

When they came upon him, he was standing against a tree trunk, his head pressed to it and his arms over his head as if trying to block out the world.

'What is it?' Hermitage asked, Wat's distress causing his own heart to race.

Wat said nothing but dropped an arm and pointed it behind him into the bushes hard by where the riverbank started its transformation to mud. 'Oh, no,' he howled again.

Hermitage and More followed the arm and stepped carefully over. Hermitage had the very strongest suspicion what he was going to find, and he would give all of creation not to find it.

'Oh,' More squeaked in excitement. 'It's some boots.' He sounded as if this trip was already proving to be worth the effort. 'Oh dear,' he added. 'They've got feet in them.'

Wat now sobbed uncontrollably.

'They're a bit big,' More observed.

'The boots?' Hermitage couldn't help but ask as he hung back. He was actually quite grateful that More was here for this awful task.

'No,' More cackled. 'The feet. They don't fit the boots. No wonder he's having a bit of a lie-down.'

Wat stopped mid-sob. 'What do you mean, he? And big feet?'

'Yis,' More's head and beard bounced happily. 'Big fellow. He really shouldn't be trying to wear boots that small in the first place. They probably tripped him up.'

Wat now sprang over and pushed Hermitage to one side. He peered at the figure lying in the bushes. 'Oh, thank God!' he cried. 'Hermitage,' he now laughed through the tears that still washed around his face. 'Look. It's a big dead man. Isn't it wonderful?'

Hermitage did feel mightily relieved. He had taken his lead from Wat and was convinced that the body in the bushes was Cwen. It was quite clearly not Cwen at all, although it did have Cwen's boots on. Wat's mistake was understandable.

In fact, the dead fellow was probably four times the size of Cwen so why he thought he could get her boots on was beyond reason. Cwen did have very nice boots and was proud of them. Perhaps this fellow had simply tried to steal them.

And now he was dead.

His investigatory experience dragged him to the conclusion of that statement. Oh dear.

From all-consuming distress that Cwen might be dead, Hermitage now worried that she'd killed someone; probably for stealing her boots.

'He looks like a Norman,' More added as he pressed closer to the body.

Cwen had killed a Norman? Oh dear, oh dear.

'And he tried to steal her boots,' Wat managed a laugh to drive away the last of his distress.

'He didn't try to steal them,' Hermitage pointed out. 'He did steal them. He's got them on.'

That did cause Wat to worry once more. 'Cwen wouldn't let anyone take her boots. No one's even allowed to touch them. What's a big Norman doing with them on?'

'A big dead Norman,' More added.

'Oh, my God.'

Hermitage let the blasphemy pass in the circumstances.

'She killed him,' Wat concluded. 'She killed him for taking her boots.'

'If she killed him, why didn't she take the boots back?' Hermitage asked.

Wat shrugged. 'Didn't want them after they'd been on some smelly Norman feet. You know what she's like about the Normans.'

'In which case, where is she?'

Wat looked about as if expecting Cwen to be simply sitting close by. 'Cwen!' he called. 'Cwen, where are you?'

There was no reply.

'Where has she got to?' he asked in frustration.

'Gone in the boat,' More nodded confidently.

'What do you mean, gone in the boat?'

'Erm.' More considered this complicated question and how best to answer it. 'The boat is gone, and she was in it. Or, to put it another way, she was in the boat and it's gone. Do you see?' He clearly thought land-folk wouldn't understand complex nautical issues like this.

'Don't be ridiculous.'

'It makes sense now,' More squeaked away enthusiastically. 'It's what I heard, see. Three people getting into the old boat, two of them with boots on. Now I think about it, the one without boots was smaller than the others.'

'You heard a small person?' Wat scoffed.

'Oh yis. The boat don't move so much when a small one gets in.'

'What the devil was Cwen doing getting in a boat in the middle of the night?' Wat complained as if this were just one more example of Cwen's thoughtlessness.

'Perhaps she had no choice?' Hermitage suggested.

'She was taken?' Wat was aghast.

Hermitage found himself slightly surprised that he'd reached this obvious conclusion before Wat.

'Who would take Cwen on a boat?'

'I did,' More pointed out.

Wat simply looked at him.

'I wouldn't do it again.' More was sombre. 'She's a bit difficult, isn't she?'

'That she is,' Wat agreed. 'And if someone took her onto a boat against her will they'd have had one hell of a fight on their hands.'

'And now a dead Norman,' More pointed out.

'Oh, hell.'

Hermitage did give vent to a slight tut at this. He knew the situation was uniquely concerning, but there were limits.

'A dead Norman,' Wat explained. 'Dead Normans generally being trouble.'

Hermitage could only agree with this, but at least he did so silently. Once this Norman was missed he would be looked for. Then, when the rest of the Normans found him, they would be very cross indeed. Which would mean trouble for everyone.

He stepped closer to the body and considered what he could see. The fellow was very large indeed, obviously having spent his life to this point eating and living well. He wore good clothes and the familiar Norman helmet lay on the ground close to his head.

'Why would the Normans want to take Cwen in the middle of the night?' Wat asked.

'What do we do about the dead Norman in the bushes?' Hermitage asked what he felt was the more urgent question.

Cwen clearly wasn't here so there was little they could do

about that at the moment. The dead Norman was most definitely here and needed their attention. 'If he's found and we're found with him?' He didn't go into the details of the likely consequences.

Wat considered their surroundings. 'He's pretty well hidden. It took us a bit to find him. If we cover the trail, he could stay here.'

'He'll probably be missed back at the tower,' Hermitage said. 'If he was the night patrol and he didn't come back, people might come out to look for him.'

'It's simple,' More said brightly.

'Oh, really?' Wat was sceptical.

'Put him in the river.'

'Put him in the river?' Hermitage was appalled by that idea. Norman or not, this was someone's body. It should be treated with respect.

'It's where all the other bodies go,' More couldn't see the problem.

'What other bodies have you had?' Wat asked suspiciously.

'Not me. It's the Normans. They're filling the thing up with them.'

Hermitage could only shake his head at that. They had already seen the very watery burial practices of the Tower of London.

Wat looked out at the stream of the river, which was now gently moving to their left. 'And when the Normans in their tower see one of their own float by they'll have a good laugh, will they?'

'We could weigh him down with something.' More offered.

Hermitage had to speak. 'We are not putting dead bodies in the river at all, let alone weighing them down.'

More grumbled that his excellent idea was being dismissed

like this.

'We can cover him up,' Hermitage went on. 'Wat's right. This is a quiet spot and he's not likely to be seen. If we bring some branches and cover him over, he might never be found.' He was horrified at the words that were coming out of his mouth.

'Good plan,' Wat agreed. 'We'd better take the boots though. Woe betide us if we haven't got them when we find her.'

They set about gathering what material they could to cover the body of the large dead Norman, More complaining all the while that it would be so much easier to throw him in the river.

'More,' Wat eventually snapped. 'Will you shut up? Look at the size of the man. I doubt the three of us could even lift him, let alone get him afloat. He'd just end up lying in the mud waiting to be spotted by the next patrol.'

More didn't shut up, but at least he helped with the cover-up.

Hermitage dragged a large branch, still heavy with foliage, that had been probably broken away by the sneakers who took Cwen. He considered the Norman who was now vanishing nicely under a pile of green and his heart sank.

How long had it taken? What was the first thing he did when he got up and started his first day as not-King's Investigator? He found a dead body. Couldn't his respite have even lasted a day or two? Did the comfort of his new life have to be snatched away so soon? Were the murders really following him around? Was he fated to now become Brother Hermitage, investigator?

If he wasn't the King's Investigator, what other sort could he be? The role hadn't even existed until Nicodemus made it up.

As usual, he referred to the Latin to give him a crumb of comfort. If you could come up with a word for something, it made the fact more palatable, somehow. He could share a word with other people and spread the burden.

He would be a single investigator. From the Latin for individual, maybe. Yes, that would do for now. Not that he relished this at all, but he felt that if he could separate the function from his own preferences and wants, it could be held responsible for the things that were going to go wrong, not him.

He breathed a heavy and heartfelt sigh. He would just have to use the Latin, privus. He would be a private investigator. At least until he could pass that on to someone else.

But then again, if he wasn't following the orders of the king, he couldn't be made to investigate anything. This situation had his friend Cwen in the middle of it and investigator or not, he was going to get to the bottom of it. After that, if people came to him with their murders, he'd be at liberty to say, no.

It wasn't even as if there was much investigation to be done here. Cwen had been taken into a boat, during which a Norman had been killed. He realised that he should have looked for the fatal wound but he had come upon this situation as a friend, not as an investigator.

It was always possible that Cwen had not done it herself. There could have been a dispute between the Normans and one of them was left behind. Still, if More was right and there were only three people in the boat, one of them must have done it.

The fact that he'd been able to identify the culprit quite quickly gave him no satisfaction.

The Norman was now comprehensively covered by such a pile of greenery that it was quite suspicious in its own right. It looked as if some monstrous animal had made a nest in the bushes.

'Now we get after her,' Wat announced.

'We get after her?' Hermitage asked. He hadn't had a chance to get his head thinking about what they did next. Hiding a dead Norman had taken all his attention.

'Of course. If More here is right, they've taken her west. That's where we go.'

'Why would they take her west? The tower is to the east and that's where all the Normans are.'

'I don't know, do I?' Wat complained at Hermitage's pedantry. 'A boat went west with Cwen in it. The boat left a dead Norman behind. The why of it all isn't really important right now. We have to go west.'

Hermitage looked along the riverbank, and while there was a path, it was small and overgrown and looked like a difficult passage.

'On the river.' Wat was impatient. 'We get a boat.'

'I've got a boat,' More piped up.

'I know you have, my friend,' Wat laid a hand on More's shoulder; a brave step. He also reached to his belt and pulled up a large purse that chinked invitingly in More's face. 'And this will be yours when we find Cwen.'

More's eyes looked as if they were trying to climb out of his face and into the purse. His mouth had dropped open and his single tooth appeared ready to gnaw Wat's hand off.

The purse disappeared again, to a sigh of pleasure from More.

'This way, gentlemen,' he said, indicating that they should head back to the village.

'Is there anything else we can learn here?' Hermitage checked.

'Such as?' Wat asked quickly.

'Signs of the boat. Confirmation that they were here and went west? Some message left by Cwen, perhaps?'

'What. Like a note?'

'No, not like a note. I hardly think she'd have time to write a note when she was being put in a boat and her boots were being taken. But she may have managed to leave some sign of her passing. She would know that we would come looking for her.'

Wat nodded that this was reasonable.

'And if she did kill one of the Normans who was taking her, the other two would have found themselves with a handful.'

'Ha, that they would.'

They very quickly stepped down to the river's edge and scoured the scene for any clues.

'Just like a real investigator, eh, Hermitage?' Wat called. 'Vestigare, to track?'

'You were listening, then?' Hermitage checked. 'But this is one investigation I actually want to do, so all the clues will be useful.' He nodded to himself. 'Of course, we don't have the first clue about when she was taken. The tide has moved the waters and may have covered all trace.'

'More?' Wat asked. 'What time was it when you heard the disturbance?'

'Dark,' More replied.

'Yes, we know it was dark, what was the time?'

'Dark time,' More specified.

Hermitage asked a heavy question. 'What times of the day do you use, More?'

The boatman explained happily. 'There's dawn and dusk

53

and in the middle of them there's noon when we eat.'

'And the bits either side?

'Dark,' More confirmed.

'No help at all,' Wat grumbled. 'I can't see anything here, Hermitage.'

'No, I think you're right. It could only be a little while since they left, the quicker we get on the river the better.' Never in his life had he thought that he would utter those words.

Leaving the Norman to his foliate grave, they quickly made their way back to the village and on towards the moat and More's boat.

'You can follow them, can you?' Wat checked. 'Only last time the tide was going out, you went with it.'

'Ah,' More explained. 'But that was with the horrible people.'

'Nicodemus and Athan,' Wat checked.

'That's right. I can row upstream when I want to.' He gave one of his cackles and Hermitage couldn't help but smile.

More led them down the slope towards the moat and his waiting vessel.

'Oh, yes?' A gruff voice with a horribly Norman accent called out. 'And just where the devil do you think you're going?'

Caput VI: Have You Got A Warrant?

'I'm going to me boat,' More grinned and squeaked and bobbed his head.

Hermitage thought it best to let More deal directly with this new Norman. Explaining himself and Wat could lead to complication and delay.

And this was a new Norman. He even looked like a new Norman, fresh from wherever it was in Normandy they were made. He looked as strong and fit as any and was clearly a man with a few years' experience behind him. But everything about him looked new. His clothes were neat and ordered, the metalwork that hung around him shone and even his helmet was pristine.

Most Norman helmets carried the dents and scars of one fight or another. Either this man's had never been in a fight, or he was scrupulous about repair and maintenance. He did not have the look of a man who had never been in a fight.

In many ways, he reminded Hermitage of Norbert.[9] He had been a very neat and scary Norman as well. Perhaps they were related?

'Your boat?' he asked, sounding quite shocked at the idea.

'That's right,' More agreed. 'Down there it is. In the moat. It's a ferry. I take people across the moat and across the river sometimes. Do you want to go across the river? It's only a penny.'

The Norman considered More as if he had encountered a talking fish. A stupid one, at that.

'No, I do not want to cross the king's river.'

---

[9] *Hermitage, Wat and Some Murder or Other*; with Norbert the Norman.

The man spoke in such an officious and confident manner that Hermitage could only think they were in trouble. Or, if they weren't now, they soon would be. And they needed to get after Cwen.

'And what do you mean, your boat?' The Norman asked this in such a particular manner that the correct answer should be clear to anyone.

More was not just anyone.

'That's right,' he nodded and smiled again. He even pointed helpfully; in case the Norman hadn't seen More's boat before.

'There are no boats but the king's boats,' the Norman announced.

More scanned the river and the moat but was obviously confused by this statement.

'What I mean is,' the man said with unpleasant glee, 'that all boats are the king's boat.'

No, still More didn't get it.

'That boat that you think is yours?'

More nodded.

'It isn't. It's the king's.'

'He stole it?' More asked in horror.

'No, of course he didn't steal it. It's his by right. Right of conquest. Everything is his by right of conquest. This land and all the things in it.'

No one had a reply to this comprehensive summary of the state of affairs.

The Norman, who had been standing very straight indeed, now straightened himself even further. 'It's a good job I got here, I tell you. Lax. The whole place had become lax. Need some good order, we do. That's what I do.' He leaned close to More. 'I bring good order.'

'That's good,' More said.

'It certainly is. So, we need to be clear that you don't have a boat, the king has a boat.'

More didn't seem too concerned about this. He looked down at his craft. 'As the king's not using it, can I just take my friends up the river?'

'It is rather urgent,' Hermitage put in, thinking it might be helpful.

The Norman now seemed aghast at a talking monk.

'Up the king's river?' The Norman asked.

'That's the one,' More confirmed.

'Of course you can.'

Hermitage breathed a sigh of relief.

'Just show me your guarant and off you go.' The Norman's accent rendered it unclear what exactly he was asking More to show him. It didn't sound very nice, whatever it was.

'My warren?' More asked.

'Guarant,' the Norman specified. 'Gua-rant. Your guarant from the king.'

More and Wat looked to Hermitage to see if he could unravel this.

'Wuarant?' Hermitage tried. He thought about it for a moment. 'Oh,' he had it now. 'A guarant. A protection, if you like. The king's protection, presumably, to allow you to move on the river without hindrance.'

The Norman did not look happy that these stupid Saxons couldn't even understand plain language.

'Sorry,' Hermitage apologised. 'To us, it sounded a bit like warrant, and we've never heard of a warrant.'

The Norman ground his teeth in More's direction. 'Your king's warrant to be using his boat on his river.' His glare now dared Hermitage to criticise any more of his words.

Hermitage didn't dare.

'I naturally assumed that you had a warrant. Otherwise, what would you be doing even thinking of getting on his boat?' The way the Norman said this made it quite clear that he knew More didn't have a warrant and was quite looking forward to having it confirmed.

'I really don't know what's become of the place,' the Norman mused for no obviously good reason. 'Saxons wandering about all over the place doing what they like without a warrant in sight. I'm not surprised this country is in such a mess.'

Hermitage thought that it had got a lot messier when the Normans came over and started killing people.

Wat had done very well to contain himself through all this but was running out of patience. 'We've got to get up the river. Quickly,' he insisted.

'Go as quick as you like, once I've seen the warrant.'

Wat seemed to gird himself up for an assault on a very neat and well-ordered Norman. Hermitage thought it was a fight he would lose, which would only make things worse.

'I've got a warrant,' More said brightly.

'Really?' The Norman didn't believe this.

'That's right. It's in me boat. Shall we go and get it?'

'No, we shall not go and get it. You will go and get it while these two stay here.'

More shrugged that this wasn't a problem and skipped off down to his boat.

Hermitage only hoped that the boatman wouldn't now give them all a cheery wave as he rowed away.

Very surprisingly, More delved into the boat obviously looking for something.

'Aha,' he called. 'Here it is.' He held a piece of parchment up and returned to the Norman.

Hermitage gaped at the material. Surely, More was not a completely legitimate ferryman? How could that be? The fellow was a mad rogue. Most of the boats he'd ever possessed had been stolen from someone else.

He appeared before the Norman and presented the parchment.

The man held it before his eyes and considered.

Hermitage had every confidence that this was not a warrant from King William for the operation of a boat on the Thames. All he could hope was that the Norman couldn't read.

The Norman could. 'This is a warrant to hold a goose fair on Blackheath common the third Thursday of October.'

More nodded as if that was exactly what had been asked for.

'And it expired ten years ago.'

'Still a warrant,' More argued.

'But the wrong one.' The Norman seemed to grow in stature as he fed off the naked error laid out before him. 'No warrant, no boat, no river.'

'We have got to go.' Wat stepped forward. 'Our friend is in danger on the river. We must rescue her.'

The Norman considered this. 'Swimming in the king's river without a warrant? What does she think she's up to? She's not fishing, is she? That's a very serious offence.'

'She's not swimming in it or fishing in it,' Wat snapped. He looked at the Norman and seemed to be considering his options. 'She was taken by someone.'

'Oh yes?' the Norman clearly didn't believe this.

'Someone who didn't have a warrant for taking people.'

The Norman frowned.

'We could get after them and bring them back.'

The Norman seemed a bit confused by this latest development and had no immediate answer.

Hermitage wondered if it was worth him speaking up. Of course it was. Cwen had been taken. If ever there was a time for speaking up, this was it.

He cleared his throat. 'I am Brother Hermitage.' He gave a short bow.

The Norman considered him. 'That's a stupid name for a monk.'

'It is unusual, I grant. But there you have it.'

'Is that it?' The Norman asked in some puzzlement. 'Is it supposed to help?'

'Brother Hermitage.'

'Yes, you said that.'

'Sorry,' Hermitage apologised. He shouldn't have so much pride as to think that everyone would know who he was. 'I am Brother Hermitage who was, until recently, King William's Investigator.'

The Norman scowled.

'From vestigo, vestigare, to track. I investigated murders for the king.'

'And Le Pedvin,' Wat put in helpfully.

The Norman stroked his chin as he thought about this. 'That's extremely interesting,' he said.

'Isn't it,' Hermitage agreed. 'So, if we could get on the boat we'd be very grateful as it is very urgent.'

'Used to be the King's Investigator, you say.'

'That's right.'

'But not anymore.'

'Well, no.'

'And who is now?'

'Oh, erm, a fellow called Nicodemus.'

'Nicodemus, I see.'

'Yes.'

'Well, there you are then,' the Norman said brightly.

Hermitage smiled.

'If this Nicodemus wants to come and use the boat, he's very welcome. As for you? Clear off.'

'Look.' Wat had had enough and strode forward, clearly intent on either going straight past the Norman or straight through him.

The Norman raised his palm, using it to warn Wat against coming any closer. When Wat did get closer, he turned his palm to a fist and used it to punch Wat hard in the face.

'I say,' Hermitage objected as Wat sat hard down on the ground.

'Oh, bloody hell,' Wat complained as he held his face.

The Norman didn't seem concerned that this was anything other than routine warrant enforcement. He stepped over and bent at the waist to look down on Wat. 'No warrant, no boat. If you want to go and get this Nicodemus to authorise a warrant, I'm sure that would be fine. Until then you keep away from the boat or I'll keep hitting you.'

Wat could only nod up at the large man.

The Norman stood and looked around. 'You!' he called to a guard who was loitering by the bridge over the moat.

The guard looked over with little interest, seemed to recognise who had called him and quickly hurried over.

If the other Normans were nervous of this man, he must be trouble.

'Yes, sir?' the guard asked.

'Stand up straight, for God's sake.'

The soldier tried to stand up straight.

'Hopeless,' his commander commented. 'And when you get off duty, I want everything cleaned.' He waved a disgusted hand up and down the soldier's appearance.

The soldier looked, as if trying to find anything that wasn't already spotless. There were many things, even to Hermitage's eye.

'These Saxons here,' he nodded towards the three of them, 'are trying to get on that boat.' He moved his nod to the boat. 'If they try again, hang them.'

'Yes, sir,' the soldier sounded full of enthusiasm for his task.

The neat Norman gave them all one last scowl before he strode off in good order, probably to shout at some more Saxons.

Once he had gone, the Norman soldier considered his charges. 'Just clear off,' he suggested quite kindly. 'Marcus is completely mad. Keep out of his way. We all do. When we can.' He turned to trudge back towards the bridge.

As he did so, he called back over his shoulder. 'Don't go near the boat,' he said persuasively. 'If you do, I will have to hang you, otherwise, there'll be hell to pay.'

Wat got up off the floor and brushed himself down as best he could. He rubbed his face and moved his jaw about, checking that it still worked. 'I know William's called the bastard,' he said. 'I didn't realise the rest were as well.'

'He's new,' More commented brightly.

'And he seems to be in charge,' Hermitage said with some despair. 'What do we do now?'

'Is there another boat?' Wat asked More.

'Oh, there's lots of boats.' The More nod and grin did their nodding and grinning.

'Good.'

'But not here.'

'Not here?'

'They wouldn't be any good over here, would they?'

'Why not?'

'People might not get in my boat if there was a choice,' More explained.

'Of course they wouldn't,' Wat agreed reluctantly.

They all looked around as if another boat would suddenly appear to them. There was a nice looking one on the other side of the moat but it was a nice Norman-looking one. Perhaps not for them.

'We go over the bridge and get another boat?' Hermitage suggested. He held an arm out towards London Bridge; the London Bridge swarming with Normans, either crossing it very carefully or directing the Saxons who were repairing it.

'I don't think so,' Wat said. 'Look.'

They looked over and there was the Norman, Marcus, talking to everyone who wanted to go over the bridge; well, every Saxon. Two of them had already received Marcus's explanation of the new rules and were sitting on the ground holding their faces.

'I don't suppose you have a warrant to cross the bridge?' Wat asked More hopelessly.

More held out his crumpled warrant.

'We haven't even got a goose.' Wat sighed. 'We'll just have to walk,' he said. We might still catch up. We don't know how far they're going.

'We need to track them on the water,' More said.

'You can't track things on water.' Hermitage said this very slowly as he wasn't actually sure what More could do.

'Oh, you can,' More assured him. 'And we need to know where their boat went. Can't track that on land.'

'Right,' Wat said with obvious exasperation. 'We need a warrant, then.'

'From Nicodemus?' Hermitage felt pale at the idea. 'I don't think he'd want to help us.'

'He might,' Wat suggested. 'He probably doesn't even know he has the power to issue warrants. He could be quite pleased.'

'I don't know,' Hermitage hesitated.

'Two more options,' Wat said. 'One, go and ask the king directly.'

Hermitage didn't like the sound of that.

'Two, you forge one.'

'Forge one?'

'You know, make one.'

'I know what forge means.'

'And you can write nicely. Should be the job of a few moments.'

'And I know what happens to people who forge king's warrants.'

'Do you?'

'Well, no, but I can imagine. I further suspect that the only thing that would make Marcus happier than a man with no warrant would be a man with a forgery.'

'Nicodemus it is then,' Wat said. 'After all, he does owe you a favour.'

Caput VII: Grabbed by The

'**I**f you don't untie me I shall come over there and rip your ears off,' Cwen snarled from her seat at the back of the boat, not really caring how she was going to achieve this feat.

'It's a tempting offer,' Peter replied languidly, 'but I think I'll decline.

'Let me go,' Cwen ordered at the top of her voice.

'That's another no,' Peter replied. 'I'll tell you what, if you don't stop shouting, I'll come over there and put a rag in your mouth. How's that?' He searched around the bottom of the boat. 'Here we are. This one looks quite revolting, would that do?'

Cwen looked at the really disgusting thing Peter was holding in his hand, holding quite gingerly, and decided that she'd rather not.

'What are you doing?' she asked quite quietly instead.

'As you can see, we have taken you.'

'What for?'

'Great purposes.'

'Great purposes?'

'That's it.'

'What great purposes?'

'Our great purposes. Ones we're not going to share with you right now, so I should save your breath.'

Cwen had plenty of breath.

'Is this because Hermitage found you out? Is that it? Revenge? Pathetic.'

'Oh, nothing so mundane, I assure you.'

She wriggled against her bonds some more. Unfortunately, they were very good bonds and didn't respond to wriggling.

'You can't just take people from their beds at night.'

Peter made a point of looking around the river, considering the boat with her tied up in it, and shrugged that Cwen already had her answer to that.

'What possible use am I going to be? Hermitage is the King's Investigator.' She paused. 'Was the King's Investigator.'

'Was?' Peter asked.

'After you left,' Cwen explained. 'Or rather, after you ran away having been discovered as a murderer, Hermitage got the king to take the job away. He gave it to Nicodemus.'

Peter only raised his eyebrows in vague interest at this development.

'So taking me is not going to get you to the King's Investigator, is it?'

Peter looked completely unconcerned about that, so Cwen assumed it couldn't be the reason. What other reason there was, she had no idea.

'Is this another killer?' She nodded towards the messenger who was propelling the boat along the river.

'Just an associate,' Peter replied.

'Another one?' Cwen asked sarcastically. 'Well, it would take three of you to capture one sleeping woman, wouldn't it?'

'Our companion was only doing his duty in helping us,' Peter said harshly. 'There was no call to do that to him.'

'I tend not to be cooperative with people who are dragging me through the woods. Or who keep me in their boat.' She kicked and struggled some more.

'There's no point fighting it. You are captured.'

'You can't do it.'

'You keep saying that,' Peter commented. 'And I don't

know why. We already have.'

'Where are you taking me?'

'Up the river.'

'Obviously. I was thinking of somewhere more specific?'

'I'm sure you were. And you will find out when we get there. We're hardly going to reveal everything to you now, are we?' Peter seemed to be thinking hard about her as he considered his prisoner.

'If I'd been awake, you'd never have got me.'

'Good job you were asleep then.'

'Why not Hermitage, or Wat? They're more important than me.' Cwen didn't like saying these words. It sounded as if she would rather they had been captured than her, which was not the case. She was actually grateful that the other two were still free - as far as she knew.

It also sounded as if she thought they were more important than her; which they quite obviously weren't.

'Or have you got them in another boat?'

'Not at all,' Peter assured her. 'They are exactly where we left them.'

'You didn't!' Cwen was horrified at what might have been done. After all, Peter was a known killer.

'No, of course not. We're not savages. We simply left them behind. I'm sure they'll be fine.'

'They'll come after me, you do know that.'

Peter waved that away. 'It could be too late by then.'

'Too late?' Now Cwen swallowed at the thought of the fate that might be in store for her.

'Why take me away to kill me?'

'Oh, for heaven's sake, why do you think everyone wants to kill someone?'

'You did.'

'That was a revolting Norman,' Peter said. 'You'd be surprised the number of people who said they were quite pleased that someone had done it at last.'

'Then I don't understand,' Cwen complained. 'What the devil is it you think you're going to achieve?'

Peter looked at her very intently. 'We are going to achieve the known world.'

The messenger gave him a warning glance, but Peter seemed happy to continue.

'And you can be part of it.'

'I don't think I want to be part of any world that takes women from their beds and ties them up in boats.'

'We don't do that all the time,' Peter pointed out wearily. 'Consider this a special occasion.'

'Charmed, I'm sure.'

'You could be.'

'What?' Cwen asked this question much more cautiously, now having even more horrible ideas about why she might have been taken.

'Oh, nothing like that,' Peter rebuked. 'Honestly, you really do think the worst, don't you?'

'Funny that,' Cwen commented. 'I'm not normally like this when I'm taken from my bed and tied up in a boat.'

'Think of this as an opportunity,' Peter said as the messenger paddled on.

'An opportunity. Silly me. There I was thinking I'd been captured. I don't know what put that idea in my head.'

'We had to act.'

'If only you'd woken me and asked if I'd like to be tied up in your boat, I could have thought about it.'

'Time is not on our side.'

'It's not the only one.'

'We had to take you. And when you find out what this is all about, you will see that it is for the best.'

'I doubt that.' Cwen struggled once more.

'You are a strong woman.'

'That I am. Untie me and I can show you how strong.'

'And you despise the invaders.'

Cwen stopped struggling and gave Peter a narrow gaze.

'I could see that from the beginning. Of the three of you, there is only one who would truly stand up and fight.'

Cwen had to admit that was true.

'That monk would not lift a hand. A word, a book, yes. But what use are those?'

'You're a monk,' Cwen pointed out, looking his habit up and down.

'Some of us are more.., what can we say, active than others?'

'Active in killing people?'

'When necessity calls. And Wat the Weaver?' Peter sounded very scornful. 'I think we all know where Wat the Weaver's interests lie.'

'He doesn't do tapestries like that anymore.'

'I mean his interests lie exclusively with himself.'

'Oh, right, yes.' Cwen nodded that this was a pretty accurate summary. 'So, you're fighting the Normans.'

'As you pointed out yourself, I did kill one.'

'Are any monks supposed to do that? Active or not?'

'Can we forget about being a monk?' Peter was starting to sound frustrated. 'The point is I was in a position to do some damage to the invaders' plans when your Brother Hermitage ruined everything.'

'Only because you were spreading the word that he'd killed Malf. You were trying to get him out of the way so that you could take his place. Except you didn't have a clue what you were doing.'

'How little you understand,' Peter condescended.

'Oh, I understand a lot. Hermitage, Wat and I have dealt with more murders than wriggles on an eel. We can recognise an idiot when we see one.

'It's just as Hermitage said; you saw how nice and comfortable it could be working for William, so you abandoned your principles for a quiet life. Damage the invaders' plans? Pah! You wanted to join in.'

Peter shook his head. 'You could not be further from the truth. Brother Hermitage was the King's Investigator. What am I supposed to think of someone who is appointed by the Norman? He could have been a close ally of William. But this is all beside the point. I don't know if I can really trust you.'

'Untie me and I'll show you.'

'Now is not the time. You could be in league with the Normans, like your monk. This could be deceit on your part and we are already taking a risk.'

'You will be when I get these ropes off.'

'I think you could have been put here by the enemy simply to lure us into taking you. Then we find that you are the traitor.'

'You think too much,' Cwen replied fiercely. 'And not very well.'

Peter gave her more appraisal as if he might be able to see her intentions.

'And it's hardly very courageous, is it?' Cwen said. 'Capturing sleeping women and poisoning a Norman. Stand up and stab them, that's the way to do it, not sneak around putting things in their food.'

Peter nodded at this. 'Which is why you will come to see that we have done the right thing.'

'You've taken me away against my will so that I can fight the Normans with you?'

Peter didn't answer but his expression said that she was not far from the truth.

'Listen,' she said. 'If King Harold had come back and sent you with a personal invitation, I wouldn't believe it. You're the trouble here. You betrayed the Saxons who were supporting you. You tried to get Hermitage executed for something he didn't do, and you tried to get his job. It's not a very nice picture. And that's if we ignore taking me from my bed.'

'There are movements greater than you or I,' Peter said portentously.

'I could give you a great movement if you let me. You seriously think that taking me like this is going to persuade me to join you?'

'Not at all. This is only the first step. You will see what is behind our actions. That will persuade you.'

'You've got me all wrong if you think I'd turn against my friends.'

'The Normans are not your friends.'

'Well, no, but Hermitage and Wat are. I'm not leaving them behind.'

'We have no interest in them.'

'You will have when they come to get me.'

'I really don't think they're the type,' Peter scoffed.

'Then you've got them all wrong as well. There is no way they're going to find I've gone and not do something about it.'

'The Normans are starting to exert their authority,' Peter said. 'People like Wat and Hermitage will find that their freedom to do what they want is severely curtailed. They can't just go wandering around the country doing what they want any more. There are new rules. And new Normans to enforce them. And you said yourself, Brother Hermitage is no longer the King's Investigator. He's just one more Saxon monk. I think you'll find Saxon monks don't have much influence anymore.'

'They'll find a way.'

'One weaver and one monk?'

'You'd be surprised what we've managed between us.'

'They won't even know where you've gone, anyway. You could be anywhere. Where will they start?'

Cwen gave Peter a smile, which he obviously found somewhat disconcerting.

'They'll probably start with my boots,' she said.

Peter looked at her feet. 'What boots?'

'My precious boots. They know I never go anywhere without them.'

'And you wear them in bed, do you?'

'When that bed is next to the wall of a Norman fortress, yes.'

'And where are they now?'

'I left them by the river. Slipped them off while you two were trying to sort out the boat between you, which I have to say you're not very good at either. Wat and Hermitage will know that I'd never be parted from my boots and when they find them by the water, they'll know which way I've gone.'

'Two boots by a big river?' Peter was unconvinced.

'Two boots at the end of the wreckage of a trail you left dragging me from the hut. It's all about tracking and clues, you see. But then you've got no idea how to investigate anything. You couldn't find your way to the bottom of your own bottom.'

Peter tried to dismiss this. 'So they know you've gone on the river? It's a big river. You could still be anywhere.'

'So many killers have made the same mistake over the years,' Cwen mused. 'Underestimating Hermitage. He works things out. I still don't really know how he does it. Right now, I bet he's saying, aha, I know where Cwen's gone.'

'Let him know. A monk and weaver will not divert us.'

'Ah, but Wat has something that can disrupt your stupid plan, whatever it is.'

'Oh, yes? And what's that, wool? Ha, ha.'

'No,' Cwen said plainly. 'Money.'

'Money?'

'That's it. He has money. Lots of it. You'd be amazed the things people will do for some of his money. Normans, Saxons, Vikings. Betray their own mothers, most of them.'

Peter did seem a little worried about this.

'The Normans may be in charge now and are stopping people going about their business, but slip a coin from Wat into their hands and they're only too happy to help.' She could see that this was having an effect on Peter.

'I imagine even some of your own closest and dearest companions would sell you for half of one of his purses.'

Peter said nothing.

'They're coming, whether you like it or not,' Cwen crowed rather. 'And when they do, I'd rather not be in your shoes.' She glanced at his feet. 'They're too big for me anyway.'

Caput VIII: Visiting The Normans

'I've got money,' Wat said holding out a purse to the Norman at the fortress entrance.

'I don't care if you've got King Harold's eyeball on a stick, you're not coming in.'

Hermitage, Wat and More wisely decided that trying to get More himself into the Tower of London was probably more trouble than it was worth. He could wait out of sight near the boat and be ready for when they came back with their warrant.

Most of all, he needed to keep out of sight of Marcus.

Despite their careful planning, they were still having trouble getting in through the gate.

'As I said, we need to see Nicodemus,' Hermitage repeated politely. 'The King's Investigator.'

'And as I said,' the guard repeated. 'I've never heard of him.'

'What about Le Pedvin?' Wat suggested. 'Heard of him?'

'Of course.' The guard's confidence did sag under the weight of that name.

'Go and tell him that Brother Hermitage needs to see him.'

The guard gave a hard and sharp laugh at that. 'Are you mad? Me? Go and speak to Lord Le Pedvin? About two mangy Saxons?'

'I am not mangy,' Wat protested. 'Lord Le Pedvin knows us well. Brother Hermitage here used to the King's investigator himself.'

'And I used to be in charge of the cart workshop.'

'Eh, what? What does that have to do with anything?' Wat was confused and becoming increasingly irritated.

The guard, meanwhile, was recalling happier days. 'Lovely

workshop full of carpenters and wheelwrights, it was. All I had to do was get the carts in, get the work done and send them out again.'

'Er.., very nice, I'm sure.'

'It was. But then William wants several carts all done at once for some big journey he's planning. Well, we don't have the capacity, do we?'

'No?' Wat asked with a bemused look at Hermitage.

'No, that's right. But does the Duke want to hear that? No, of course he doesn't. Just get the carts ready on time, he says. I tried to tell him, but he wouldn't listen.'

'And did you get the carts ready on time?' Hermitage couldn't help but be intrigued.

'In a manner of speaking. But one little mishap with a wheel and it's no more workshop for me.'

Hermitage and Wat nodded with what sympathy they could raise for the guard who was being so difficult.

'A wheel fell off,' Wat concluded.

'It did. But then wheels fall off carts all the time, don't they?'

'Not when they've just come out of William's cart workshop, I imagine,' Wat speculated.

'It wasn't the wheel falling off, it was where it went.'

'Where it went?'

'How can I be held responsible for a wheel rolling down a hill? I mean, hills are the work of God, aren't they?' He seemed to be looking to Hermitage for confirmation of this.

Hermitage could only move his head around in a non-committal sort of way.

'It was an act of God.' The guard sounded as if he was reciting an old argument; an unsuccessful one.

Wat just raised his eyebrows to get the rest of the tale.

'And a dog.'

'A dog?' Now Hermitage was completely lost.

'An act of God and the act of a dog. If William's favourite hound hadn't gone chasing after the wheel the accident wouldn't have happened. It was his fault for not controlling his dog.'

'The dog caught the wheel.' Wat concluded.

'That it did. Then it tried to bite it.'

'I see. Being a hunting hound, I suppose it would.'

'And once it had hold of the thing, it wasn't going to let go.'

'Quite.'

'But the wheel didn't know it had a dog holding on. It just kept going.'

'Good for the wheel, not so good for the dog.'

'That's right. Round and round it went. The dog was howling and growling at the same time.'

'Must have been a well-made wheel.' Wat nodded.

'Certainly was. But the Duke wasn't so interested in that.'

'And when the wheel eventually came to a halt, the dog was no more?'

'Oh, no. It was a bit giddy, that's all. Couldn't stand up straight, or know where it was trying to go.'

There was a horrible pause.

'Which is when the wheel fell on it.'

Wat rubbed a hand over his face. 'So William dismissed you.'

The guard grunted acknowledgement. 'And the dog hates me now as well.'

They had no sympathy to offer.

'And that's how come I end up in this horrible place.'

'Guarding William's tower.'

'England,' the guard specified with a shiver.

Wat was trying extremely hard to maintain his calm. 'I can't immediately see what this has to do with us?'

'It's him,' the guard nodded at Hermitage. 'If he used to be the King's Investigator but isn't any more, he must have done something horribly wrong. Take some advice from me and keep your head down. If they see you again, it only makes things worse.'

'It's nothing like that, I assure you,' Hermitage said. 'I did lots of investigations for the king, but my time was over and Nicodemus took my place. I just need to have a word with him about an, erm, investigation.'

'Not past me, you don't.'

'And you won't even take money?' Wat checked.

'There's a new captain arrived from Normandy,' the guard explained. 'Name of Marcus.'

'We've met him.'

'Then you know why I'm not taking any money. I don't actually know what job is worse than this one, but I'm not going to find out.'

'Could you just send word to Nicodemus that we're here?'

The guard shook his head. 'Guard, they told me. Didn't say anything about sending word. Especially to people I've never heard of.'

Wat sighed and drew Hermitage away slightly.

'We're not getting anywhere with this one.'

Hermitage could only agree. Having spent so much effort trying to get away from the king and his tower, he felt somewhat bemused that he was now trying to get back in again.

Wat whispered quietly. 'I don't suppose we should mention the dead Norman?' He held up Cwen's boots that he was now carrying as if they were precious cargo.

Hermitage was very worried by that suggestion. 'I don't think so. Imagine the trouble there would be. They probably would take us into the tower and then never let us out again.'

'Hm,' Wat had to agree with that. He snapped his fingers. 'John.'

'John?'

'Le Pedvin's son, John. We can ask to speak to him.'

Hermitage was encouraged by that idea. John had been positively helpful; not like a Norman at all.

They returned to the guard. 'Can you let John know that we're here then?'

'John? John who? There's lots of Johns.'

'John, the son of Le Pedvin.'

'Oh, John!' The guard seemed pleased to mention the name. 'You know John?'

'Yes, yes we do.'

'Well, why didn't you say so in the first place? He stood aside and beckoned them welcome. 'Any friend of John's.'

Wat and Hermitage walked past the guard cautiously, half-expecting him to call them back.

Wat sagged as he walked. 'And we had to put up with all that nonsense about the dog.'

Hermitage scanned the inside of the fortress grounds, hardly expecting to simply spot Nicodemus wandering about. Activity was bustling all around them as people commenced the work of the day, dawn still being only a recent prompt to get on with things. Normans were shouting, Saxons were complaining, and the few animals about took no notice of anything.

'Up to the keep?' Wat suggested, indicating the large wooden building on top of the hill towards the back of the compound.

'Oh,' Hermitage hadn't really thought that far. The keep had William and Le Pedvin in it. The William whose service he had only just managed to escape. If the king saw him back again so soon, he'd wonder what was going on. He might even be tempted to give Hermitage his old job back, and that would never do.

'Nicodemus will probably be in there,' Wat said. 'You know, nice and close to the king, just to show how important he is.

'I'm not sure,' Hermitage said in a rare moment of insight. 'Being near to the king is a pretty horrible experience. He gets you to do things. I suspect Nicodemus doesn't want to be doing things. He just wants to have a title and some authority.'

'He could probably order people about more effectively from in there. And we do need our warrant so that we can find Cwen.' Wat reminded him of the urgency of their mission.

'Of course. You're quite right. We must do whatever is necessary.' Hermitage took a breath and step towards the keep.

'Hello,' a piercing voice rattled into their heads and they turned quickly.

'More!' Wat hissed 'What the devil are you doing here? We told you to wait by the boat.'

'And I did,' More nodded that he had complied completely with his instructions. 'But then cousin More went by and asked if I'd like to come in.'

'Through the secret passage down by the river.' Wat sighed at his own stupidity at trying to get in through the front door.

'Oh no,' More said. 'Tide's too high. We came in through

the hole at the back.' He gestured to where the walls of the stronghold were still being built.

'Well, you're here now.' Wat tried to ignore the complete waste of time they'd just had. 'We need to find Nicodemus.'

More looked around the place, screwing his eyes up as if this would make spotting Nicodemus easier. 'Can't see him,' he reported.

'We know that,' Wat snapped. 'That's why we're going to the keep.'

More looked up at the keep. 'I wouldn't if I were you.'

'We don't have much choice. We need our warrant.'

'Oh yes,' More nodded as if he only now remembered what they were doing here. 'Why don't we ask a More?' he suggested.

'A More?'

'Yis. There's always one nearby.' He nodded over towards a crowd of Saxons who didn't appear to be doing anything constructive. In the middle of this band, they saw nothing more than a grey beard nodding up and down.

'A More,' Wat accepted.

'That's right.'

'Any More in particular?'

'Doesn't matter really.' He beckoned that this new More should come over and join them.

Disturbed. That was the only word Hermitage felt appropriate as he saw this new More come over. And it was the perfect word. To see another version of More walking towards the first was simply disturbing. It wasn't like looking in a glass, there were differences between the two men, but equally, the differences were not as different as seemed quite natural.

'Hello More,' the new More squeaked.

'Is this a More we've met before or yet another one?' Wat checked.

'This is More of Lambehitha.'

More of Lambehitha gave them all the More nod.

'Lambehitha?' Wat checked

'Far off to the west,' More gave the land a mysterious aura.

Hermitage didn't like to point out that it wasn't that far off to the west. And the Normans, who couldn't manage the Saxon names, had started calling it Lambeth anyway.

'And he knows where Nicodemus is?'

'He knows where everyone is, don't you?'

The beards on the two Mores seemed to exchange their own communications during the nodding that went on.

'I know there's a lot of Mores,' Wat complained quietly. 'But one of each type would be best.'

'Oh,' More comforted him. 'More and I are hardly related at all. Very distant cousins, we are.'

Wat considered them both. 'I think you might want a word with Mummy More about that. Now, Nicodemus.'

'Oh, yis,' the new More grinned his grin. 'He was heading for the guardhouse. Looking for John, they say.'

'You do know who Nicodemus is?' Wat checked carefully.

'Oh yis,' More Lambehitha confirmed. 'Newly appointed King's Investigator. Previously Bishop's amanuensis from Lincoln. Accompanied by Prior Athan of De'Ath's Dingle, but then you'd know all about that, Brother Hermitage.' The new More acknowledged Hermitage's past. 'Rumour is that he originally came from York and was the son of a pig drover.'

Wat gaped. 'How do you know all this?'

'I keep my ear to the ground.'

Wat shook his head in bemused amazement.

'And the rest I make up,' More grinned and nodded.

'Right,' Wat said. 'To the guardhouse. Thank you More.'

Both he and Hermitage gave More Lambehitha a modest bow of the head. When they looked up there was only the one More left, still grinning at them.

Hermitage's disturbance told him not to enquire too far into where the other one had gone or how he had done it so quickly.

It was only a short step to the guardhouse, which was, quite understandably, surrounded by guards.

'I think I'll wait outside,' More said.

'Good idea,' Wat agreed. He whispered to Hermitage. 'Just look confident.'

Wat should know that was a ridiculous thing to suggest. Hermitage simply tried to freeze all expression from his face in the hope that that was what confidence looked like.

'What do you want?' One gruff guard demanded as they drew near.

'John,' Wat replied with equal gruffness. 'Or Nicodemus, whichever comes first.'

That seemed to soften the guard's demeanour and he nodded that they could enter the simple building.

Ducking their heads under the low entrance, they walked into a simple but very dark room. Guards lounged here and there, and the smell of cooking wafted about, largely defeated by the smell of lounging guards, which wafted with much more strength.

Hermitage brightened as he saw John facing them. Two dark shapes had their backs to the door and were engaged in conversation with the Norman.

John raised his eyes and smiled at the sight of the two of them.

The other two turned.

'Well, well, well. If it isn't Brother Hermitage,' said Athan. 'Brother Hermitage the king's nothing at all. We've been looking for you.'

Caput IX: Go West

'**W**ill you stop struggling,' Peter was getting quite cross with his captive. He knew that capturing people was not a trouble-free process, but you would think once the capturing had been done, things would calm down a bit.

'Absolutely not,' his captive snapped back as she wriggled yet more.

'Look,' Peter explained. 'There's no point being difficult now is there? We're nearly at our destination and we'll be getting off the boat.' His tone darkened. 'I wouldn't want you to fall off and drown, or anything.'

Cwen simply glared.

'It would be so difficult to explain,' Peter said, as if her drowning would only be a minor inconvenience.

'You're going to have to take these ropes off sometime.'

'I prefer you with them on, but when we arrive I am sure they will be removed.'

Cwen had to accept that she was not going to escape her bonds by simply being angry with them or the people who had put them on. It was quite a new experience for her, as being angry with things usually made them go away.

'And where is it that we are arriving?'

'Our destination.'

'Very informative.' Cwen looked around the waters of the river. The north and south banks were still some way off, although they were a lot closer to the north. 'We've left Westminster behind, so, if there's a village along here on the north, I'd say it might be Chelchea?'

If Cwen had hoped that this information would disturb Peter, she was disappointed.

'Well-off little village, Chelchea,' Cwen commented. 'I think we've done tapestry business down this way.'

'How lovely for you.' Peter and the messenger exchanged nods and the boat was turned towards the shore.

'People there might know me,' Cwen went on. 'And wonder why I'm arriving tied up on a boat. Heaven forfend that they should try to rescue me and, I don't know, kill you? That would never do.'

Peter sighed heavily. 'Chelchea is our outpost, no one is going to rescue you. We are coming to the end of your journey now and the situation will be explained to you by people who are more important than you or I.'

'I imagine people more important than you are pretty easy to find.'

'Before we go our separate ways, can I just say what a horrible experience this has been?'

Cwen was a bit surprised by that.

'I've done all sorts for our cause, as you well know. Capturing you and bringing you here will go down as one of the worst.'

'I'm glad you think so.'

'How those other two put up with you, I will never know. If I were them, I'd have tied you up with some rocks and thrown you in the river long ago.'

'Oh, really?' Cwen's anger was getting up again.

'You were captured and tied up and put in a boat. I can understand that was unpleasant and unexpected, but did you have to go on and on about it for the entire journey? Most people, when they're captured, have a bit of a struggle and then settle down until they can do something about it.'

'I'll remember that when this all goes wrong and we've got you captured.'

'You've done nothing but complain and issue threats and demands. And you're tied up!' Peter seemed to be getting quite excited.

'I am sorry I've been such a difficult prisoner,' Cwen sneered.

'I tell you this for good reason,' Peter said fiercely. 'We're going to get off the boat in a moment or two and you might think of making an escape attempt of some sort.'

Cwen said nothing, but escape was her main idea at the moment.

'If I have to hit you on the back of the head with an oar, or simply kill you, I will happily explain to my masters that it all went horribly wrong and I'm terribly sorry.'

Cwen's glare did not back down in the face of this threat.

'And that will be that,' Peter concluded. 'I shall get on with my life, you won't. Our plans may be diverted, but quite frankly, it'll be worth it.' He gave Cwen a very hard look.

At that moment, the boat gently nudged the shore and the messenger climbed forward to secure it to a post.

They had come round a corner of the riverbank and arrived at a well-developed landing spot. The bank here was chalky, rather than the ubiquitous Thames mud, and several boats were pulled up.

A number of people were going about their business, none of whom paid any attention to the vessel that had just arrived with a woman tied up in it.

'I shall tell them that we have arrived,' the messenger called as he walked up the shoreline, leaving the prisoner in Peter's care.

Cwen scowled. It seemed that she had come to the heart of the enemy, whoever that enemy was. If she did manage to run off, she'd likely be quickly captured.

She still thought that this was Peter's revenge for their exposing him. But if that were the case, he was being very well organised about it.

What else could it be? He'd talked about fighting the Normans, which she was all for, obviously, but this was not the way to recruit to the cause.

Peter took Cwen by the wrists and hauled her up from her seat.

She stumbled down the boat and tripped as she climbed over the bulwark and onto the shore.

Peter issued a word of caution. 'And don't even suggest I untie you because you can't walk with your hands tied. I'm not stupid.'

'Can I disagree?' Cwen asked, mid-trip. As she straightened herself up, she clenched both fists together and swung them into Peter's habit.

The spot at which she swung them was carefully selected and Peter was unable to even cry out. The pain that coursed through him robbed him of all power and demanded that he simply clutch the damaged region and collapse onto the floor, screwing himself up into a ball.

All sorts of thoughts were rushing to get his attention, but the winner was the one that said if he relaxed any single one of his muscles right now, the pain would take over the rest of his body and never leave.

His mind even told him to stop breathing as it had a lot more important issues to deal with right now. He knew that when he did manage to produce a sound, it would be a high-pitched squeak of little use in summoning help.

The sound of Cwen crashing away reached his ears but prompted nothing but a measure of despair to go with his discomfort.

Footsteps did draw near and one of the fellows who had been tending his boat appeared in the periphery of Peter's vision.

His mind said, "get her" and he knew that his lips moved. Unfortunately, no sound emerged.

His attendant crouched down and said the words that come naturally on occasions like this but are seldom helpful.

'Are you all right?' the new arrival asked the monk who was doubled up in pain on the riverbank.

Peter did manage to move his head slightly from side to side to indicate that no, funnily enough, he was not all right. He tried to nod in the direction of Cwen's departure, but this was misinterpreted.

'Have you hurt your neck?'

Peter did now manage to groan, which was a help.

'She's caught him right where it hurts,' a knowledgeable female voice now spoke. She then shouted at Peter, as it is well known that injured people become suddenly deaf. 'I bet that's painful,' she imparted her knowledge of the subject.

'My Wilfrid got butted there by the goat once,' she informed what seemed to be a small crowd that had now gathered for whatever entertainment this was.

'He was never the same again,' she added somewhat wistfully.

'Get her,' Peter managed to croak.

'Don't look at me,' the woman protested. 'I'm not tending to that. Not with him a monk and all. It wouldn't be right.'

Peter now managed to get himself onto his hands and knees and his breath was starting to return in bursts. There was no way he was going to try and stand up yet. 'Get the woman who did this,' he panted.

The small crowd stood up straight from their

consideration of the prostrate monk.

'She's gone,' the woman reported. 'Can't say I blame her.'

'Get help, then,' Peter growled.

'Oh, it's Peter,' one of the men said. 'I didn't recognise him with his face all screwed up like that.'

'Who did you think it was?' Peter managed to sound angry. 'Get help now.'

One of the men scurried off.

'A poultice,' the woman said thoughtfully. 'That's what you need, a poultice.' She nodded to the crowd. 'I'm not putting it on though.'

. . .

Cwen was entirely satisfied with her escape. She was well aware that she may be captured again at any moment, but the escape itself had been very good indeed. Brother Peter would remember Cwen for the rest of his days. And for a very good reason.

With her captor well and truly incapacitated, she got into the undergrowth along the riverbank before the crowd had even gathered to share their gratitude that they weren't the ones who'd been hit like that.

Her hands were still tied though, and she needed some means of freeing herself. Naturally, she had no knife to hand; the one she normally slept with having been left behind. Perhaps there was some sharp rock she could rub the rope against.

She scoured her surroundings with little success. Loose bits of chalk were lying here and there, but they would crumble to dust.

There was no point trying to find someone who would

help. She was obviously in the midst of Peter's band, whoever they were, and would only be taken once more.

But she was a Saxon and they were Saxons. Someone would help, surely? It would only be natural to assume that the Normans had done this to her.

Whatever the true motivation behind Peter's actions at the Tower of London, she was sure that this was a case of simple revenge. If these people knew that she hated the Normans as much as they did, they would let her go.

They'd have no choice but to release her even if it did upset Peter's plans.

She would simply explain her position to whoever was in charge and things would be fine. Peter was the problem. He just needed to be ignored.

She worked her way on down the shore, heading east for no other reason than the undergrowth had been closer when the time came to run away from Peter.

She realised that if she went too far in this direction, she might bump into a Norman patrol and they would be most unlikely to help a tied-up Saxon.

As there was no obvious pursuit, she took a moment to stop and consider what she was doing. Heading back to Chelchea was no good. If the people there really were with Peter, she'd be going straight into the hands of the enemy.

Continuing east had the risk of the Normans, but at least it was the direction from which Wat and Hermitage would be coming; she had no doubt at all that they would be coming.

They would have found she was gone soon after dawn. Then they would have looked around and seen the trail leading away from her hut. She'd caused enough trouble for her captors that there was no way they could have moved discreetly.

Then they'd find her boots, and probably the stupid one who had been the third of Peter's band. She chortled as she thought about what she'd done to him.

They would have worked out that she'd been taken on the river and would have set off straight away. All they needed was a boat. And there was More, of course. Wat would have paid the fare and they could be on the river looking for her even now.

This train of thought convinced her to go down to the riverbank. She knew it was unlikely that Wat and Hermitage would be passing just at that moment, but she might see someone who would take her back towards London. She did think that a woman with her hands tied up, trying to wave down a passing boat might not have much success.

Pushing through the rough grasses and small shrubs, she pressed on in the direction of the river. Emerging by the side of the water she saw that this wasn't going to be quite so simple.

There was a good reason Chelchea had sprung up where it was; there was absolutely no way of getting down to a boat just here. The trees grew cheek by jowl with one another, and then there was about an eight-foot drop onto a bank of horribly soft-looking mud.

There was traffic on the river, but it was no good to Cwen as she couldn't make herself seen anyway. She turned back and set off east once more. If she and Wat and Hermitage passed one another on the way, they'd have to sort it out later.

It now felt even more urgent to get these ties off her hands.

Before she had pressed on more than a few paces, she came to a halt when she heard a voice. She crouched down and tried to see who was coming.

When she heard more voices and the tramping of many feet, she felt that her chances of remaining free were slight. This was clearly a patrol of some sort, Norman or Saxon, it probably didn't matter.

Now, through the gaps in the trees, she even caught sight of a shining helmet. Curse her luck. She lay down flat on the ground and just hoped that this force would not spot her.

A word was barked out that she couldn't understand and the tramping came to a stop.

Without looking up, she could tell that someone had appeared through the trees and was standing looking at her.

There was no point pretending anymore. She raised her head and considered the feet in front of her, which wore some rather odd-looking sandals. She looked higher and the view did not get any less odd.

She decided that all she could do was stand up and face her discoverer.

'Good Gods,' the soldier said. 'You're tied up.'

Cwen held her hands out to show that this was the case.

'There's no need to worry,' the man stepped forward and drew a short sword with which to cut the bonds. 'You're safe now.'

Caput X: Persuasion

'Aha,' Hermitage said, and not in the usual manner.

'Aha, indeed,' Athan smiled in that way he had; vaguely human. 'We were just talking about you.'

'Really?' Hermitage swallowed.

'Not in a good way,' Athan assured him.

'If it isn't the new King's Investigator,' Wat observed brightly.

Nicodemus and Athan frowned deeply at his exuberance.

'We were just talking about you as well,' Wat went on. 'And your new exalted status.'

Now Nicodemus and Athan actually looked a little worried.

'What do you want?' Nicodemus asked carefully.

'Nothing of significance,' Wat shrugged. 'We were talking to a new Norman captain, or something, fellow by the name of Marcus.'

John sighed.

'You know him?' Hermitage asked.

'Everyone knows Marcus,' John said wearily. 'Ranulph de Sauveloy has brought him over from his Normandy estates. Apparently, we all need someone who'll bring a bit of order to the place.'

'He seemed very ordered,' Wat agreed. 'And he sent us to see the king's own investigator, Nicodemus.' Wat even gave a little bow, which caused Nicodemus and Athan to take a step back, as if he were about to steal their legs.

'He sent you?' Clearly, Nicodemus did not believe this. 'I've only just been appointed. How did this Marcus know who I am?'

'Marcus knows everything,' John complained. 'And no one knows how.'

Still, Nicodemus was not convinced.

Wat continued. 'This Marcus said that you'd be the one to issue our warrant.'

'Your warrant?' Nicodemus could smell when he had an advantage over someone, and Wat was now the smelliest thing in the room. Not having a clue what that someone was talking about didn't mean you couldn't take advantage of them.

'That's the one,' Wat spoke as if this was nothing more than an irritating formality.

'I can issue your warrant? And what does this warrant do?'

'It's just a permission, that's all.'

Nicodemus seemed to grow in stature as he absorbed the fact that someone had to ask his permission for something. Permission frequently turned out to be a very profitable commodity.

'A permission for what, exactly?'

'We're leaving, yes?' Wat said with a smile.

Hermitage had no idea what was going on but knew enough to keep quiet. It was clear that the disappearance of Cwen was not going to get a mention.

'Possibly,' Athan said, which was a rather worrying development.

'Hermitage not being the King's Investigator anymore,' Wat bowed to Nicodemus again.

'Get on with it,' Nicodemus instructed.

'Apparently, according to this Marcus, we need one of these warrant things to go anywhere these days.'

'Sounds like Marcus,' John admitted.

'And as I said,' Nicodemus reminded them, 'this Marcus

doesn't know who I am.'

'But he knows about the King's Investigator. He said that the holder of that high position would be able to issue the warrant.'

Even Hermitage thought that Wat was laying it on a bit thick now.

'This warrant is going to give you permission to go home?' Nicodemus sounded as if he didn't believe such processes existed, but if they did, he quite liked the sound of them.

'That's it. In a nutshell,' Wat agreed.

Nicodemus considered for a moment. 'I'm not sure,' he said slowly.

'Not sure?' Wat's frustration was barely contained.

'Lord Le Pedvin has charged us with finding Peter,' Nicodemus explained.

'What's that got to do with anything?' Wat asked rather too quickly.

'You were among the last to see him. I'm not sure that having you going back to Derby will help in my, erm...,' he searched for the word.

'Investigation?' Hermitage offered.

'Just so. I don't think you should leave town at all.' Nicodemus had a little wallow in his authority.

'Oh, that is a shame,' Wat shook his head, as if only now being able to give Nicodemus some bad news.

'Why?'

'It's Cwen, you see.'

Nicodemus frowned. 'Yes, where is she? It usually takes the three of you to do anything at all.'

'She went on ahead.' Wat said.

'Without a warrant?' Athan asked with a sneer.

'She went early before we knew you needed a warrant.

She'll be well on her way by now. So, if we could have the warrant we can get after her.'

Athan now considered what Wat was trying to slide behind his back. 'What are you doing with her boots then?'

'Boots? Wat asked innocently.

'The pair of women's boots you've got in your hands?'

'Oh, these,' Wat held them out. 'This is her best pair. She didn't want to get them dirty on the road.'

'Didn't want to use them to walk in, eh?' Athan's disbelief in all of this was becoming palpable.

Nicodemus said nothing.

'So, if we could get off, we can bring her back,' Wat offered.

Eventually, after what appeared to be much deliberation, Nicodemus slowly shook his head. 'I don't think so. It's bad enough that she's gone, if the two of you go after her we'll never see you again.'

'If she's gone at all,' Athan sneered. 'And hasn't simply decided to leave these two fools.'

Hermitage noticed that Wat now had his fists clenched but was maintaining the calm in his voice.

'We were supposed to get straight after her until this Marcus interrupted. I'm not sure she'll be safe on the road alone,' Wat speculated.

'We are talking about the same woman?' Nicodemus checked, clearly thinking that Cwen was more capable of taking care of herself than the other two put together.

'What with Peter out there,' Wat added suggestively.

'What do you know about him?' Athan demanded.

'Nothing,' Wat assured him, sounding as if he wished he'd never mentioned the name. 'Nothing at all. Haven't seen him since he left the tower.'

Athan's eyes narrowed. 'But you know something.'

'Me? No, not a thing. I don't know anything.' Wat emphasised the "I".

'But you know someone who does.'

Hermitage couldn't help but liken this exchange to fishing. He could see that Wat now had them on his hook and was slowly hauling them in. Any moment now he'd have exactly what he wanted, while Nicodemus and Athan would be thrashing around thinking how well they'd done to snag themselves a fisherman.

'Not at all,' Wat assured them. 'One hears things, obviously, but who can say if it's just gossip?'

'You can say,' Athan instructed him with a pointed finger. 'What have you heard about Peter?'

'Nothing,' Wat repeated. 'I assure you that I have heard absolutely nothing about Peter specifically.'

'And generally?' Nicodemus asked.

Wat shrugged, as if very reluctant to pass on what was bound to be only idle rumour. 'There's the river.' He said this as if he'd never even seen a river in his life.

'What about the river?' Athan snarled. 'I suggest you get to the point before we give you a warrant to try and walk across it.'

Wat finally surrendered to the intensity of their interrogation. 'There was talk of someone taking a boat and heading off on the river. There, I've told you.'

'It's a big river and there are lots of boats,' Athan pointed out.

'This was in the middle of the night. And it was not far from the tower, in a spot people don't normally take boats from. Some of the locals reported that there had been a bit of a struggle and there were signs of a hasty departure.'

'Don't know anything, eh?' Athan was triumphant that he had wrenched this information from the weaver.

John was nodding. 'If he did get away on the river it would explain why I couldn't find him.'

'You know where this spot is?' Nicodemus asked.

Wat shook his head. 'Not exactly. Only reporting what I heard. I suppose we could go and look if we had to.'

'You may have to,' Athan said with his horrible glee.

Wat shrugged that he would simply have to do as they told him. After all, they were in charge.

Hermitage saw that John was looking very thoughtful and was passing his gaze from Wat to Nicodemus. Fortunately, there were no words to accompany his thoughts.

'Of course,' Wat said with a light laugh. 'I expect that Marcus will make you have a warrant simply to get on a boat.'

'We won't need a warrant if the King's Investigator is there in person,' Nicodemus's self-importance said.

'Very good,' Wat was impressed. 'Having you in the vanguard of the search for Peter the murderer will have a real impact.'

Nicodemus suddenly looked as if making a real impact was not really his thing.

'Athan shall go with you,' he said.

'I'll what?' Athan snapped.

'The King's Investigator will need to be at the king's command.' Nicodemus explained.

'Le Pedvin just commanded you to go and find Peter,' Athan reminded him.

'I am doing, I'm sending you. It's called, erm..,' Nicodemus screwed his face up to help it find the right word.

'Delegation?' Hermitage suggested. 'From delegare, to send

on a commission?'

'Perfect. I'm delegating you.'

Athan did not look happy with his delegation. 'While you stay behind and away from any trouble?'

'Not at all. There will be trouble aplenty here.' He tried to reassure Athan. 'What would you rather be doing, chasing Peter down the river and bringing him back after a struggle, or loitering around court making sure you say the right things to the right people?'

Athan grumbled his admittance that the latter sounded truly appalling.

'There you are, then,' Nicodemus concluded. 'We each have our talents. Yours are chasing and struggle.'

'And yours is loitering.'

'We are agreed.' Nicodemus clapped his hands that it was all settled.

'You'll definitely need a warrant,' Wat put in. 'Marcus is not going to let the three of us just go wandering upriver.' He snapped his fingers. 'Come to think of it, we'll probably need More as well. He's got a boat.'

'That loon?' Athan complained. 'I'm not getting in another boat with him.'

Nicodemus ignored the complaint. 'What does one of these warrant things consist of?'

Wat shrugged as if he had no idea and was only taking a wild guess. 'Some sort of parchment saying you give your permission, I assume.'

John was now rubbing his face as his thoughts about all of this crystallised. 'I think I'll go with them,' he said.

'Really?' Nicodemus asked, clearly unable to understand why anyone would volunteer for a job like this.

'Yes. My father told me to find Peter in the first place, so it would be good to make some progress. And Marcus won't ask for a warrant from me. I'd also like to see Peter brought back in one piece.' He gave Athan a cautious look. 'And not accidentally dropped in the river on the way back, or something.'

Athan simply shrugged, clearly not that offended by the implication.

Hermitage couldn't help but admire the way that Wat had got exactly what he wanted, while simultaneously making Athan and Nicodemus think that they had got exactly what they wanted.

His admiration was very short-lived as he now realised that he was going to have to get in a boat with Athan. A boat that was supposedly chasing Peter when it was doing nothing of the sort.

And the boat was going under the direction of More.

Being in the boat was going to be bad enough. Getting out of it and letting Athan know that they'd come after Cwen and not Peter at all was going to be worse. Perhaps Wat would be able to make Athan believe that it had all gone terribly well. He could only hope.

'Let's get on with it, then,' Athan instructed. He gestured that Wat should lead the way. 'I assume you can take us to the vicinity of this spot on the river?'

'I think I've an idea of where it might be. From what people said, you understand.'

'I don't really understand why we're believing anything you've said, weaver,' Athan replied. 'But we've got to find Peter and this seems as good as anything.'

Wat smiled that he was only too happy to help.

'But when I find out that this is some scheme of your own making, I shall do something really quite horrible.' He passed his look over to Hermitage. 'To both of you.'

Hermitage was used to Athan saying things like that. He'd just thought that those days might have passed by now.

As they left, Nicodemus beckoned Athan to join him and they engaged in a private discussion.

'Lining up our fate, I imagine,' Wat said to Hermitage and John as they waited.

'I must say,' John was nodding gently to himself. 'For someone who wanted a warrant from a man who didn't even know what one was, you have done remarkably well, Master Wat.' He gave a little laugh. 'Might I further suspect that you really wanted a warrant to travel on the river all along?'

'What a suggestion!' Wat said.

'It further seems highly unlikely that Cwen would have gone ahead to Derby on her own. Perhaps she took a river trip and you are anxious to find where she's gone?'

They started to slowly make their way towards the gatehouse, leaving Athan to catch up when he was done.

'You give me too much credit.' Wat said. 'Mind you, it was very tempting to sell them a tapestry or two while I had them.'

Caput XI: Dead Nuisance

As they left through the tower gate, Hermitage would really rather Athan didn't walk quite so close or look at him with such intensity. It was bad enough that there was a deception going on here. To expect him to maintain it with the awful prior breathing down his neck was too much.

He tried to tell himself that they really could be going after Peter. They didn't know who had taken Cwen at all when he thought about it.

There was a dead Norman in the bushes, obviously, but perhaps that was a different dead Norman altogether and nothing to do with them. He just happened to have Cwen's boots on by coincidence. He'd have to work pretty hard to come up with the right coincidence, but he was sure there could be one.

And maybe Normans died in the bushes all the time. When their moment came, they went off into a bush. It was possible.

What was not possible was that he had forgotten there was a dead body of any sort in the bushes.

He hadn't been engaging with Athan's gaze since they left the tower; now he engaged with it even less.

There was a dead Norman in the bushes. In the bushes that they were taking Athan and John straight to. Could he hope that they might not spot it? They had covered the body quite well, but perhaps tell-tale signs had been left. He needed to get a warning to Wat who may not have thought of this.

'Was it this way?' he asked as he stepped over to Wat's side and pointed down towards the river.

Wat frowned at him. 'No, of course it wasn't. At least, not from what I heard,' he added for Athan's benefit.

'I suppose not,' Hermitage agreed. 'After all, there's a lot of Normans down there.' He tried to emphasise the word, Normans, without making it too obvious. 'One of the Normans would be bound to spot Peter running away in a boat.'

Wat still didn't seem to get the message.

'And I expect the Normans patrol all up and down the river anyway. You know, checking all the hiding places. Little culverts, bushes, that sort of thing.'

Now Wat got it and his eyes widened. 'That's a good point, Hermitage.' He turned his face to John. 'Perhaps one of the Norman patrols saw something useful?'

'We can ask Marcus,' John nodded forward to where the very upright and organised-looking Marcus was striding towards them; probably wanting to ask why people were walking on the ground without a warrant.

'What's going on here, then?' Marcus asked officially. He directed the question at John.

'And you are?' John asked nonchalantly.

'I am what?' Marcus was confused.

'Yes,' John said. 'You are what? Why are you interrupting?'

'Why am I interrupting?' Marcus couldn't believe his ears.

John took a pace forward and looked Marcus up and down. 'Do you know who I am?'

'Well, yes,' Marcus was hesitant. 'Of course. You're John, son of Le Pedvin.'

'Son of Lord Le Pedvin,' John corrected. 'And if you'd care to explain to him why you're getting in the way of his business, I'm sure that can be arranged.'

Marcus clearly had the urge to lash out at something but

would have to save it for later. 'Saxons,' was all he could say as he considered the others.

'Well done,' John congratulated the observation. 'I can see you're going to have an easy time of it in England; the place is full of them.'

'Those two are the ones who wanted to get on a boat.'

'Quite right too,' John said.

'Without a warrant,' Marcus protested at the truly outrageous nature of such a request.

'I shall be on the boat as well now, so we won't need a warrant, will we?'

Marcus could only splutter a bit at the very idea of a warrantless boat going anywhere.

Wat gave John a nodded prompt to enquire about movements on the river.

'Have any of the patrols reported unusual activity on the river last night?' He asked the question just like any commander expecting a report from his subordinate.

'Erm.' Marcus seemed confused by the question.

'Come on, man. You must have heard the night reports by now.'

'Yes, that is no.'

'Well, which?'

'Yes, the reports are in and no unusual activity on the river.'

Hermitage chanced a glance at Wat. How could the reports miss a dead Norman in a bush? Perhaps he had only been done very recently?

Wat gave an imperceptible shrug that there wasn't much they could do about it now.

John moved quickly on. 'We're going down to the riverbank. Find a boat and send it round to us.'

Marcus had no words for this situation.

As if by magic - a rather peculiar magic that didn't bear thinking about - at the words, "find a boat", More appeared in their midst.

'This is our boatman,' John said, coping with the surprise very well. 'See that he's properly equipped.'

More grinned and nodded at Marcus. He obviously had a very clear idea what being properly equipped was going to be like.

John beckoned that the small party should now follow his lead.

'Not so bad yourself,' Wat said to him quietly as they walked on.

'It could come back to haunt us,' John said. 'Once the boat is sorted, the first report will be to de Sauveloy.'

'He will get the boat, will he?' Hermitage asked, thinking that Marcus didn't seem very happy about the whole situation.

'Marcus?' John asked. 'Not follow an order? Unthinkable.'

As they entered the village and Wat led the way to the start of the trail to the river, the conversation between More and Marcus drifted over.

'But that's your boat,' Marcus was shouting.

'No, no,' More's squeak travelled through the air. 'Never seen it before. That big one over the other side, that'll do.'

'That's a Norman boat,' Marcus protested even louder.

'It'll be nice and comfortable for the Norman then.'

They let the argument drift into the background.

'Now,' Wat mused as he considered the undergrowth. 'I think they said it was around here somewhere.' He looked left and right, and Hermitage followed suit. Maybe they could divert the group away from the troublesome bush.

'You mean somewhere near all this track that's only just

been trampled?' Athan asked with his customary contempt. 'I know Hermitage is an idiot. Until now, I only thought you might be one.'

'I've not been here before,' Wat said. 'Just following what I heard. This could be a regular route for all I know.'

Athan shook his head. 'If Peter made his escape from the tower this way, he's a bigger idiot than the two of you put together. He's hardly covering his tracks, is he?'

'He was probably in a hurry,' Wat said.

'Just like the rest of us. Now get on with it.' Athan gestured for Wat to lead the way.

That did give the chance for Wat to lead the party slightly away from the bush with the not-so-little Norman problem. As it was hard by the trail, it was impossible to avoid, but when they arrived, he kept his back to it and considered the river swirling beneath them.

'Hm,' Athan grumbled as he considered the obvious fact that someone had been here. 'How do we know which way they went?' he asked. 'And how do we know it was even Peter?'

'More reckoned he heard a boat going west,' Wat said.

'Him!'

'Think what you like of him, he does know about boats and rivers.'

Athan folded his arms and addressed Wat very directly. 'Are you telling me that the things you heard about Peter came from the mouth of that, whatever he is?'

'He's only reporting what he heard. He's not making it up.'

'I suspect everything he does is made up. I don't believe this.' He clapped his arms to his side and turned to John. 'We're supposedly chasing Peter because the weaver here reports what the mad boatman of London has gabbled.

Probably in his sleep.'

'There is a trail,' Wat retorted quite sharply, pointing out the damaged undergrowth around them. 'Or can priors tell what made a path thanks to their divine guidance?'

Hermitage drew breath at what sounded like a blasphemous insult.

'Oh, I beg your pardon,' Wat went on. 'You're not really a prior at all, are you. That would require a monastery to be prior of; and no one will have you.

'As for the trail being Peter? Well, we don't know, do we? But it could be him. He's obviously not here and this is the only clue we've got. Unless you've got something stuffed up your habit?'

Athan took a decisive step forward at this, only to be blocked by John.

'We are following a real trail which might, or might not, be Peter,' he said. 'We are doing so at the behest of my father, Lord Le Pedvin. If you two want to divert from that, Hermitage and I can leave you here to get on with it.' He gave them both firm stares.

Athan shrugged as if he would get Wat later.

Wat bowed his head to John. 'Priorities,' he said. 'First things first.' He smiled at Athan. 'Second things second.'

'We know someone came this way recently,' John summarised. 'And we have More's word that a boat left for the west. We shall follow and see what we can find. There may be some landing place further upstream where we can ask if Peter was seen.'

'We don't know if he crossed the river,' Hermitage suggested. He felt it important to keep the conversation going, in case Athan and Wat got back to their personal business.

'We shall see what More reports,' John said. He looked out onto the river and towards the tower, perhaps hopeful that More would appear soon. 'There really isn't much more we can do here.'

Hermitage was extremely grateful to hear that. If John kept looking out to the river, he would be less likely to spot the body in the undergrowth.

Athan was not so helpful. He was nosing around the shoreline as if hopeful of finding something helpful.

'If Peter was in such a hurry, he might have dropped something,' he explained.

'Such as?' Wat enquired sarcastically. 'A map, perhaps?'

'Anything at all,' Athan replied. 'With any luck, something sharp.'

'Prior Athan,' Hermitage squeaked like More as the prior approached the fateful bush.

'What?'

'Oh, erm, nothing. I just, erm, thought you might be about to fall into the river.'

Athan simply looked at Hermitage.

'And that would never do.'

'Idiot,' Athan mumbled and resumed his examination of the surroundings.

Hermitage gave Wat an urgent glance for some assistance in diverting Athan.

'The filthy waters of the Thames would probably throw him out,' Wat said. 'It'll take the dead but even it draws the line somewhere.'

'That's it, weaver,' Athan turned towards him. 'It's way past time you were dealt with.' He clenched his ample fists and took two long steps towards Wat.

'Good God,' John called out. 'There's a body in here.'

Everyone stopped, and Hermitage felt himself sag as he saw that John had turned away from the river and had gone over to the bush, obviously to relieve himself. The relief had not even started before he discovered that his chosen spot was already occupied.

'A body?' Wat called in horror. 'Really? It's not just someone asleep?'

'If he's asleep he's covered himself very well in branches. It looks like someone has tried to hide him.'

They all came over and joined John now, peering into the bush to see if he was right.

'Good Lord,' Wat said. 'You're right, there is a body. Can you see who it is?'

'Of course he can't see who it is,' Athan snapped. 'I thought you two were supposed to be the investigators.'

John had reached down and was pulling back the branches that Wat and Hermitage had carefully put there very recently.

Hermitage was so frozen by all this that he couldn't say anything. True, no one had asked if there was a body in the bush, so he hadn't lied. But he was pretending to be surprised by the discovery, which was just as dishonest.

He could only pray that John didn't ask if any of them knew anything about this.

Wat could obviously see his dilemma. 'Oh, no,' he said with mock shock. 'It looks like a Norman.'

John turned his head back to Wat. 'No, it doesn't,' he said as if so much should be clear to the casual observer. What sort of casual observer would be examining bodies in bushes would have to wait for later.

'There's a helmet,' Wat pointed out the helmet that lay on the ground.

'So, he's got a Norman helmet,' John said. 'Probably stole it.'

'Not a Norman?' Wat sounded genuinely confused and gave Hermitage a subtle puzzled look.

'Of course not. His clothes are all wrong, his hair's positively peculiar and he's no one I recognise.'

'Do you know all Normans?' Hermitage couldn't help but ask. There was an awful lot of them and to know everyone seemed quite a feat.

'No. But I know all the ones that are his size. He's huge. Almost a giant.'

'He is pretty large,' Wat acknowledged.

'It's not Peter,' Athan pointed out unhelpfully.

John was thinking. 'Could be another of Peter's victims. Or an accomplice.'

'Why would he kill his accomplice?' Hermitage asked.

Wat gave a snort. 'Would you want a man this big getting on a small boat with you?'

'Hardly reason to kill him,' Hermitage said before he realised he shouldn't really be defending Peter; not if Cwen was the real killer.

'Could be ruthlessly covering his path,' John speculated. 'Doesn't want anyone left behind to say where he's gone.'

'What an awful man,' Hermitage managed to say; which was true, just not in this context.

There was a clatter off on the water and they looked over to see More approaching in a very nice-looking boat. This one even had a small mast and simple sail as well as the oars that More was using to manoeuvre the craft towards the shore.

Hermitage was relieved that they'd soon be on their way from this awful scene. He was almost trembling with the expectation that someone would ask him what he knew about the dead man in the bush.

As More rowed closer he had another terrible thought. A terrible thought that became reality before his very ears.

'Oh,' More called happily across the water. 'You found the body, then.'

Caput XII: Rescue of Sorts

'What do you mean, safe?' Cwen asked as she stood and considered the peculiar man before her. If this was safe, she worried about how danger was going to present itself.

He was a tall man who towered over Cwen as she examined him. Most people towered over Cwen, but she never let that get in her way.

From the peculiar sandals upwards, the dress was most disconcerting. He wore tight brown leggings bound with strips of leather, which was fine, but around his top half, he seemed to have some sort of tunic which came down almost to his knees. And it was bright red; a very expensive colour.

He even had a similar coloured cloak hanging from his shoulders. This was a very well-equipped soldier.

Cwen had to conclude that he was a soldier of some sort, if only because of the sword. The Normans were very particular about who carried swords these days; it was only them.

This man was clean-shaven and relatively young, looking fit and strong. His hair was close-cropped and not in the least Norman-like. On top of his head was a helmet of some sort, but not one Cwen had seen before. It was close-fitting and had panels on either side that came down and were tied under his chin.

He still held the short sword in front of him but had at least used it to cut Cwen's bonds.

She looked a little wider and saw that this man had four others with him, all of them dressed the same.

'Who are you people?' Cwen asked. She'd seen a lot of Normans but never any like this. Perhaps they were a special force of some sort.

'We are your rescuers,' the soldier replied in a rather odd accent, also not Norman. But if they weren't Norman, who were they? Certainly not Saxon. No Saxon would be seen dressed like this.

'That's very nice of you.' Cwen rubbed her wrists. 'You're, erm, not from around here, are you.'

'We have come from our city, far off in the west.'

Cwen thought about this for a moment. The west eh? That would explain things. She nodded to herself; Irish.

She'd never met an Irishman before but had heard all about them, of course. The magical powers, the druids, the flying. The closest she had got was Wales and even they spoke in awe about the Irish. Apparently, they used to walk over the sea in the night and leave babies behind. Or so a lot of Welshmen said.

'What are you doing here?' Cwen had to ask. She didn't know if the Irish were actually any safer than the Normans. Still, this one had cut her ropes; it was a good start.

'We have come to deal with the invaders,' the soldier replied.

Cwen appraised the small band. 'I hope there's more of you.'

'Of course,' the soldier gave a light laugh.

'Because there's a lot of invaders.'

'We know that,' the man seemed nothing more than slightly irritated that the Norman invasion was turning out to be such an inconvenience.

'Why now?' Cwen asked. 'They've been here for a while, you know.' She thought that anyone coming to fight off the Normans constituted a good thing. The Irish cure might turn out to be worse than the Norman disease, but that was for later.

'We know that too. We have been too lax.' The soldier shook his head slowly. 'We should have moved earlier, much earlier, but we are here now.' The soldier paused as if thinking that he might be saying too much. 'But what are you doing tied up stumbling through the woods?'

'I was taken,' Cwen said.

'I imagine so. Tying yourself up would be foolish.' There was not a hint of humour in the man's voice.

'Erm, foolish, yes. It's a long story.'

The soldier gestured that she should follow him as they moved back to the trail. He indicated that he was prepared to listen. 'You don't look like a Norman.'

'Well I'm not,' Cwen snapped, offended at the very idea. These Irish didn't know much if they thought she was a Norman. 'I'm Saxon.'

'Ah,' the soldier nodded as if this explained exactly what she was doing tied up in the woods. 'And the Normans did this to you?'

'Not exactly, I think.'

'You think? You're not sure who tied you up?'

'I know who tied me up. A stinking rat called Peter.'

The soldier frowned.

'Not a real rat,' Cwen explained impatiently. 'He's called Peter, but I'm still not sure whose side he's on. He was supposedly working for the Saxons and had got close to the Norman king. Now, I think he's simply working for himself.'

'Peter,' the soldier repeated the name.

'There were two others with him. One didn't say much and just rowed the boat, the other, erm, had a bit of an accident.'

'Accident?'

'He died.'

'Sounds like a bad accident.'

'You could say.' Cwen cast her eyes to the floor for a moment.

'And why did this Peter take you?'

'We upset his plans.'

'We?' The soldier cast an urgent look around the woods for any more tied-up Saxons who might be stumbling about.

Cwen sighed that she was going to have to explain all this. 'Brother Hermitage and Wat. They're my friends, see. Hermitage, funny name for a monk, I know, was made to investigate murders for the king.'

'Investigate?' The soldier tried out the word. 'Vestigare?'

'Exactly.' Cwen nodded. At least this soldier had some Latin. 'He had to track killers. He didn't want to,' she emphasised. 'King William made him do it. Anyway, he found that this Peter had killed someone and so he ran off.'

'Brother Hermitage?'

'No, Peter. Why would Hermitage run off, for goodness sake?'

'Why would Peter take you?' the soldier retorted. 'Why not take the monk?'

'Oh, I don't know,' Cwen moaned. 'Look, I was the one who was taken, you'd have to ask Peter. He said something about fighting the Normans and how I would be persuaded to join him.'

'By being tied up?'

'Quite,' Cwen agreed.

The soldier looked bemused by all this and his fellows were exchanging shrugs that they didn't have the first idea what was going on. They probably didn't even speak English.

'However,' Cwen went on. 'You've freed me now, which is truly kind, thank you. I can get back to my friends who'll be looking for me.'

'I can't allow that,' the soldier said blankly, with no hint of threat.

'I beg your pardon,' Cwen said with quite a heavy hint of threat.

'I can't let you go back. You know that we are here.'

'I won't tell, I promise.'

The soldier shook his head. 'I can't take that risk. We have come now and are preparing to drive the invaders away. The element of surprise is essential.'

Cwen coughed at that. 'If there are as many of you as you say, the Normans will already know you're coming. They have people everywhere.'

'And you could be one of them.'

'I am not,' Cwen bridled.

'So you say, but this could all be a clever ruse.'

'Believe me, the Normans don't do clever ruses. It's as much as they can manage to hold their swords the right way round.'

'Nevertheless, it is safest if you stay with us.'

'Safest for who?' Cwen demanded.

'Safest for us,' the soldier made the position very clear.

'What are you going to do, tie me up again?'

'If you like. Either way, you come with us.'

Cwen fumed but could see that she didn't really have much choice. There were five men here and hitting them all where it hurt without being stopped would not be easy.

'My friends will still be looking for me,' she said, trying to make it sound like some sort of credible threat.

'Then they can join us as well. If, as you say, you are a Saxon, you should be pleased that the Normans are to be dealt with.'

'Well, yes, I am,' Cwen admitted. 'I just don't like being told what to do.'

'I can tell,' the soldier said with a bit of a sigh.

He gestured to his men and two of them came over to stand either side of Cwen. These two held long spears, at least seven feet tall. If she tried to run, they could finish her off without even stretching. The whole band started to move.

A suspicion crossed her mind. 'You're not with Peter, are you?' she asked as they moved on.

'Never heard of him,' the soldier said. 'Another peculiar name. You all seem to have them. What are you called?'

'Cwen.'

'Cwen.' The soldier shook his head as if Saxons really were the most ridiculous people.

'And you?' Cwen asked.

The soldier was about to reply when they emerged from the woods onto a broad trail. Several local folk were about who didn't give the soldiers a passing glance. They must have been here for some time now and people had got used to them.

They did stare at Cwen though as she was bundled along the road.

'Where are you taking me?'

'To our commander, he'll know what to do with you.'

'Do with me?' Cwen's question was full of concern.

'Keep you until our business is over, or release you,' the soldier explained wearily. 'We're civilised people.' The way he emphasised this made it clear that he thought they were the only civilised people in the whole country.

'Well, that's good,' Cwen tried to sound a little grateful.

As they walked on, Cwen discerned no threat from the soldiers. It seemed as if she really was just a bit of a nuisance

117

who had got in the way of their patrol.

This was a huge relief as all the other soldiers she had come across were Norman, for whom threatening was a way of life. Even in the old days, when Saxons had ruled the land, the soldiers were not above a bit of threat now and then.

Perhaps these Irish really were here to get rid of the Normans, after which they'd go home. But then she'd never heard of a group of armed men, Norman, Saxon or Viking, who went home again.

'Why do you want to get rid of the Normans anyway?' she asked.

'Why?' The soldier obviously considered this a completely bizarre question.

'Yes. I mean, they're not really bothering you, are they?'

'Not bothering us?' the soldier was aghast and looked at Cwen as if she was talking about some other Normans altogether. 'They threaten our very existence.'

'Do they?'

'Yes, they do. They dealt with the Saxons, which was a bit of a surprise, to be honest, and now they move to the rest of the country. It won't be long before they reach us. Before that, they must be dealt with.'

'Very good,' Cwen nodded. 'I'm all for dealing with the Normans, believe me.'

'We have let too much go by.' The soldier seemed to be recalling old arguments; unsuccessful ones, by the sound of it. 'We should have acted sooner, much sooner.'

'Why didn't you?'

The soldier appeared to be holding back. 'That is for our leaders to answer.'

'Ha,' Cwen laughed sympathetically. 'Leaders eh? We're told we have to have them, but they don't do much for us, do they?'

The soldier looked rather alarmed to hear someone speaking out like this.

'Old King Edward wasn't too bad,' Cwen went on. 'but then he'd been king forever. Then Harold just took over because he wanted to be king and look what happened to him.'

The soldier had nothing to offer.

'I sometimes wonder why anyone wants to be a leader. It seems an awful lot of trouble.'

They had come back to the landing at Chelchea now and Cwen was grateful to see there was no sign of Peter; although if he had still been writhing on the floor in agony she'd have been quite pleased.

They carried on, following the path further west and Cwen started to wonder how far they had to go. She was confident that Wat and Hermitage would follow her trail and know that she had gone on the river. But if the soldiers went on and on into the west, they might never find her. And if she was taken to Ireland, no one might ever find her again.

'How long does it take to get to this city of yours?'

'We're not taking you to the city.' The soldier scoffed at that ridiculous idea. 'Just to our camp. It is not far.'

'Ah, good.' Cwen turned her head back in the direction of Chelchea. 'Perhaps we could leave word here for my friends. So they know which way to come?'

'Our patrols will find them.'

Cwen thought that might be a bit risky, particularly if Wat was in a difficult mood, which he should be if he knew what was good for him.

'Here,' the soldier announced.

They turned off the path and entered a reasonably

substantial encampment. It was also very well ordered. Neat tents stood in rows and there was even a wooden stockade set up around the place.

These Irish were very well organised, she'd give them that.

She considered the size of the place and thought that this was probably an advance party, come to scout out the land for the main force. Which made it even more impressive if this was how advance parties organised themselves.

At the back of the space, there was a large single tent, akin to something King William himself would have. It was very well presented, and more soldiers stood outside, their long spears at the ready.

As they passed the guarded entrance, two soldiers standing by the side clapped their right hands to their chests, and Cwen's man replied in similar fashion. He then led the way straight through the middle of the camp, up to the large tent.

As he drew close, the tent flap was thrown aside and a figure appeared. It was stooping slightly and walked with a bit of a limp.

Cwen felt the blood drain from her face.

'Excellent,' the figure said. 'You have her.'

The soldier clapped his hand to his chest once more and bowed his head. 'Petruvius,' he said.

'Petruvius?' Cwen stammered. 'This is Peter.'

Caput XIII: More Madness

'What does he mean, oh, you found the body then?' Athan asked.

'Who knows with More,' the noise Wat made was more pain than laugh.

Athan's natural scowl took on a deeper intelligence as he looked hard at Wat and Hermitage. He clearly had some horrible thoughts but hadn't quite worked out what they were yet.

'He probably heard it,' Hermitage suggested, his own words taking him by surprise.

'Heard it?' John asked. 'He heard a dead body?'

'He hears lots of things.' Hermitage tried nodding, to see if it would help him agree with what he'd said.

He couldn't help but notice that More and his boat were drawing closer and closer and it wouldn't be very long at all before the boatman was here to give his own explanation for his cry; the one that included Wat and Hermitage covering up the dead body in the first place; just at the spot Cwen had been taken.

Hermitage found that his life-long craving for honesty and openness in all things, including murder and investigation, had been thrown in the river to float away as fast as it could.

Cwen was his main suspect here, but he just knew that she couldn't have done it. Well, he knew that she could have done it, but she hadn't. It was true, he had no evidence that she hadn't done it, and if she was asked herself, she'd probably insist that she could have done.

Equally, there was no hard evidence that she had done it. That was a bit of a comfort. Apart from the boots, obviously.

Perhaps best not to mention the boots. And the fact that Cwen had been here and was taken in a struggle. And would have put up one devil of a fight as it happened. Apart from all that, there was no evidence at all.

Weak. That's what he told himself. It was a very weak case against Cwen. Weak-ish. Bordering on the weak. Weak in comparison to finding her standing over the dead body shouting, "there, I killed him".

The problem was that as soon as More arrived and started talking, which he always did, the case might get a lot stronger. And it would happen right in front of Athan, who Hermitage knew would be more difficult about it than John.

After all, it had turned out that the body was not even Norman. Which was a huge relief.

Hermitage really felt as if he was in danger of losing control of himself completely as he called out loudly to the approaching More.

'That's right, isn't it, More? You hear all sorts of things. And you hear them very well.'

More's nodding head told that he could hear what was being said. Whether he would understand what was going on, let alone take any notice of it was just a chance Hermitage would have to take.

'More heard the commotion in the night and could even tell the number of people getting on the boat. That's it, eh, More?' Hermitage shouted at the top of his voice, even though More was quite close now.

'That's right,' More gabbled his agreement.

'And he probably heard the body as well.' The way Hermitage said these words was so obviously an instruction to More that he couldn't believe the others hadn't stopped him to ask what on earth was going on.

'Heard the body?' More asked as he drove the craft straight into the bank; his normal method of berthing a boat.

'Absolutely,' Hermitage tried to make it sound as if he were only agreeing with More. 'You heard the body. That's how you know that there is one. After all, you didn't kill him.' Hermitage gave a little laugh that was so false it could have been found guilty of the murder all on its own.

'I heard the body?' More asked.

'There you are,' Hermitage confirmed the explanation to the others.

Just down to Hermitage's left, he could swear that he heard the chink of Wat's purse for some reason.

'Oh, that's right,' More nodded happily, hearing the sound of money very well indeed. 'I heard a body, so I knew there'd be one.'

Hermitage was now drowning in a bog of his own dishonesty. He didn't really understand how he'd got into it, so there was no way he was going to find his way out.

First a dead body, now paying someone to withhold evidence. What next? Drown Athan in the river?

He was quite shocked at where that awful thought had even come from. He tried to regain his equilibrium and get back to all of the real problems that the world had lined up for him.

'He heard the body?' Athan asked with his natural contempt.

'I did,' More confirmed as he jumped ashore. 'I heard all the commotion. People going to the boat, it setting off west. And there was one left behind. Big fellow he was.'

'You could hear his size?'

'Only when he landed.'

'It's just a good job Cwen's not here,' Hermitage said too

quickly and too loudly.

They all looked at him. Even Wat gave him a despairing glance.

'Dead bodies,' he explained.

'Just the one,' Athan corrected.

'One's enough.' Hermitage said. 'Wouldn't want Cwen exposed to this sort of thing.'

'If she didn't do it herself.' Athan said with a snorted laugh. 'I never liked that girl.'

Wat growled. 'As soon as I meet someone you do like, I'll eat a tapestry; a big one.'

The two men exchanged fierce glares.

'Never mind anyone who likes you,' Wat added for completeness. 'That's not going to happen in this world.'

'Can we get back to the matter in hand?' Hermitage asked, trying to sound impatient to get on. 'The problem we face is that Peter may well have escaped onto the river, with, erm, others, leaving this body behind.'

Athan's face was now a deeper shade of frown. 'This is all getting a bit too much for me.'

'A dead body at your feet?' Wat asked. 'Surely not.'

'You two,' Athan specified his problem. 'I've always said that there was something wrong with Hermitage.'

Hermitage had to agree that was true; Athan had always said it.

'And we all know what's wrong with the weaver,' Athan added. 'Now we find the two of you, along with the mad boatman and a body in a bush.'

Hermitage swallowed. He could only hope that Athan's intellectual powers required their usual nourishment; something to hit. Without something to hit it was so hard for him to tell truth from falsehood.

'We just came here with you,' Wat pointed out with a roll of the eyes.

'We don't know you weren't here before,' Athan's suspicions were getting dangerously accurate.

'We don't know you weren't here before either,' Wat said.

'Eh?'

'You could have come out here, killed this man, and then gone back to the tower to wait for us.'

Hermitage relaxed.

Athan now looked completely confused. 'Why the devil would I do that? I've never seen the man before.'

'Neither have we,' Wat replied. 'But of you and Hermitage, who's the most likely to have killed someone, eh? Answer me that. Have you ever known Hermitage do harm to a living creature?'

'That's just one of his failings,' Athan complained. 'I still don't like it,' was all he could come up with. 'You two turn up close to dead bodies far too often for my liking. I wonder if the King's Investigator should look into this.'

Hermitage felt slightly sick. If Nicodemus got his hands on this situation, things might not go so well at all.

'The point is Peter,' John interrupted, sounding quite weary at this chatter. 'We have been told to find him and he may have gone on the river. We need to follow. I don't think the body is going to go anywhere and it's no one we know so we leave it.

'It could be part of the whole Peter problem or something completely different. For now, we get on the boat and see if we can follow Peter. We'll deal with the body later - if we even have to.'

More nodded happily at this suggestion and stood by his vessel, waiting to welcome his passengers aboard.

Wat went first and muttered to More as he passed. 'If I were you, I wouldn't try asking the Normans for a penny to travel on their own boat.'

More seemed to get the message; probably that Wat would pay him later.

At least this boat was large enough for them not to have to sit close together. It even had a steering oar at the back and More took up his position there. Athan went to the prow and the others settled on either side.

The boat was even big enough to prevent some of Hermitage's normal apprehensions upon boarding a boat; the main one being death. Waves, lightning, sea monsters; he knew they were usually waiting for him on any body of water. The sea monsters probably even came upriver especially for him.

Perhaps it was that he had his mind on other things; Cwen going missing; Cwen having possibly committed murder; him lying about both of the aforesaid. He tried to concentrate on being scared for his life instead.

'Off we go then,' More said. He gave Athan a pronounced nod, indicating that being in the prow, it was now the prior's job to get them on their way.

With a scowl and a growl, Athan took an oar from the floor of the boat and used it to push them away from the shore.

More then nodded encouragement to Wat and John, who it seemed were there to row.

'What is that you actually do in this boat?' Wat asked.

'I'm tracking,' More replied brightly. 'Can't track and row at the same time, I'd get confused.'

'You'd get confused?' Wat sounded as if More being confused would be a sight to behold. 'What's wrong with the sail?' he looked up at the mast and the cloth that was currently furled tight.

'I don't trust 'em.'

'You don't trust sails? Of course you don't. Why would you?'

'It's the wind,' More explained. 'Whisk you off to Africa before you know it.'

Wat said nothing but rowed and shook his head. More doubtless thought Africa was just beyond the Isle of Sheppey.

'Which way, then?' Wat asked rather hopelessly. 'Up, down or across. Three to choose from. More said west, but is that any guide?'

Hermitage looked towards More to see if the boatman was actually going to have any idea at all where they should go.

The wind from the river rustled through the grey More beard and stirred it in a worrying manner; as if the strands had life of their own and were feeding off the breeze.

The eyes turned to the sky and then rolled down to the surface of the water in a manner that made Hermitage remember his seasickness.

A great sniff was drawn into the nose and exhaled with the satisfaction of a cook preparing a fine meal.

Hermitage sniffed and got a head full of river odours, which only confirmed that he wanted to go no closer.

'They went this way,' More said confidently, pointing upstream.

'Really,' Wat scoffed with a shake of the head. 'I suppose they're hardly likely to go back past the tower or risk being spotted from the bridge. West it is.'

More readily agreed. 'It's in the wind.'

'Something certainly is.' Wat rowed on.

As they moved slowly up the river, the two oarsmen doing well against the flowing tide, More's attention to their surroundings was quite intense. It was certainly a change from the usual More, who seemed to find everything in the world around him a bit of a surprise.

'Aha,' he called out at one point.

'What is it?' Hermitage asked.

'The stick,' More cried triumphantly.

Hermitage thought this must be one of the more obscure parts of the boat that now needed urgent attention.

He saw that More was pointing to the water.

As he followed the gaze he saw what was indeed a stick, drifting languorously in the stream.

'Do you know it?' Wat asked. 'Sticky More?'

'See how it spins,' More said excitedly.

Hermitage saw that it was indeed turning in the river as it made its way to the sea.

'It's going the wrong way,' More informed them.

'The wrong way?'

'Oh, yis. Outgoing tide, this side of the river, it should be going around the other way. Someone's been by in a boat. They've left a trail.'

'In a river?' Wat checked.

'That's right.' More scampered down from his steering oar and leant over the side to dip his fingers in the stream.

'There's been a disturbance,' he reported.

'I think it's still with us.' Wat rolled his eyes at the others.

Hermitage felt a gag rise to his throat as More dipped his hand further into the water and then extracted it to taste what he'd got.

'Hm.' The boatman smacked his lips. 'Small boat, definitely.'

'The river tastes of a small boat?' Wat checked, looking quite anxious that they were stuck in a boat with More.

'That's right. Big boats stir up the muck. River doesn't taste too mucky at the moment.'

'Which means you know what it tastes like the rest of the time.' Wat looked positively disgusted.

'It's not very nice,' More agreed brightly.

'If we believe any of this, we now know that a boat went upriver,' Wat pointed out. 'Which is hardly a surprise, given that it's the Thames and it's full of boats.'

'Ah, but this one was sneaking.'

'A sneaking boat?'

'Yis. They were trying to go quietly and the trail is very subtle. Only a real expert could follow it. You're lucky I'm here.'

'It's not the word I'd use.' Wat shook his head. 'Perhaps you can tell if Peter was in it? That would be helpful.'

More turned his head back to the breeze as if that were just what he was going to do.

Wat addressed the other passengers. 'If he says. "yis", we throw him overboard.'

'Can't tell,' More finally concluded.

'Oh dear. Your powers failing you?'

'No.' More was unconcerned by Wat's scepticism. 'It's just that they're too far ahead. Must have set off a while ago.'

'Of course. If only we'd left earlier you could have told us what they were wearing, then we'd know who to look out for.'

'I can tell you one thing though.' More took another breath of the air, as if confirming a suspicion he had.

'Oh yes, what's that? One of them has a limp?'

'No,' More didn't seem to think that was a ridiculous

suggestion. 'One of them is a woman.'

Caput XIV: Doing What He Does Best

Nicodemus prowled the corridors of the Tower of London like a cat who has it on good authority that all the milk is stored around here somewhere.

If More's tracking abilities worked as well on land as water, he'd have been able to tell that someone had passed this way and left a trail of ingratiation in their wake.

Treading silently, the new King's Investigator pressed his ear against doors and listened intently for a few moments before moving on.

Eavesdropping on one particularly useful conversation, he heard that Lord Le Pedvin was to depart for the north soon; the best information always came from those who didn't know you were listening to them. If that were the case, Nicodemus should take steps to secure his position with those who remained in authority. All he had to do was find them.

Coming to one entrance more imposing than most, he paused for slightly longer. Seeming satisfied with the result, he straightened himself, brushed down the clerical robe that he was not entitled to wear and knocked.

It was a crafted knock honed through years of practice. Strong enough to attract attention, it was not so impertinent as to be demanding. It caught the attention but did not rouse the irritation. His knock had helped get Nicodemus where he was today.

'Enter,' a voice called from within. The perfect answer.

Nicodemus pushed the door open, his head bowed to show that a very humble supplicant was on his way in.

'What do you want?' Ranulph de Sauveloy asked with his

calm and dismissive manner; he'd have used the same tone with the cat.

'My Lord,' Nicodemus bowed some more.

'Yes, yes,' de Sauveloy acknowledged the greeting and got on with considering the parchment on the desk in front of him.

'I wonder if I might seek a word of advice, my lord?'

Ranulph did glance back up at this. Advice was only asked from one's betters; Ranulph liked being a better. Nicodemus knew that Ranulph would like being a better.

'On a matter of some delicacy?' Nicodemus piled it on.

De Sauveloy even pushed the parchment to one side now. He was intrigued. This was all going very well indeed.

'Proceed.'

Nicodemus took steps into the room and closed the door behind him, taking the very obvious step of making sure that there was no one around to observe this encounter.

He moved up to the desk but did not even think about considering sitting on the chair that was in front of him.

'Well?'

'I have a concern, my lord, and I don't really know who to discuss it with, being so new to my position.'

'King's Investigator,' Ranulph said, indicating that he didn't think much of it.

'As you say.'

'And what have you investigated that causes your confusion? I'm sure it can be straightened out with a few words of guidance.' Ranulph offered guidance to everyone and anyone, whether they needed it or not.

'It is very early days, hours, even,' Nicodemus acknowledged. 'But already, I have tried to serve the king by assisting in the finding of Peter.'

'Pah,' Ranulph dismissed the name that had caused him so much inconvenience.

Nicodemus seemed to draw some satisfaction from this response. 'I have despatched my own man, Prior Athan, to follow what may be a trail.'

'Sounds like the sort of thing an investigator should do.'

'Thank you, my lord. News of Peter came from Brother Hermitage and the weaver and my problem is this: I now have a concern.'

'I think you'd better get to the point of your concern before you become tiresome.' It was quite clear what happened to people Ranulph found tiresome.

'There could be more going on than I have discerned.'

'I don't doubt that at all.'

'This Peter may have allies.'

'Most people do.' There was a hint of wistfulness about this as it was well known that Ranulph de Sauveloy didn't have any allies; apart from the king, who was the only one anyone needed, really.

'And I may have inadvertently aided him in his endeavours.'

'Oh dear.' This was said very seriously. The sort of, "oh dear", that had dire consequences.

Nicodemus now shook his head in self-recrimination. 'I may have played straight into his hands.'

'How, exactly?' Ranulph was staring quite intently now, which was quite disconcerting but very rewarding at the same time.

'I have sent his allies to his aid.'

'Why the devil have you done that?' Ranulph didn't rise or shout his anger; he never indulged in such outward displays. Instead, he made it perfectly clear that the person in front of him was now half a step from a very unpleasant experience.

'I didn't know, my lord. It has only now occurred to me as I think about it.'

'Explain.'

Nicodemus took a breath but still didn't sit. 'Brother Hermitage,' he said. 'The previous incumbent of my role.'

'Yes, yes,' Ranulph waved this away.

'He is a simple fellow who has little guile or understanding of the ways of the world.'

'He investigates murders,' de Sauveloy pointed out.

'He did,' Nicodemus corrected. 'But always with the assistance of the two weavers. Wat the Weaver, a man of such disrepute that his own guild has turned against him, and latterly the girl, Cwen. Quite frankly, a nasty creature given to threats and violence.'

Ranulph's expression said that he could be quite a nasty creature when the call came.

'And she has a deep hatred of the Normans, I am sorry to say.'

'A lot of Saxons do.' De Sauveloy looked straight at Nicodemus.

'Some do, my lord, some do. Others of us see that the world has changed and we welcome the new order.'

'Hm.'

'All of which set me to thinking.'

'Well done.'

'Poor Brother Hermitage is easily influenced by the two weavers and could be led along the wrong path.'

Ranulph got this straight away. 'The path with Peter on it.'

'Just so. I fear that they may be in league.' Nicodemus hung his head. 'Far from sending them off to chase down this Peter, I may have sent them to join him.'

'It was Brother Hermitage who identified Peter as the killer of Malf,' de Sauveloy pointed out. 'Hardly the sort of thing to do if you're in league with the killer.'

'But that was only to defend himself in the presence of the king and your noble self. I now suspect even that was a ruse. Brother Hermitage made his accusations precisely to give Peter the chance to escape.'

De Sauveloy raised his eyebrows.

'It hardly seems credible that the King's Investigator would let a killer simply walk out of a room without noticing, or perhaps mentioning it to someone? I know I wouldn't.'

'They planned it all along?' Ranulph sounded doubtful that Saxons could come up with something as clever as this.

Nicodemus simply nodded.

'But you have sent this Prior Athan as well.'

'I have, my lord.' Nicodemus emphasised the hesitation in revealing his next worry. 'But I fear that Athan is another very angry Saxon.'

'Angry with the Normans.'

'No, just generally angry. He could be tempted to join any sort of active campaign if there were a chance to take his anger out on someone.'

'This seems simple enough.' De Sauveloy sounded slightly disappointed that this wasn't a very meaty problem at all. 'Just send a handful of guards after them.'

'Would that it were so simple, my lord,' Nicodemus simpered.

'What else?' Ranulph sighed as if Nicodemus was now going to confess that he'd accidentally killed the king.

The King's Investigator looked carefully around the small room, checking that there was no one to overhear his next words.

So effective was his caution that Ranulph found himself looking round as well before he shook his head and clicked his fingers at Nicodemus to get on with it.

Taking a deep breath, Nicodemus breathed the word. 'John.'

'John?'

'John, son of Lord Le Pedvin.'

'What about him?'

'He went with them, my lord.'

Ranulph took a pause before he spoke; as if the cat had just figured out how to milk a cow itself. 'Did he now?'

'He insisted upon it, my lord. He said that he was going to go with them. And who was I to question the son of Lord Le Pedvin?'

'Who indeed?' de Sauveloy was now very thoughtful.

Nicodemus went on. 'I have heard that John is rather sympathetic and helpful to the conquered people.' He added a shrug for good measure.

Ranulph nodded. 'He insisted on going, you say?'

'He did, my lord. I made no suggestion of it at all. I simply sent Athan.'

'My, my,' Ranulph said with the sort of satisfaction that even the widely reviled know to keep to themselves. 'And the monk and weaver went with him?'

'That's right. They said they had news of where Peter might have gone.'

Ranulph allowed himself a small frown. 'Why would they come and tell you this if they were in league with him?'

Nicodemus gave a modest bow of enormous pride. 'I managed to get it out of them, my lord. They came seeking a warrant to travel on the roads.'

'Ah, Marcus,' Ranulph nodded contentedly.

'But I could see that there was something going on. Naturally, I refused the warrant and managed to get the true reason out of them. They needed to travel so that they could go and join Peter. Perhaps they thought I could be trusted.'

'I see that you cannot,' Ranulph said with no hint of criticism.

'It depends who is doing the trusting, my lord.'

Ranulph indicated that this was the right answer. 'The last person I trusted turned out to be a killer called Peter,' he warned.

'He was a mere newcomer, my lord,' Nicodemus reassured him. 'I have been seeking the king's service for some time now.'

'Yes, I've seen you skulking around.'

'And now that I am the King's Investigator, I can devote myself to the king. The king and his most important advisers.'

'And did these people give any indication of where Peter had gone?'

'Not specifically, my lord. And I couldn't appear to be too difficult as I wanted them to speak freely. I did manage to extract the fact that they wanted to go to the river.'

'The river?'

'On a boat.'

'I imagine one would be necessary. Peter left on the river, eh?'

'So it would seem.'

Ranulph sat and let his hands writhe themselves together like a nest of snakes squabbling over the last mouse. 'I see your dilemma.'

Nicodemus acknowledged the problem. 'I could not possibly go to Lord Le Pedvin or the king with this, think of the embarrassment.'

'I am.' Ranulph smiled.

'And they may simply not believe me.'

'Let alone give you a small force to get after the lot of them and bring them back.'

Nicodemus looked as though he had never thought of that. In truth, he had never thought of going anywhere. Small forces were for sending, not accompaniment. The chances of a small force ending up in a fight of some sort were really quite high. Nicodemus would be happy to read a report of the fight; he didn't need to be in it.

'Well,' Ranulph was thoughtful. 'When I say bring them all back, I mean John. He is the son of the king's noble friend, despite the very numerous errors of his ways. The others are Saxons.'

'Who might get lost on the way,' Nicodemus suggested.

'Perhaps best if they did,' Ranulph suggested nonchalantly. 'Don't want them muddying the waters when all of this is reported to the king and Le Pedvin.'

'The small force could be suitably instructed,' Nicodemus agreed.

A smile played on Ranulph's face, the sort of smile that played in places other smiles tended to avoid. 'In fact, muddying the waters might be the absolutely best thing they could do, what with already being on the river and all.'

Nicodemus bowed his acquiescence.

'I shall make the arrangements,' Ranulph said. He picked up and rang a small bell on his desk that was supposed to summon the lacklustre and slovenly servant he had been given. 'I know the very man for a job like this.'

He considered Nicodemus for a moment as if trying to discern true motives. 'This Prior Athan?'

'My lord?'

'I thought he was a confidant of yours.'

Nicodemus showed little interest. 'An irritating fellow who has had his uses in the past.'

'But not best suited to being at the side of a man with a position to maintain?'

'I couldn't have put it better myself.'

'Then he had better find himself muddied with the rest of them.' Ranulf waved that Nicodemus could leave now. 'Not a word to anyone,' he cautioned.

'Of course not, my lord.'

'Because only you and I know any of this and if I hear of it from another source, I will know that it has come from you. And I am told there is a lot of mud in the River Thames.'

Caput XV: Who Would Do Such A Thing?

'**O**ne of them is a woman,' Athan repeated as if the secret he had long suspected was now revealed.

'According to More,' Wat tutted that only a fool would believe another fool.

'Called Cwen,' Athan concluded.

'I don't think he can tell names.'

'I'm not stupid, weaver,' Athan snapped. He continued before Wat could offer an opinion on this. 'The two of you turn up asking for a warrant because the third one has gone ahead. Now we find that we're chasing a boat that has a woman in it.'

'There are other women in the world,' Wat pointed out, naturally thinking that Athan wouldn't know that.

'Not in coincidences like this, there aren't. Your Cwen has gone missing, has she? Run off, more likely. And now you've got us chasing after her.'

'She has not run off,' Wat protested.

'But she hasn't gone ahead, has she?'

Wat didn't reply.

'Taken then. Ha. Who'd want to take her?'

Wat paused at his oar. 'Listen, you disgusting..,' he searched for the word. 'Prior. We are on a boat on the river going after Peter. If Cwen is involved in some way, it's only good that we're on our way.'

'Ha!' Athan crowed. 'I knew it. I knew you were lying. And you, Hermitage.'

Hermitage dropped his head.

'Deceiving your old prior like this,' Athan shook his head in mock sorrow. 'And I doubt that this is anything to do with

Peter.' He gestured towards John. 'You've even dragged the son of Lord Le Pedvin into it. That's not going to go down very well when we find there's no Peter, is it?'

Wat's face was grim.

'I knew it was mistress Cwen we were after,' John said with little concern.

This clearly bothered Athan, from which Wat took great pleasure.

'It was pretty obvious,' John pointed out, clearly quite surprised that Athan had only just worked it out. 'And if she is taken, who would do it?'

Hermitage was about to say Normans, when he recalled that John was one. The pause also gave him time to consider the body in the bush, which they now knew was not Norman after all.

Could it be that it wasn't Normans who had taken her at all? In which case, who? There wasn't really anyone else in the country at the moment who went around taking people. He felt that even if he were proved to be wrong about the Normans, it had been a very reasonable assumption

'Could have been anyone who didn't like her,' Athan suggested. 'Which gives us a whole world to choose from.'

'I'll come over there and do something to a prior with this oar in a moment,' Wat threatened.

Athan gave a dry laugh. 'Even you have to admit that she's not easy to like. Rude, threatening, aggressive.'

'Which is a bit rich coming from you,' Wat retorted. 'Cwen's fierce and stands up for herself. You're supposed to be a man of God, what's your excuse?'

'She probably just said the wrong thing to the wrong person who decided they'd had enough.'

'In which case, why not simply deal with her?' John asked.

'Why take her anywhere?'

Hermitage chanced his question. 'It is usually the Normans who take people,' he said as meekly as he could.

'True,' John admitted. 'But no one has any interest in Cwen. However, you were the King's Investigator. There could be reason to get at you through her.'

Hermitage frowned as he tried to understand that.

'If you'd done someone harm?' John prompted.

No, Hermitage couldn't see that.

'Found out that they'd committed murder, perhaps? And brought all the subsequent trouble down on their head?' He seemed to be waiting for the right answer.

'Oh, right, yes.' Now Hermitage got it.

'Good,' John said. 'Such a person might think that the King's Investigator himself would be too risky a target. Get Cwen though and they could get you.'

'A trap of some sort,' Hermitage suggested.

John nodded at what could be a very good idea. 'Or a hostage to get you to come forward, that sort of thing.'

'Ha,' Athan laughed again.

'What is it now?' Wat asked wearily.

'A hostage,' Athan said. 'But not for Hermitage.'

'Who then?'

'The rich weaver.' Athan gave a horrible grin.

'Oh, my God.' Wat breathed. 'They want money.'

'I don't think..,' John began.

'They know I'm rich and they've taken Cwen to get my money,' Wat wailed at the passing water. 'This is all my fault.'

Hermitage saw that this was a truly horrible situation for Wat. If it was the case that Cwen had been taken as a hostage simply because Wat was a wealthy man, he would be feeling awful about it.

'Erm..,' John tried to interrupt the moaning that Wat had now started.

Hermitage knew that Cwen and Wat cared very deeply for one another, even if they had a rather odd way of showing it. He also knew that Wat cared very deeply for money. This was going to be a tricky situation.

'They shall have it,' Wat said without further hesitation. 'Whatever it costs.' He patted himself in various spots. 'I just hope I've got enough on me. I can always send to Derby for more.'

'That wasn't..,' John started again but was ignored.

'I am sure we will find her safe and well,' Hermitage said. In his heart, he knew that "safe" and "well" were not words generally associated with hostages but saying that they'd find her unsafe and harmed would not be helpful.

Wat looked plaintively at Hermitage.

'If it is for your money they will need to keep her, won't they?'

Wat nodded grimly. 'I could always sell the workshop,' he said.

'Who'd buy that?' Athan asked. 'The workshop of Wat the Weaver? No one's even going to admit to knowing where it is, let alone giving you money for it. You do have a reputation, you know.'

Wat could only sit at his oar and fume.

'We need to keep rowing,' More said. 'Well, you do. We'll end up back at the tower if we leave the river to take us.'

They looked around and realised that this argument had taken their minds off the boat. They were being slowly turned by the current back the way they'd come.

Wat dug his oar back into the water and pulled hard.

143

'Why now?' he moaned as they got back on course. 'We've been going around the country dealing with murders for ages now. Why choose this moment?'

'Like I said,' Athan put in, 'maybe it's just someone who doesn't like you and wants your money. And if they don't like you, they probably don't like her either. Come to think of it, there's probably a bit of a queue.'

Hermitage couldn't help but think that Cwen did have a tendency to, how could he put it, make people remember her? And not in a good way. But as Wat had said, why would anyone choose this moment?

'Her mother?' he suggested.

'Her mother?' Wat asked in some shock.

'They don't get on. And Eadgyth was after money the last time we met her.'[10]

'I don't think her mother would take her hostage to get money out of me.' Wat dismissed the idea.

Hermitage then tried to think of all the people in Derby who Cwen had upset in one way or another. He quickly came up with several names but again, he couldn't see any of them coming all the way to London just to take her. Surely, they'd wait until she got home?

And the more he thought about it, the more he realised that anyone who actually knew Cwen wouldn't dare take her hostage; it would only make her really cross.

As he pondered the various generally useless ideas he was having, he noticed that John was smiling slightly and seemed to be shaking his head in amusement.

'Do you have an idea, John?' he asked, genuinely looking for any help.

'It is as I said at the start,' John explained, 'and have been

---

[10] *A Murder for Mistress Cwen*: for her, not of her, obviously.

trying to say ever since, this could be someone who you have caused great trouble.'

'Me?' Hermitage checked. 'Not Wat's money?'

'Unlikely. As Master Wat says, why now?'

'Oh, my.' Hermitage was horrified at the thought that Cwen's predicament could be his fault. And there were so many situations to choose from. So many murders for one young monk to have dealt with.[11]

'Someone quite recent?' John suggested.

Hermitage tried to think who his most recent killer had been. 'Oh,' he said. 'Peter.'

'Peter,' John said with some relief that they'd got there at last.

'So we are after Peter.'

'I suspect so. Who else would have the most urgent interest in taking Cwen?'

'To what end?' As Hermitage said this, he thought that it might be his end.

'You did ruin his plans,' John pointed out. 'He had killed Malf and got himself close to the king. He thought he was going to get rid of the King's Investigator and settle to a life of comfort in the royal circle.

'Instead, he had to run away from the scene of his crime and go into hiding. Presumably, he's had a bit of time to plot his revenge on the one who did all this to him.'

'But he was a killer,' Hermitage complained. He thought it most unreasonable that killers should complain when they were caught. After all, it was the most awful of the mortal sins. If they were prepared to contemplate the deed in the first place, they should think through the consequences.

'He was, or rather is a killer. In which case a bit of revenge

---

[11] 19 Chronicles, see if you can count all the murders....

will be nothing.'

Hermitage saw the reason in this but didn't like it very much. 'But why Cwen? Why not just take me?'

'For all he knew you really were close to the king. It's risky to attack a king's favourite servant.'

'Ha,' Hermitage gave a helpless laugh at that thought. 'So, unless I give myself up to him, he will harm Cwen.'

'I imagine that's the plan.'

'Not if I get to him first,' Wat growled.

'If we even know this is anything to do with Peter,' Athan huffed. 'This is nothing but speculation. All we know is that we've been tricked into a boat trip so that we can see where your Cwen has gone. If you looked after her better we wouldn't be out here in the first place.'

'I really am going to fill the nearest prior with a long piece of wood,' Wat said, half-standing to begin the process.

'Perhaps when we're off the water?' John suggested.

Wat sat with a reluctant grumble.

'What does Peter expect?' Hermitage asked, trying to put himself in the position of a hostage-taking killer. 'He's sent no message. Isn't that usual in this sort of situation?'

'It is,' John said, sounding sadly familiar with the business of hostages. 'It could be that we are simply quicker on his trail than he expected.'

'If it's him at all,' Athan repeated with irritation.

John ignored the interruption. 'You only found Cwen gone at dawn?'

'That's right.'

'In which case, Peter may not even have got to his final destination yet. Word could be on its way to you right now.'

'And I won't be there to receive it,' Hermitage wailed. 'I won't know what my instructions are.'

'I'm sure we'll find out.' John didn't seem concerned.

'I should think he'd want me to come alone,' Hermitage went on. 'When he sees a whole boat-load of us, he may do something rash.'

'You sound like you've done this sort of thing before.'

'Ask our nearest prior,' Wat sneered. 'He was the last one who actually tried to kill Hermitage.'[12]

'Really?' John sounded intrigued.

'Completely different situation,' Athan dismissed the matter.

'The point is,' Hermitage went on, 'that if Peter sees us all turn up, he may harm Cwen.'

'Where, exactly, are we going to turn up?' Athan asked. 'We don't even know where we're going. A row up the river with the floating beard back there is hardly a threat to anyone.'

'We're nearly there,' More piped up from his steering position.

'Smells from the river or a conversation with a fish?' Athan asked.

'No,' More replied happily. 'I can see the dock.' He pointed forward and they followed his gaze to the landing. 'That's Chelchea, that is. It's where I'd come if I was going upstream.'

'With a hostage?' Athan asked.

'I've never had one.' More sounded as if he'd like to give it a try.

'The best we can do is go ashore and see if anyone has seen anything unusual,' John said.

'Follow the trail,' Hermitage said, reminding himself that

---

[12] *A Murder for Brother Hermitage* - that one's spoiled as well now.

this was investigation after all.

'Or we can ask if a madwoman went by being rude to anyone she met,' Athan offered. 'That should be a pretty clear trail.'

'We can follow it,' Wat said. 'Because once you and I are on dry land I'm going to do something very sinful to a prior. You won't be capable of walking anywhere.'

'Words, weaver. And no more decent than your tapestries.'

'Perhaps we should concentrate on Cwen and Peter?' John said. 'After all, my father has said Peter must be found, and Wat and Hermitage want to find Cwen. You two having a fight is not going to get us any closer to either.'

'Quite right too,' Hermitage added his own admonishment.

Wat and Athan still looked ready to fly at one another as soon as the boat touched the shore.

'And,' John added, making the very persuasive noise of a large weapon being drawn, 'of us all, I'm the Norman with the great big sword. Yes?'

Wat and Athan considered the great big sword that was now in John's hand.

Like two boys who had been pulled apart by the ears, Athan and Wat switched their gaze to the approaching shoreline, each blaming the other for their predicament.

'One moment alone,' Wat hissed at Athan as they disembarked. 'That's all I'll need to remove one very irreligious prior.'

'When I rid the world of Wat the Weaver,' Athan replied, 'they'll probably make me a saint.'

Caput XVI: Infinite Cunning Explained

'Are they with you, or are you with them?' Cwen demanded of Peter who, she was pleased to see, still looked a little pale from the low blow she had struck.

He was no longer dressed in a monk's habit but was wearing some sort of long robe, cast around his body and over his shoulder.

'How little you understand,' Peter said. 'But I suppose that as you're still alive it is time you were informed.' He sounded disappointed about this. The delivery of Cwen's body would probably have cheered him up.

'Come,' he gestured. 'The masters will see you now.'

'The masters?' Cwen mocked the title. 'Oh, I am worried.' She pointedly turned her back on the soldier who had brought her and walked up towards the tent as if she owned it.

As she drew level with Peter she gave a quick dart towards him and said "boo". He clamped his hands to his groin and jumped backwards.

'Ha,' Cwen laughed. 'Come on then, let's see the masters. I hope you've warned them.'

Peter followed behind. 'I have told them everything and suggested that a better idea than their own would be to throw you in the river. But they are the masters, they have to find out about you for themselves.' He paused for a moment. 'Perhaps I'll get a boat ready, just in case. And some rocks.'

Cwen coughed her contempt and walked on into the tent.

Even she had to admit that it was very nice inside. She was fully prepared to be mocking and dismissive of whatever was displayed, but this was quite impressive.

A large space in the middle of the tent was completely clear, although three flaming torches burned on either side. This would be a foolish way to light a tent, but these torches had chimneys on stands above them that exited through the roof of the tent.

The walls of the place were hung with coloured panels of extraordinary vibrancy; and price, to Cwen's eye. Simple blank fields of red and blue and yellow were decorated with fine borders creating images of huge pictures.

That sort of thing might well be appropriate for a castle, but a tent? These masters had some money, that was for sure. She thought about Wat catching her up just at this moment and being struck dumb at the sight of such wealth, as well as the thought that he might be able to get his hands on some of it. What to do first, he would fret, rescue Cwen or sell some tapestry? She found herself smiling at the thought.

At the far end of the space, there was a raised dais with three chairs on it. These too looked expensive, covered, as they were, with red padding. These were chairs fit for a pope, or what Cwen imagined were the sorts of things popes sat on.

All of this opulence put her off her stride somewhat; the stride that was going to see her march up to these masters and give them a piece of her mind; as well as a piece of anything else that came to hand.

She was positively disappointed to see that the occupants of the chairs were as old as old people could get. Three men, at least she assumed they were men, were sat above her, considering her arrival with interest. They were so wrinkled, thin and bent that there could have been anything under their clothes.

Damaging Peter, fighting soldiers and defeating masters was fine. She couldn't attack old men like this though. It wasn't decent. The sight left her nonplussed for a moment. Perhaps she could just run away. There was no way any of these three could catch her. The problem would be all the soldiers outside.

The old figures wore the same robes as Peter, but theirs looked as if they were the only things holding them down in the chairs. One whiff of a breeze and these three would blow away. Unlike Peter, their robes had stripes of colour on them and she now realised what looked odd about all of these robes; they were clean. And the people who wore them were clean as well.

She'd got an idea in her head about what these fighters of the Normans would be like, and it was nothing like this. She'd met Hereward the Wake in the east as he put up his resistance to the invasion and he had been more like it.[13] He and his men had been disgusting. They spent a lot of their time avoiding the attention of the Normans in ditches. And it wasn't too long before they looked like ditches themselves. And smelled like them.

This was no fighting force of any sort. They obviously spent far too much of their time washing things. And one another, by the look of it.

She had to admit that she had never seen anything like these people. None of the tales of Ireland had given even a hint of the truth.

The man in the middle chair now gestured that Cwen should come and stand before them. With nothing better to do, she sauntered over and did so.

'Salve,' the man said.

'Save what?'

'Salve,' the man repeated with a slightly disappointed sigh.

---

[13] *The Case of the Curious Corpse*; yes, it's another murder.

'It means greetings.'

'Does it?' Cwen's first word of Irish was at least a useful one.

'And you say Salve back.'

'Do I?'

'You do.'

'All right,' Cwen grumbled. 'Salve.'

'Thank you,' the man nodded his head towards her.

The old fellow's accent worried Cwen. She had never even met any Irish people doing trade, but for some reason was sure they didn't sound like this when they spoke English. Still, Ireland was a big place and a magical one. These could be one of the supernatural Irish; it would explain the robes. Mind you, Peter didn't feel very supernatural when she hit him.

'You have come to us.' The man stated

'I was dragged, actually,' Cwen corrected.

'A necessary step to maintain confidentiality, I assure you.'

'Hm.'

'Petruvius informs us that you have talents that ideally suit our plans.'

'You mean Peter,' Cwen corrected.

'His true name is Petruvius, but Peter fits in better.'

'You do know what he's been up to, do you?'

'Of course.'

Cwen huffed her contempt for this. 'I doubt it. He killed a Norman.'

The man simply looked as if he were waiting for Cwen to tell him something new.

'And then tried to blame someone else, a Saxon monk.'

Now the old one nodded as if this sounded like quite a good idea.

'And when he was found out, he ran away.'

'Eminently sensible, I should say.'

The old one to the right now spoke up, the one who looked like he'd only just recovered from the exertion of walking to his chair. 'This Saxon monk ruined carefully laid out plans.'

'If Peter hadn't tried to blame him for the murder, he wouldn't have had to,' Cwen snapped back. 'On top of that, he tried to take the job of King's Investigator for himself.'

'King's Investigator,' the one in the middle confirmed.

'From the Latin,' Cwen explained to these idiots. 'Vestigo, vestigare. It means to track.'

'Does it now?' The old one had a slightly mocking tone in his voice that annoyed Cwen no end; not that she wasn't already annoyed enough.

'Yes, it does. And Peter was trying to get the job so that he could live a life of comfort with King William, betraying everyone in the process.'

'You are right,' the one on the left addressed Peter, ignoring the accusation. 'She is a fierce one.'

'I am standing here.' Cwen put her hands on her hips.

'Perhaps we should name her Ferox?' the old one suggested with a wry smile shared by the others.

Cwen had no idea what they were talking about, but she quite liked the sound of that name. It had a certain worrying aggression about it.

'Is someone going to tell me what's going here?' she demanded. 'If you Irish are coming over here to fight off the Normans, all well and good. You could even have asked for some help. There's no need to simply drag us into your convoluted schemes.'

'Irish?' That did seem to surprise the old one in the middle.

'What on earth makes you think we're Irish?'

'You're not from around here, that's for sure.'

'We are more, "from around here", than you think.'

Cwen frowned at that idea. She didn't know the country as well as Wat did, but this was only Chelchea. People weren't that odd down here.

'You're not like any Saxons I've met.'

'Saxons? Pah!'

'Yes, Saxons,' Cwen said proudly. 'The people who have had their land taken from them by the invader.'

'Their land?'

That seemed a very odd question.

'Yes, their land.'

'Hardly,' the man scoffed. 'What are Saxons doing in Britain? Why aren't you all in Saxony?'

'Eh?' Cwen was confused now. Perhaps these people were just plain mad. Mad rich people. There were quite a few of them about, and it might explain things.

'You can't just cross the sea and claim that this is your land, you know.' A finger now pointed. 'Let me tell you, Mistress Cwen, there is only one people who can rightfully call themselves Britons; us. The Romans.'

Cwen could only gape. Yes, she was right; they were mad. The problem with mad people was that they behaved, well, like mad people. There was no telling what they might do to her for no good reason at all.

She tried a smile. 'Romans, eh? Of course you are.'

'I am Magnus Theodosius Maximus.' The man spoke the name as if Cwen would recognise it immediately.

'Very nice,' Cwen tried.

'Nice?' Magnus Theodosius Maximus obviously took his name very seriously. 'I am a direct descendent of the

Emperor Magnus Maximus.'

'Well,' Cwen hesitated. 'That's good.'

'Yes, it is good.' Magnus was starting to sound a little irritated. 'And my two consuls here, Lucius Quinctius Crassus and Agrippa Sempronius Medullinus are descended from Romans of noble birth.'

'That's a lot of names,' was all Cwen could think of.

'A lot of..?' Magnus was finding this hard to deal with. He looked to Peter for some help.

'She is a weaver,' Peter assured them.

'A weaver?' Cwen asked. 'What's being a weaver got to do with anything?'

Cwen waited while Magnus Theodore Mucksy, or whatever his name was, took a deep breath.

'You are right about one thing; we have come to deal with the invader.'

'Right.' Cwen had complete confidence that this lot stood not a single chance against the Normans. Mind you, it wouldn't be the old leaders who did the actual fighting, would it? It never was. Perhaps all those soldiers out there could achieve something.

'We have waited too long,' Magnus seemed to be confessing to something people had been telling him about for quite a while now. 'Safe in our city, we ignored the comings and goings of savages.'

'Who are you calling a savage?'

'Well, you, of course.' Magnus didn't seem to think there was any question. 'Our records show the arrival of so many wandering rogues it was hardly worth keeping up. Angles, Saxons, Jutes, Frisians, Vikings. No sooner had one lot turned up than a new band came along to throw them out.

'But we ignored it once too often. Honestly! Turn your

back for a moment and you find the whole country has been taken over.'

'That's Normans for you,' Cwen agreed.

'Not the Normans,' Magnus protested. 'The Saxons.'

'Saxons? We're not invaders.'

'You are from where we're standing.'

'Wait a moment,' Cwen tried to recall one of the things Hermitage had told her. He told her so many things, most of which were completely useless, that she tended not to hang on to them. There was one that had stuck though.

'The Saxons came here hundreds of years ago.' Hermitage had read it in one of his books and had told her exactly how many hundreds of years it had been. Exact numbers were one of his most useless things.

'And we came here a thousand years ago,' Magnus retorted. 'We got here first. The great Julius reported that the place was nothing but squabbling tribes when he arrived.'

'I think you'll find it's the person who got here last who ends up owning the place. And what about the Celts?' Cwen asked impudently.

'Now we really are talking savages,' Magnus dismissed the entire race.

'How can you not have noticed the Saxons?' Cwen asked. 'It's too late to start complaining now.'

'We are magnanimous when it comes to dealing with new people. You don't have an empire that covers the known world without putting up with a few oddities here and there. Anyway, you spent most of the time fighting amongst yourselves.'

'I don't think you do have an empire that covers the known world anymore. Hermitage said so.'

'And Hermitage knows everything, does he?'

'Pretty much, yes. Anyway,' Cwen went on, thinking about this more as she went. 'What about all the roads and Roman castles? They're ruins now. They have been for as long as anyone can remember. Why haven't you been looking after the roads if you think the country is still yours?'

Magnus sighed. 'We know that the main force returned to Rome a while ago.'

'Hundreds of years,' Cwen reminded them.

'But we are still here.'

'Yes, where is here, exactly? Can't say that anyone else has noticed that the Romans are still with us.'

'Our land is in the west. The sea separates us from you.'

'You are Irish,' Cwen said.

'We are not Irish. We live in the last remnant of true Britannia. True, we are reduced to one island now, but that will change.'

'An island? What's this island called then, Ireland?'

Magnus ignored the suggestion. 'Our name for it is Avallonis.'

'Never heard of it.' Cwen hadn't, but that didn't mean it didn't exist. These people had obviously come from somewhere.

'It lies between the coasts of Wales and Mercia, and it is our stronghold.'

'Must be a pretty small stronghold to have been there all these years without anyone noticing.' Cwen was very doubtful.

'Well, it isn't,' Magnus snapped. 'And we have come forth to deal with the latest invader. We'll get to the Saxons in due course.'

'I think you'll find it's a bit late for that. If I were you, I'd have mentioned something to the last few Saxon Kings who thought they were in charge.'

Magnus waved this away as a minor inconvenience.

'Well,' Cwen shrugged. 'I suppose you have got some men and they seem well ordered. An attack on the Normans might work, you never know. They're a difficult lot though.'

'Attack?' Magnus asked. 'Oh, nothing so primitive as that. We have a plan to destroy their rule from its roots.'

Despite her contempt for these people, Cwen wanted to know what the plan was; it sounded like a good one.

'And that is where you come in.'

'Me?' Cwen had forgotten that she'd been brought here for a reason.

'Exactly.' Magnus leaned forward and delivered the detail of the plan of infinite cunning that they were putting in place. He looked her straight in the eye. 'We are going to make a tapestry.'

Caput XVII: Pursue The Pursuers

$\mathfrak{N}$icodemus's satisfaction with developments was tempered by the concern that he had wound up in the middle of them.

He was much more comfortable watching developments from some distance, before stepping in to take any credit that might be left lying around; or avoiding any blame that went flying.

When developments involved troops of Norman soldiers chasing rebellious Saxons on a river, they should really be left to the experts.

It was clear that Marcus was an expert.

Summoned by de Sauveloy, the straight and proper Norman had grasped the details of his mission very quickly indeed. A bit too quickly for Nicodemus's taste. It was quite clear that the man had done this sort of thing before. And the look he gave the King's Investigator said that he was quite happy to do it to him if necessary.

Nicodemus harboured a brief hope that the gathering force would be so significant that they wouldn't notice he had sadly slipped behind and been left on the shore.

Unfortunately, de Sauveloy dashed that hope as he said that this needed to be a subtle mission. In order to avoid any questions, Marcus could take just two men with him. He simply had to select a pair that he could trust with something like this.

That worried Marcus. Finding two men to trust on a mission that might make Le Pedvin angry was not straightforward. He hummed a bit and considered the ceiling for a few moments.

'I have it,' he said eventually. 'There are two who would follow instruction.'

'Then be about it,' Ranulph instructed.

Marcus gave a brief bow to de Sauveloy and a glare to Nicodemus indicating that the Investigator should lead the way.

'I knew they were up to something,' Marcus complained as they made their way out of the keep. 'And I've never trusted that John. He's got some very funny ideas.'

Nicodemus thought it best not to say anything. He knew he was taking a risk siding with de Sauveloy, but the possible gains were enormous. And if Le Pedvin could head north quite quickly, so much the better.

For all he knew, they could be out chasing Hermitage and the others for days. As he was now caught in the middle of his own plan, he thought that might be for the best. The last thing he wanted to do was take any responsibility for his own suggestion; at least until Le Pedvin was a lot further north than he was just at the moment.

'This way.' Marcus led the way to the gatehouse and through it onto the bridge over the moat. 'You there,' he called.

All of the half-dozen guards who were on the bridge snapped upright at the sound of Marcus's voice. Most of them tried to look the other way and hope the words weren't intended for them.

One did turn to face them and had a worryingly expectant look on his face.

'Ah,' Marcus said. 'Hugo, I've got a job for you.'

'Yes, sir,' Hugo said with worrying enthusiasm.

'Some Saxons to chase down.'

'Best thing to do with them, sir.' Hugo gave Nicodemus a

rather disgusted look.

'This one's brought us some news,' Marcus explained.

'I see.' Hugo clearly thought that news brought by a Saxon was probably revolting.

'Where's Justan?'

'Justan, sir?' Hugo was not enthused by the name.

'Yes. We need him as well.'

'Really sir? Do we have to?'

'Yes, we do. This is a delicate matter.' He beckoned Hugo to draw near. 'There is the suggestion that John, son of Le Pedvin may be involved in something and we need to follow him.'

Hugo considered this information. 'May I say that I am not at all surprised, sir.'

'And it doesn't worry you?'

'Worry me, sir? Why would it worry me? If Lord Le Pedvin himself took up with the Saxons the way his son does, he should be brought to justice.'

'Quite. So you see why we need Justan.'

'I suppose so,' Hugo said reluctantly. 'Shall I gather a good force together, sir?'

'Not this time. Just us.'

'Us?' Again Hugo looked as if he'd been asked to deliver a load of old hags to a witches' coven. 'We need a force, sir. A job like this, involving, erm, certain people? Needs to be done properly. Don't know what we might come up against.'

'It'll be just John and some Saxons,' Marcus said. 'And two of them are monks and one's a weaver.'

'A weaver?' Hugo clearly thought that being a weaver was even worse than being a Saxon. A Saxon weaver was simply unthinkable.

'So they won't give us much trouble.'

'No sir. Shall I fetch horses?'

'No. We're going on the river. We think that's the way they went.'

Hugo seemed to consider this and his next words carefully. 'If I might comment, sir, a mission of this nature without men or horses? Well, I mean to say. Got to do a job like this properly.'

'The horses won't be much good in the river, will they?' Marcus observed.

'No, sir, but still..,'

'Just go and find Justan.'

'Yes, sir.' Hugo obeyed his order with only the slightest shiver of concern.

'He's a good man,' Marcus said to Nicodemus.

'I'm sure,' Nicodemus agreed. He had met Hugo's type before. The ones who wanted to do everything properly and thoroughly and as a result annoyed everyone else intently. This was mainly because they seemed to think that only they knew how to do things properly and thoroughly.

There was frequently a risk that they spent so much time making sure that proper and thorough were attended to that they never did anything at all.

He dreaded to think what Justan was going to be like.

It wasn't a few moments before he found out.

Hugo returned in good order and had a follower. This creature was plainly Norman because he was dressed as one, but his resemblance to Marcus and Hugo was passing at best.

For one thing, he was eating as he walked. Marcus and his ilk would only do one thing at a time, and Hugo would make sure that it was done correctly. Eating was for eating time, walking was entirely separate, and the two should not be mixed up.

This man's uniform was on his body, but it looked as if it was simply kept there while its owner got on with more interesting pastimes. What weapons he carried were in very poor condition, and the hands he was using to eat with were covered in something that didn't bear close examination.

The two Normans could not disguise their contempt for the new arrival.

'What is it?' The figure that must be Justan asked in a rather impudent manner.

'Work is what it is,' Marcus said.

'Oh, what?' Justan complained.

'Work for Lord de Sauveloy.'

'God,' Justan now sighed.

'That's enough of that,' Hugo intervened. 'You know how much you owe his lordship.'

'I've paid my dues.'

'Not for what you did, you haven't.'

Nicodemus raised his eyebrows at Marcus.

'Justan here is our best tracker,' Marcus explained. 'And he is in debt to Lord de Sauveloy.' He turned his attention to Justan. 'A debt that cannot be repaid by simple money.'

'I told you it was an accident,' Justan complained. 'I told everyone it was an accident.'

'And no one believes you,' Marcus replied. 'So you have to do as you're told, don't you?'

Justan just grumbled at this.

'We are chasing some Saxons,' Marcus said. He gave Nicodemus a warning glance at this, which made it clear that there should be no mention of John. 'And you're going to tell us where they went.'

Justan sighed and considered the bread he was holding in his hand. He took a bite and then threw the remainder on the ground. 'Let's get on with it then,' he said through a hail of crumbs that got Marcus and Hugo stepping smartly back. 'Where do we start?'

Marcus gave Nicodemus a prompt.

'I'm told they went on the river.'

Justan looked at Nicodemus as if only just noticing that he was there. 'Here you are,' he said. 'This is a Saxon. Can I go now?'

Marcus simply reached out and smacked Justan round the head.

'Ow.'

The grumble from Hugo said that it should have been a lot more than a smack.

'The river,' Hugo issued the command.

Grumbling, complaining and rubbing his ear,' Justan led them down to the riverbank, considering the ground at his feet as he went. 'What time did these Saxons leave?'

'Only recently,' Nicodemus said. 'Earlier this morning.'

Justan let his eyes wander around the area. 'And who are they?'

'Does that help?' Nicodemus asked, wondering how knowing someone's name helped you track them.

'I mean what are they?' Justan corrected. 'Fighters, servants, escaping slaves?'

'Erm,' Nicodemus still didn't quite understand. 'Two are monks and one a weaver.'

'Weaver, eh?' Justan now sounded a little bit interested in his task. 'Well-to-do weaver?'

'Yes, I suppose so. Name of Wat. Wat the Weaver.'

'Name's not much good, is it?' Justan scoffed. 'Not unless he's written his name in the dirt. And monks, two of?'

'That's right.'

164

Justan nodded. 'This way.' He pointed off away beyond the Saxon village.

'Really?' Nicodemus was impressed.

'Simple. Two pairs of sandals, one pair of good boots. All of them together and heading this way.'

Marcus nodded while Hugo seemed to reluctantly accept that this was some help.

'They've got a Norman with them, though,' Justan said suspiciously. He cast a glance at Marcus. 'Or am I not supposed to know that?'

'You just concentrate on the Saxons.' Marcus instructed.

'Very good boots indeed,' Justan commented. 'Almost noble, you might say.'

Marcus issued a growl of warning.

'And he was definitely with them. Not following or chasing. Now, which noble do we know who spends too much time with the Saxons? And who hasn't been seen for a little while? Or should I say, which son of a noble?'

'Remember how you got in trouble in the first place?' Marcus asked pointedly.

Justan said nothing.

'Don't do it again,' Marcus instructed. He gestured that Justan should continue to follow the trail.

Keeping his peace, Justan did as he was bid and led them around the back of the village.

'Don't think you need me anymore,' he said, indicating the blatant trail of flattened undergrowth that led on. 'Even Hugo could follow this one. Proper trail that is.' He chortled.

'You needn't think we're letting you go back to the tower.' Marcus said. 'This is a sensitive matter and the last thing we want is you opening your mouth to one and all.'

Justan didn't even try to suggest that he would never do

such a thing. 'Sensitive, eh? Ha, I can see John's boots from here.' Justan neatly dodged another slap from Marcus.

Once down at the water's edge, with the tide now noticeably receded, everyone could see that there had been a flurry of activity. Multiple footprints and the clear scrapes of at least one boat were obvious, even to those who'd never tracked a thing in their lives.

'Quite a little harbour,' Justan commented as he examined the muddied surroundings. 'There's our little band, and one before them, I'd say.' He pointed to the area under consideration. 'Later footprints covering earlier ones. Ones made since the last high tide so they haven't been washed away.'

Nicodemus had to admit he was quite impressed.

'My, my,' Justan commented as he squatted down on his haunches.

'What is it?' Marcus sighed at Justan's air of superiority.

'A child,' Justan said. 'Or a small woman. Barefoot, for some reason.' He scanned about. 'And two others. No, three. That's odd.'

'What's odd?' Hugo demanded an explanation.

'The earlier boat, a smaller one,' Justan explained. He pointed to the relevant marks in the mud. 'There were three people and the woman. But then two of them stop at the side of the boat. Probably to get in.' He turned his head carefully from side to side examining the shoreline to left and right.

'Ah,' he said. 'Got it.'

'That's excellent,' Marcus said brusquely. 'Going to share it?'

'Of course,' Bertram said brightly. 'The third one is dead in that bush.'

There was no response to that. Marcus, Hugo and

Nicodemus simply looked at the tracker as if he'd announced that a fairy boat had then come and taken everyone away.

'Dead in a bush?' Marcus asked as if people weren't allowed to be dead in bushes without a warrant.

'You can see where the branches have been dragged to cover him up. You didn't tell me there were going to be bodies.' Justan clearly blamed Marcus for not explaining the task fully.

'I didn't know there were going to be any bodies,' Marcus said as he went over to the bush.

'Anyone we know?' Justan asked.

'No,' Marcus shook his head. 'Big fellow, but no one I recognise.'

Hugo went over and confirmed that the corpse was a stranger.

'Well, here's a fine to do.' Justan said. 'A sensitive matter with a dead body in it. What have we got ourselves into?'

Marcus gave Nicodemus a hard glare.

Nicodemus was quite capable of glaring at himself in this situation. It was bad enough that he had had to come on this mission at all. If he'd had the first idea that there would be a dead body involved, he'd have feigned illness and stayed behind.

'So now we have to follow on the river,' Marcus said with heavy resignation.

'Don't look at me,' Justan said. 'I can have a guess they went upstream from the marks in the mud, but I don't do water.'

'Hello,' a bright and hideously squeaky voice called.

They all spun and watched as a bizarre, bearded figure emerged from the undergrowth.

'You following More?' the figure asked brightly. 'More the

boatman?'

Marcus was very cautious. 'Possibly,' he said.

'That's good. I can help.'

'Why would you do that?'

'Money.' The figure held out a grey and grasping hand.

'How do we know you can help?' Hugo asked. 'You look like a loon.'

'Because I'm More of Lambehitha and I can follow More easily. Leaves a trail a mile wide, he does. He's an idiot, see?'

Caput XVIII: I Don't Want To Go To Chelchea

The people of Chelchea watched with some interest as another rather odd boatload disembarked. The one with the sword appeared to be herding a monk and a merchant, while another monk and a mad man followed behind.

They were used to seeing strange things come up and down the river. Sometimes the strange things went up the river and then floated back down again a few hours later. Being prudent folk, anything of value was quickly retrieved and put to better use. If it were found not to be of value or was really rather nasty, it could always be put back in the river for the less fortunate folk downstream.

Living at a landing post gave them an equitable nature. All sorts of people came and went and there was no point making a fuss about any of them unless they caused trouble. Visitors were always welcome, and the village headman made his way down to the shore to greet this new batch in the traditional manner.

'That's a penny.' he smiled.

'What's a penny?' John asked.

'The landing fee.'

'Landing fee?'

The headman smiled and seemed accustomed to giving the explanation. 'It's the fee for landing, see.'

'A fee for rowing our boat up to the shore and getting out.'

'Now you've got it.'

'And what do we get for our penny?'

The village headman seemed not in the least concerned that this fellow with all the questions was carrying a large sword.

The last lot who turned up from the west had all been carrying swords. They still paid.

'You get to land and get out.'

'Which we've already done.'

'Hence the penny.'

John folded his arms and started to look very much like a Norman conqueror; a Norman conqueror who's just been asked to pay a penny for landing his boat at Pevensey.

'Things did not go well the last time someone tried to stop us landing where we wanted.'

'Here,' Wat stepped smartly forward and handed a penny over to the headman, which was gratefully received. 'We've got more important things to worry about,' he reminded John.

He turned to the head man. 'We're looking for someone. Not sure if they came this way...,'

'They did,' More piped up.

'Oh, God,' the headman took a step back. 'It's him. What have you brought him for?' He pointed a shaking finger at More and clasped his penny close to his chest. 'I thought it was just some loon with a beard, but it's that one.'

'He brought us,' Wat explained. 'Have you met?'

'Have we met?' the headman asked. 'Have we met? Every time he comes here it ends up costing us money. And we still don't know why.'

More nodded and gave his cackling laugh. 'I like it here,' he burbled.

'Take him away,' the headman said. 'You can have your penny back. How's that?'

'We are looking for someone,' Wat repeated slowly. He beckoned that More should come and join him. 'A young woman came this way in a boat. If we find out which way she went, we can be on our way. And we can take More with us.'

'A young woman?' the headman asked.

It was a village tradition not to give information away about other peoples' movements. If everyone felt free to come and go as they pleased without too many questions being asked, the pennies would continue to flow. Where and how people got their pennies was none of his business. Taking them was most definitely his business.

'That's right. Of course, if you don't know, or can't help, I suppose More and the rest of us will just have to wander around the village for an hour or two. See what we can discover.'

The thought of More wandering around anywhere was clearly more than the headman could bear. 'A young woman, you say?'

'We've said it three times between us now. I think you've got the idea.'

'I could go and knock on some doors,' Athan offered helpfully.

The headman considered him and immediately registered the sort of monk who knocked doors down.

'It really is most important,' Hermitage pleaded. 'You will be doing us a great service.'

The headman didn't do great services without great recompense; it was one of Chelchea's most important rules. It came just behind "don't let the village get burned to the ground or sacked."

'There might have been a young woman,' the headman said cautiously.

Wat held another penny up in his hand.

The headman looked around his demesne, just to make sure that everyone could see that he was taking money. Woe betide him if the people of Chelchea thought he was doing something disreputable for nothing.

Hermitage tutted at them both. He wondered what trust could be placed in a man who gave answers to questions for money. He could say anything.

And Wat was just as bad. Tempting people into the sin of avarice, simply to get what he wanted.

It worked though.

'There was a young woman,' the headman said quietly.

Wat breathed a great sigh of relief. 'Was she all right?'

'She was fine, it was the one with her who wasn't so good.'

'Why?'

'She hit him.'

'It was Cwen,' Wat grinned at them all.

'She hit him most horribly.' The headman gave the male grimace that described exactly where the blow had landed.

'Definitely Cwen.'

'Who was the one with her?' Hermitage asked. 'The one she, erm, struck?'

'One of your lot.'

'My lot?'

'You know. A monk'

'A monk?'

'Yes, a monk. You all look alike to me.'

'That is the general idea,' Hermitage explained gently. He tried to think why Cwen would be hitting monks. Obviously, he had annoyed her, but then Hermitage annoyed her and she'd never hit him. Wat annoyed her and she had hit him, but never, "down there".

'Was there anyone else with them?' he asked.

'A young chap who ran off.'

'Before she could hit him as well,' Wat suggested.

'No. I think he's a messenger of some sort. Always coming and going, anyway.'

'The three of them got off a boat,' Hermitage summarised. 'The messenger left, and the woman hit the monk.'

'That's it,' the headman confirmed.

'What did she do then?' Wat asked, looking around as if expecting to see Cwen coming down to the shore.

'She left as well. Quite quickly.'

'Which way did she go?' Wat demanded.

'Back east, along the riverbank.'

Wat turned his head and scoured the direction with no luck.

'Any Normans at all?' Hermitage asked.

'Normans?' the headman cast a careful glance at John.

'There were no Normans in the boat?'

'One monk, one messenger, one woman. That's your lot.'

John had a look of, "I told you so" on his face.

All of Hermitage's early thinking had been that the Normans had taken Cwen and that was a perfectly reasonable suspicion and consequently hard to cast off. Despite the earlier discussion and the very reasonable conclusion that this would be Peter, he still almost wanted it to be Normans. It was the sort of thing they did and so the world would be in order.

Mind you, the dead Norman in the bush was not a Norman at all according to John. And he should know; he was one.

And a monk? Cwen hit a monk. Who else could it be?

'Peter,' he said. 'It really is Peter, then.'

'More by luck than good judgement,' Athan complained. 'And why am I not surprised that your woman hit a monk?'

'My woman hit a killer,' Wat said. 'And when we find her,

I'll ask her if she'd mind hitting you as well.'

'Which way did the monk go?' John asked the headman.

The headman shrugged. 'Sort of clutched himself and fell to the ground.'

John sighed. 'Not immediately. Which direction did he take when he recovered?'

'I don't think he did recover, really. He sort of staggered off after the others.'

'What others?' John now sounded impatient that he wasn't being given the whole tale in one go.

'The others who've set up camp on the hill. He's one of them.'

John cast his gaze away from the river up the rise of the land. 'Who are they? These others?'

'Odd,' the headman said.

'Not what are they, who are they?'

'I don't know, do I? They came from the west, paid their landing fees nice and prompt, and then set up camp on the hill. As long as people pay their landing fee they can do what they want.'

'Are there many of them?'

'Oh yes, lots. They're very well-behaved though. Very ordered. Nice robes.'

'Nice robes?' John looked to the others to see if this meant anything. No one had anything to offer. 'And Peter's one of them.' John was thoughtful. 'Are they armed?'

'They certainly are,' the headman nodded happily. 'Big load of swords and the like they had.'

'Did they?'

'That's extra. Landing swords and cargo.'

'Armed monks?' John asked Hermitage.

'Hardly,' Hermitage said. 'Not the sort of thing monks go

in for.' He considered Athan for a moment. 'Most monks,' he corrected.

'Saxons, then?'

'No,' the headman said. 'Not like any Saxons I've ever seen. And I'm Saxon,' he added as an afterthought. 'They even gabble amongst themselves in some strange tongue.'

John considered their options for a few moments. 'We need to go and see who these people are. If Peter is in with a large band, he may be hard to take. We'll get the lie of the land before deciding what to do next.'

'Well, good luck with all that,' Wat said. 'Hope it works out for you. We'll get off and find Cwen now. Perhaps see you back at the tower. Or not.'

'I think we need to keep together,' John said. 'If this is a large group it may be more than we can manage.'

'And,' Athan added much more directly. 'Our mission is to find Peter, not go chasing your troublesome wench.'

'Troublesome wench?' Wat ground out the words very slowly.

'That's right.' Athan pointed his finger. 'It's about time you started doing what you were told. John here is in charge and I represent the King's Investigator, so I can tell you that you are coming with us. If your woman wanders off and drowns in the river, it'll be one less thing to worry about.'

In the face of this, Wat seemed very calm to Hermitage's eye. Which was worrying.

'Hermitage,' he said. 'Could you hold this?' He took his purse from his belt and handed it over; something Hermitage had never seen him do in all the time he'd known him.

'John?' Wat asked, nodding towards Athan. 'If you don't mind? This won't take long.'

'For goodness' sake,' John complained with a sigh. 'I don't

think you two are going to be much use in any situation. Perhaps we'll all just leave you to it.'

Athan had rolled up the sleeves of his habit and was cracking his knuckles and rubbing his fists. 'Come on then, weaver. It's time you were taught a lesson.'

Wat rolled his shoulders, stretched his neck this way and that and simply stood in front of Athan.

The prior gratefully stepped forwards and put his hands on Wat's shoulders. He leaned back and was obviously preparing to drive his head into Wat's face.

'Both of you!' Hermitage cried. 'Stop this.'

But it was too late.

Athan lunged forward, but as he did so, Wat seemed to collapse in his grasp and sink towards the ground. Once down on his haunches, he swung his right arm back and drove it hard into Athan's midriff.

Prior Athan doubled up. He stayed doubled up while Wat stood and took half a step away.

'I said it wouldn't take long,' Wat reported as he held a hand out for his purse back.

There was no sound from Athan.

'I'd breathe out first if I were you,' Wat suggested amicably. 'Trying to breathe in doesn't work for some reason.'

There was a wheezing sound from Athan, followed by a painful gasp.

'You see,' Wat explained. 'This is what happens when you get used to hitting people who don't hit back.'

Hermitage bent close as he detected a word coming from Athan.

'Unfair,' the prior croaked.

'I'm glad we've got that over with,' John said. 'Perhaps now we can get after Peter.'

'We've got to find Cwen,' Wat said, sounding disappointed that his treatment of Athan was not being effective.

'We will,' John assured him. 'It sounds as if she is quite capable of taking care of herself, though.'

'She is that,' Wat acknowledged.

'And our prime task is to find Peter. That's the one my father, Lord Le Pedvin, remember him, has given us?'

'Yes, but...,'

'And if I hit you with my big sword it'll do a lot more damage than a fist in the stomach.'

Hermitage looked at John, who had seemed such a nice fellow. There was an implacability about him.

'For all we know, your Cwen has followed Peter to continue her retribution,' the Norman said.

'That would be like her,' Wat admitted.

'In which case, we will find them all in the same place.'

'Or she could be heading east looking for us.'

'Then she is safe and we don't need to follow.'

Wat didn't look happy with this very reasonable argument.

'Either way, we are here to find Peter,' John declared as he strode off up the hill. 'And bring the damaged prior,' he called back over his shoulder. 'Once he gets his breath back, he might be useful.'

Caput XIX: Is That The Best You Can Do?

'A tapestry?' To say that was the last thing Cwen expected to hear would be an understatement. She hadn't expected to hear it at all, so it couldn't be the last. 'What do you mean, a tapestry?'

Magnus frowned. 'It's an image woven into cloth. Peter said you were a weaver? Or are you the wrong sort?'

'I am a weaver,' Cwen snapped. 'A very good one. Very good. And I make tapestry so no, I am not the wrong sort. What I mean is, why on earth are you talking about tapestry?' She narrowed her eyes and looked around. 'Are you all mad?' she asked seriously.

'Certainly not,' Magnus said, although Peter didn't look quite so sure. 'We are full of cunning and wiles.'

'Cunning and wiles, eh? Very handy when it comes to a big Norman on a horse with a sword in his hand.'

'We are more subtle than that.'

'Subtle, cunning and wiles? It sounds to me like the Normans aren't even going to notice when they trample over you.'

'They will not notice us until it is too late.'

'And a tapestry is going to achieve this, is it?'

'It is.' Magnus looked quite smug.

'Come on then,' Cwen hurried him along. 'I'm dying to find out. Is this tapestry going to be so big you can throw it over all the Normans and then hit them with sticks?'

Magnus shook his head at her. 'The tapestry will tell a tale. It will tell the tale.'

'Hm,' Cwen considered this. 'Do carry on, although I think I may have some bad news for you.'

'Consider,' Magnus instructed. 'How do the Normans rule?'

'However they like,' she shrugged.

'I mean, why do the people submit to their rule? What is it that makes people believe that the Normans are in charge?'

'They hit people. Kill them. That sort of thing? They killed the last king and that's usually how a new one takes over.'

'But they haven't hit or killed all the people.'

'There wouldn't be anyone to rule if they did. Anyway, they don't have to kill all the people, just the important ones.'

'Exactly. The ordinary folk are left carrying on just as they were. The fields are tilled, the animals cared for, life continues.'

'Apart from the Normans,' Cwen reminded him. 'Don't forget them.'

'All they do is tell people that they're the rulers now.'

Cwen was wondering where all this was going. These people had soldiers with uniforms and swords. Attack. That was what they needed to do, not make a tapestry. 'They tell people quite often, quite loudly and frequently accompanied by violence.'

'But what if we told the people that the Normans do not rule. What if we told them that we do?'

'You could have a go. I expect William would disagree though. And when he disagrees he can be very disagreeable.'

'We wouldn't concern ourselves with him, we would go straight to the people with a message they can understand immediately.'

Now Cwen got it. What a pathetic idea. 'A tapestry,' she snorted. 'You have a tapestry made showing that the Romans rule the country and that the Normans are what?'

'Simple usurpers with no rights to rule at all.'

'It's an idea, I'll give you that,' Cwen shook her head which she hoped indicated that it was also a bad idea. 'Can I just point out a few problems?'

'Problems? What problems?'

'What problems? Really? Let's start with how long it would take to make the tapestry you're describing. I assume you'd want it big?'

'Of course.'

'Naturally. Be more impressive for the tillers of the fields and the carers for the animals.'

'Quite.'

'Years. It would take years to make something like that. Even if you had a host of weavers it would still take years. Me on my own? I'd probably die before it was finished. By which time, the Normans will be on to king number two or three. Very much too late to tell the folk that they aren't in charge at all.'

Magnus looked somewhat irritated that Cwen was being so uncooperative about this.

'Second, once you've waited years for your tapestry to be ready, you have to take it around the country. The whole country. Everyone would have to see it.'

Magnus nodded that this was expected.

'So there's some more years for you. By the time the whole job has been done, we'll probably have been invaded three more times. Then you'll have to start the whole business all over again for the new lot. It'd be never-ending.

'You'd end up with parties showing contradictory tapestries wandering up and down the land for eternity.'

'You are getting completely carried away.' Magnus retorted.

'But there's an even bigger problem.' Cwen smiled horribly.

'And what's that?'

'It's already been done.'

'What?' Magnus looked around the room for someone to blame for not telling him this.

'The Normans have already started their own tapestry telling people precisely that they are the new rulers. Not only that, but they're the rightful ones. Harold having betrayed his word.'

'How do you know this?'

'I've seen it. And it's not actually a tapestry, that would take far too long and the Normans aren't stupid.' She looked at the three men on the dais making it perfectly clear who, in the current company, was stupid.

'It's an embroidery. And they've got nuns making it.'[14]

'Nuns?'

'Lots of nuns. Be finished in no time. Then they're going to display it in a church somewhere and everyone will come to marvel at it.'

Magnus was taken aback by this news and sagged in his chair.

'I suppose that means it is quite a good idea,' Cwen acknowledged. 'Using simple pictures to tell people what's going on. Or rather, to tell them what you want them to think is going on.

'It's dangerous to let people make their own minds up about things. Goodness knows what awful conclusions they'd come to if they stopped to think for a moment. Just tell them something easy. Harold traitor; William king. There you are. One bad thing, one good thing and no possibility of anything in between.

'King Harold was a bad man quite frequently and good one

---

[14] *The Bayeux Embroidery:* A tale of murder and coloured wool.

now and again. Does that make him a good king or a bad king? Come on, he's got to be one or the other. You're not allowed to mix the two.

'And William? He's been bad all the time so far, but he might do something good one day. I don't hold out much hope, but you never know. Does that make him a bad king? Well, yes,' she thought about it. 'It does. So there you are.'

Magnus looked quite confused now.

She shrugged that this was simply the way of the world. 'You want to give the people your own simple answer. Normans bad, Romans good. You're just far too late and were going about it the wrong way to begin with.'

Magnus now had his head in his hands.

'And there's one more thing that I ought to add,' Cwen said quietly.

'Really?' Magnus asked. 'Do you have to?'

'I wouldn't have done it anyway.'

Magnus seemed to think that was the least of his problems.

'I have trouble doing what other people tell me at the best of times. At least, that's what they tell me.' She spared a glare for Peter. 'Drag me from my bed and tie me up and there's no chance.'

'But you hate the Normans,' Magnus pleaded. 'Peter said so.'

'Peter says a lot of things,' Cwen observed. 'But in this case, he's right. I do hate the Normans, but making a tapestry isn't going to drive them away. You don't know them like I do.'

'And what would your wisdom suggest?' Magnus asked quite sarcastically.

'Violence.'

'Violence?' Magnus didn't sound keen.

'It's the only thing they understand. From what I hear of

the battle near Hastings, they got lucky. The Saxons mucked it up and then the Normans managed to shoot Harold; leader fallen in the mud, battle over.'

Magnus didn't look so sure that being a leader required falling in mud.

'And you've got men,' Cwen pointed out. 'Some quite big ones with uniforms and swords.'

Magnus nodded slowly that this was true.

'And the time to strike is now,' Cwen said.

'Really?'

'You're right. You've spent too long in your stronghold letting the world go by. If you'd stood up for yourselves in the first place, we probably wouldn't be in this mess.'

'You mean we should have driven the Saxons away when they invaded?'

'Yes.' Cwen then thought what she was saying. 'Well, no, but the Normans have only just got here really. They're not fully settled. Even William's Tower of London is barely started.

'If you wait much longer it'll be hell to get rid of him. You need to strike now, while there's still some weakness to exploit.'

Magnus looked very doubtful.

'What do your soldiers do all day? Just wander around looking like soldiers?'

'They are there for our defence.'

'But your stronghold is so well hidden you haven't had to defend yourself. Probably in living memory?'

'We are respected,' Magnus said rather grandly. 'And so left alone.'

'You've been forgotten about, you mean. I've travelled pretty far in this country and I've never heard of you. Wat's been everywhere and he's never mentioned the Romans. And if Hermitage knew you were still here, he wouldn't stop going on about it.'

'I think you've got two choices,' Cwen said. She now took to walking up and down in front of the dais, lecturing the men who sat above her. 'Go home, close the doors of the stronghold and wait for the Normans to arrive. It could be years before they find you; no one else has managed it. You can just carry on as you have up to now. It'll all come to a horrible end eventually, but with any luck, you won't be alive to see it.'

She considered the state of the men before her. 'I mean, you definitely won't be alive to see it. You three might not even make it home.'

'And the other choice?'

'Fight. And do it now. Gather your forces, march on London and defeat the Normans. You've got one major advantage.'

'And what's that?'

'Surprise. Believe me, when a troop of Romans come marching out of the west, everyone is going to be very surprised.'

'Hm,' Magnus was thinking about it.

'The Normans have defeated the Saxons,' Cwen went on. 'William has no idea that there is any other reasonable force to stand against him.

'Yes, some of the barons are a bit rebellious, but they're nothing compared to the might of the Roman army.'

The gloom in the room seemed to lift slightly at this thought.

'And you will have the people on your side. The Normans are ruling, but they're not doing it well. Everyone hates them.

If people can rally to your cause, it will give them some hope.'

Magnus beckoned to the other two old men, and they leaned their heads together to discuss the options Cwen had presented.

'And there is one important thing to consider,' Cwen called up.

'Oh yes?' Magnus asked although he was sounding as if he wished she'd stop talking now.

'You won't have to fight. You just sit in your chairs and issue some orders. Then, when it's all over you find out what happened. Good or bad. And it really is one or the other when it comes to battles. One side seldom only wins a bit, from what I understand.'

The three heads got back together but it didn't stop Cwen. 'Think what an opportunity this is. It's far too late for you to defeat the Saxons, but the Normans have done it for you. William has removed all opposition and now you can remove him.

'One strike and the whole Romans-rule-the-country-really problem is solved.'

'And there could be some people who think it's right and proper that you're in charge. As you said, you were here first. Might be nice to get back to how things used to be.

'Granted, the last person to actually remember probably died five hundred years ago, but that's history. Ask Hermitage; he thinks that sort of thing's important.'

The discussion on the dais was completed and Magnus turned back to Cwen. 'You really think these Normans could be defeated?'

'Of course. They nearly were by the Saxons. Like I said, you've got surprise on your side and a pretty well-prepared fighting force, by the look of them.'

'The Normans are not prepared for battle?'

'Absolutely not. They're always ready for a bit of a fight, but battles are planned, apparently. One lot turn up, wait for the others to arrive and then get on with it. If you simply appear at the gates of the tower you could march in and have the place in an hour.'

The heads nodded at one another that their minds were made up.

'Petruvius, assemble the legion.'

'Oh,' Cwen was impressed. 'Legion, that sounds good.'

'Are you sure about this?' Peter asked.

'We are.'

'Don't worry about him,' Cwen said brightly. 'He's still quite young. With any luck, he'll be killed in battle.'

Peter gave Cwen a very odd look. One that said he was not as worried about this as he should be. He left the tent to do as he was bid.

'Come then,' Magnus said as he stood from his chair. 'You are the one with the intelligence on the Normans, it is best that you address the legion directly. Your information on the Norman dispersal and situation will give us a vital edge in the battle to come.'

Cwen could do that. She could address a legion as it went to war against the hated Normans. In fact, she felt as if this were now one of the high points of her life. From being taken and threatened, she was now encouraging her captors into a defiance that might just succeed.

Wait until Wat and Hermitage found that she was in charge of a legion of Roman soldiers and was sending them out to battle William's forces.

She stood tall and proud and followed the old men out of the tent.

Still assembling themselves, a very modest gaggle of soldiers spread itself out before her. She recognised the group who had found her by the river.

She sighed at her own stupidity. This was a simple outpost; an expeditionary force that had left the stronghold in the west probably weeks ago.

Still, word could be sent, the massing of the army might still be achieved before William got any wind of what was going on.

'Ah,' she said. 'Perhaps we do need to wait until you can summon the rest of your forces to join you.'

'Rest?' Magnus asked. 'What rest?'

Caput XX: In Luke Warm Pursuit

'Are we really going to trust our lives to this,' Nicodemus searched for the word to describe the new arrival. 'Thing?' he came up with.

'This is your mission,' Marcus reminded him. 'On behalf of Lord de Sauveloy. Missions get completed. You don't turn around and go home at the first sign of trouble.'

Nicodemus had a fundamental problem with Marcus over that philosophy. Trouble was the prime indicator that the time for turning around and going home had arrived.

'We don't have a boat.' Nicodemus tried to sound disappointed at this insurmountable difficulty.

'We can get the other one,' Marcus said. 'The one the other loon left behind.'

The new More nodded enthusiastically at this and without instruction skipped off.

'Upstream?' Marcus asked Justan.

The tracker considered the mud at their feet. 'Possibly. That's the direction the boats were pushed from the shore. But who knows once they were afloat? They could have crossed to the south.'

Marcus was obviously frustrated that he was not getting the information he needed and that the pursuit of his quarry was being stymied.

'I don't suppose you want to tell me why we're tracking some Saxons and John?' Justan asked.

'Why?' The thought was a new one to Marcus.

'If I know why I'm tracking someone it tends to help. Are they running? Are they hiding? Have they simply gone for a walk and need to be brought home? It all makes a difference.'

'You said you couldn't do water,' Hugo reminded him brusquely.

'I imagine they only travelled on the water to get somewhere.' Justan spoke as if to an idiot. 'There will be more tracks when we arrive. And now we've got two boatloads to deal with.'

'There's probably no connection,' Marcus said sharply.

'No connection?' Justan clearly didn't believe this. 'We're on a spot on the riverbank that no one comes to. A path has been trampled through just to get here. Then we find a boat has headed off with a bare-footed woman on it.

'That was followed by another boat with our monks, weaver and Norman on board. Oh, and there's a dead body in the bush? No connection? Really?'

Marcus leaned over and spoke very clearly in Justan's face. 'No connection that is any of your business.'

'Please yourself,' Justan shrugged. 'If you don't want to tell me, that's fine. It'll just make the job harder and will risk it failing altogether. I'll leave you to explain that one to de Sauveloy.'

That did seem to cause Marcus some concern. 'You will be told what you need to know when you need to know it.'

Justan rolled his eyes at Nicodemus. 'Not if no one knows anything, I won't.' He gave a hopeless laugh.

There was a clatter of oars on the river and the boat of More, now piloted by an almost identical More, swung into view.

'How did you get here so quickly?' Marcus demanded.

'Yis.' New More nodded agreement that he had got here quickly. He rowed as close as he could to the shore. 'You'll have to walk from there,' he called.

Nicodemus considered the mud at his feet with distaste.

Marcus simply strode forward as if the mud would know that it had better not get in his way.

Hugo followed promptly and Justan set off with another shrug for Nicodemus.

Hoisting his robes up to his knees, he gingerly stepped forward and grimaced as the mud immediately climbed up the side of his fine boots and slithered down the inside to coat his feet.

As he climbed into the boat with three Normans and a mad Saxon, he asked himself why it was that all his good ideas went wrong so quickly. They were good ideas, he had no doubt about that, but the moment he put one into action other people ruined things.

It was other people; they were the problem. As soon as anyone else got involved in one of his schemes, the whole thing fell apart. A scheme with no people involved couldn't really be called a scheme at all. He simply had to find better people.

Athan had had his uses but was a very blunt instrument. In the position of King's Investigator, he needed someone much sharper. He could see that Ranulph de Sauveloy would be a good friend to have in high places; well, not friend, obviously. Either of them would escort the other to his execution if there were gain to be made, but that was perfectly understandable. At least de Sauveloy would protect him while it was to his advantage.

No, what Nicodemus needed was an accomplice. A competent and capable accomplice. And he hadn't met a suitable candidate yet.

Their More heaved them away from the shore and headed upstream.

'Did they go this way?' Marcus demanded.

More sniffed the air. Then he rested one oar while he licked his finger and held it up in the breeze.

Nicodemus gagged slightly at the sight of More putting that disgusting finger in his mouth.

The boatman now turned his head to left and right. Then he coughed twice and spat over the side of the boat. He leaned over to examine how the spit moved in the stream of the river.

Finally, he closed his eyes and muttered something incomprehensible to the sky.

He turned to face Marcus. 'Yis,' he said.

'Yis?' Marcus asked.

'It's Saxon for yes,' More explained cheerfully.

Marcus looked to Justan to see if any of the convolutions made sense to a seasoned tracker.

Justan shrugged. 'As I said, I don't do water.' He considered More at his oars. 'And I don't think I'll ever bother.'

With no better suggestions, the boat continued its slow passage upstream, with More pulling strongly against the tide.

Nicodemus took the quiet moments to take his boots off. He considered his mud-caked feet and wondered if this wasn't simply all he deserved. Perhaps, if he couldn't find his perfect accomplice, he should just give up scheming and apply himself to honest toil.

'Ha,' he even laughed out loud at that ridiculous idea.

'What?' Marcus asked.

'Nothing. Just looking at my ruined boots.'

'They'll wash, you useless man.' Marcus leaned over and snatched the boots from Nicodemus's hand. He leaned over the side of the boat and dunked them in the passing water.

He then swirled the water round inside the boots and tipped the muddy residue out.

'There you are,' he handed them back with a snort of contempt for this ineffectual and hopeless individual.

Nicodemus now considered his completely ruined boots and made a note; when he was firmly ensconced in Ranulph de Sauveloy's inner circle, he would send some punishment the way of Marcus.

With no other option, he swung sideways and dangled his feet over the side of the boat to get the worst of the mud off.

Back on his seat, he considered the prospect of putting his soaking feet back in his wet boots and shivered. Where was the warm fireside in Lincoln he had once enjoyed? How had all that been taken away from him?[15]

Hermitage. Perhaps Athan was right and the reason for his failing was not other people in general, it was one in particular. If Brother Hermitage was no longer in the world, things would start to go well. He was intelligent enough to see that this was highly unlikely, but it had to be worth a try.

He might need Athan for a bit longer after all.

He grimaced his disgust as he started to slide his left foot into the boot. Then he paused and realised that they would have to get out of the boat at some point, which would doubtless involve more mud.

This was followed by the thought that he should have taken the boots off in the first place and carried them to the boat. That was probably Hermitage's fault as well.

He leaned forward to rest them on the boat floor in the cold and meagre sunshine. Perhaps they might dry a bit.

Before he could set the first one down it was slapped from his hand and thrown to the side of the boat.

---

[15] Find out in *The Heretics of De'Ath.*

Doubtless, the wretched Marcus was sick of him tending to his footwear.

He looked up and saw that the Norman was sitting still and staring intently upstream. That was odd.

He then looked at his boot which was hanging on the inside of the boat, not having dropped at all. Which was even odder.

Then he noticed the arrow that had pinned it to the woodwork.

My word. They were being shot at.

'Good God,' he cried in alarm. 'We're being shot at.'

'What?' Marcus clearly thought Nicodemus was imagining things.

Another arrow thumped into the side of the boat.

'We're being shot at.' Marcus sounded mainly offended by the idea.

Justan ducked immediately down behind the bulwarks of the boat. Hugo stared intently in the direction the arrow had come from, daring someone to try and hit him.

More continued to row on.

The third arrow narrowly missed Marcus.

The shoreline here was thick with trees and bushes and there was no obvious sign of anyone. Not that Nicodemus could have spotted them from where he was lying, face down in the bottom of the boat.

Marcus drew his sword as if it were going to help.

'Stop,' a deep voice called from the shore. 'Stop the boat and row over to the shore.'

'We will not,' Hugo cried his defiance.

He then cried again as an arrow nicked his ear.

'What do you think you are doing?' Marcus called back.

There was a brief pause before the deep voice explained

with some disappointment that an explanation was necessary. 'We're shooting at you to make you stop and come to shore.'

Nicodemus considered that this was clearly an English voice. Mind you, he thought it would be a bit odd if the Normans were shooting at one another. This gave him some comfort that the people with the arrows might not want to shoot him.

'How dare you,' Marcus retorted. 'Do you know who we are?'

'Oh yes.'

'We are Normans on a mission from King William.'

'I said we know who you are. Now get over to the shore before we actually shoot one of you.'

'You wouldn't dare,' Marcus challenged.

They shot him.

'Ow.' Marcus looked with disbelief at the top of his left leg that now had an arrow sticking out of it. 'You shot me.'

'I said we would.'

'You can't do that.'

'I can do it again if you like. It's a good job you're a fair distance away. That'll only be a wound. Now, if I aim for your head..,'

Marcus grumbled loudly at this outrageous behaviour but indicated to More that he should turn to shore.

'We're not going to do as they say?' Hugo asked with some horror.

'I'll ask them to shoot you next,' Marcus warned. 'Just get your sword ready.'

Hugo did as he was told and drew his sword as the boat approached the shore.

'And throw your swords out,' the voice on the riverbank instructed. Another arrow thudded into the boat as encouragement.

With huge disappointment that their cunning deceit had been uncovered, the two Normans threw their swords as far they could. Hugo looked like he hoped his would hit someone.

More drove the boat into the mud and Nicodemus and Justan cautiously raised their heads above the parapet.

'Now come ashore,' the voice instructed.

Hugo helped Marcus get his leg over the side of the boat and the two Normans led the way through the mud and up towards the dry ground.

Nicodemus and Justan exchanged glances that said they had no choice but to follow. Nicodemus retrieved his now damaged and soggy boot and carried the arrow with him. He thought that if he gave it back their attackers might think better of him.

He was already planning how he was going to explain the deaths of the Normans to de Sauveloy and come out of it well.

More seemed quite happy to stay in his boat and watch the goings-on.

'And you, boatman,' the voice called out.

More looked up as if only now realising his boat had been attacked and one of his passengers shot. He looked as if this sort of thing happened all the time and clambered out.

As they pushed their way through the undergrowth, their attackers appeared. There were four of them, and they were well armed with swords, knives and the longbows that had delivered their message so effectively.

Their dress and appearance made it immediately clear which faction they belonged to.

'Danes?' Nicodemus asked in surprise.

'Aye, Danes,' their leader replied confidently.

He was as big as a Dane should be but somehow looked even more Danish than legend. Long hair flowed from under a metal helmet and a huge beard made it look as if his face really was peering out from behind its own bush.

The chest was broad and criss-crossed with leather strapping. The leggings were tight and functional and the boots were firm and strong. His arms looked as if they could simply carry the boat out of the mud. Across his back, an axe was strapped.

He stepped towards Marcus, reached down and promptly pulled the arrow from the Norman's leg.

'Ow, hell,' Marcus cried out.

'A scratch,' the Dane dismissed the complaint as he wiped the arrow on his leggings and put it back in the quiver at his waist.

'What are you doing shooting at people?' Marcus demanded as he hobbled about clutching his leg.

'We are shooting at invaders.' The Dane obviously thought such an action was entirely reasonable.

'Conquerors, you mean,' Marcus corrected. 'The Normans have defeated the Saxons and now rule this land. You will pay dearly for what you have done.'

'Ha,' the Dane snorted at this. 'Invaders I said and invaders I mean. Normans, Saxons, you're all the same to me.'

'Erm.' Nicodemus was quite keen on not being counted with the invaders.

'First, the Saxons invade our land, and now the Normans. The Danelaw is the only rightful rule.'

'Danelaw?' Nicodemus couldn't control his surprise. 'I thought the Danes invaded the Saxons first.' He didn't like to insist on historical accuracy in the circumstances. 'And there hasn't been Danelaw for a hundred years.'

'And that's what's wrong with this country.' The Dane seemed very sure of this. 'Now's the time to get things back as they ought to be; while the Normans are at their weakest.' He gave Marcus a sneer. 'We shall take back control.'

Caput XXI: Sneaking Up

With directions from the headman, John's little band now followed him up the hill away from the river.

Athan had recovered enough to start muttering threats about what he was going to do to Wat when he had a fair chance.

'I'm not going to give you a fair chance then, am I?' Wat replied. 'You're used to jumping out on people when they don't expect it, or hitting innocent monks who wouldn't dream of hitting back, or even defending themselves, probably.'

Hermitage recalled that some of Athan's worst temper was reserved for those who defended themselves.

'I shall have my eye on you prior,' Wat said in quite a threatening manner. 'And next time I won't be so gentle. I didn't survive this long in my particular branch of the tapestry business without being able to defend myself. Worse than you have had a go and failed.'

This was another side of Wat that Hermitage had not really seen before. Of course, it was Wat who rescued him from attack all those years ago; and that had been with some very handy fighting.[16] But he never came across as an aggressive weaver. He was well able to defend himself, but now he sounded as if he was willing to attack as well.

Even Athan, who was renowned for his willingness to attack, seemed cowed by the weaver's manner.

As they approached the first rise of land from the river, John stopped walking and gestured that they should do

---

[16] *The Heretics of De'Ath*; again. It really is the cause of most of this trouble.

likewise. He even crouched slightly, perhaps expecting the enemy to be over the ridge.

Hermitage had no idea how crouching helped if the enemy was over the ridge, but he did as he was told. He assumed it was something to do with not being spotted; not being spotted and then killed. When he thought about it, he supposed crouching might be quite a good idea.

Wat and Athan followed suit, but More simply walked up, gazing around as if he'd never been anywhere so interesting before.

'Get down,' John commanded.

Wat reached out and pulled More down by the shoulder.

Now on hands and knees, John crawled forward, using some low shrubs as cover.

Hermitage could see his shoulders sag. 'Nothing,' he called back, standing up. 'They must be further on.'

Everyone stood now and followed John once more.

'Are we nearly there?' More asked loudly.

'Quiet,' John commanded. 'I don't know, do I?'

'Oh. Only if we have to do any more crouching can I be excused? It's me knees, you see.'

John stopped, turned and considered More. 'What are you doing here anyway?' he asked sharply.

'I'm More,' More explained. 'I brought you in the boat.'

'I know who you are. I mean why aren't you still in the boat?'

'Oh,' More sounded very critical of that suggestion. 'You couldn't get a boat up here. Too dry, see?'

'It's all right,' Wat said before John could do something rash. 'I'll deal with it.'

John turned away again and Wat addressed More. 'You go back to the river and wait for us there.'

More nodded that this sounded like a good idea.

'Get in the boat and wait for us,' Wat specified. 'Don't just stand in the river.'

More looked grateful for the clarification.

'If we do find Peter and Cwen, we may need to get away quickly.' Wat examined More's face to see if the message was understood. 'And so we'll need you, in the boat, on the river, ready for us to get into, yes?'

'Oh, yis,' More nodded happily, but Wat looked as if he had little confidence that this would turn out in any way they could possibly imagine.

More scampered back down the hill, while Wat gave Hermitage a shrug and they followed John.

'Who are these people likely to be?' Hermitage asked as they continued. 'The headman said they gabbled some strange language.'

'That'll be for you, then.'

'Me?'

'Languages and things.'

'I don't know many. I can't imagine they'll be chattering in Greek.' Hermitage gave the question some thought. 'Welsh,' he concluded.

Wat nodded slowly. 'You could be right. Although this is a long way east for them to venture. And why?'

'Come to deal with the Normans?'

'They were keeping to their hills the last time we met any.'[17]

'They've come to negotiate?'

'Peter didn't seem Welsh. And murdering Normans is an odd way of negotiation.'

'That's true. And why would the Welsh take Cwen?'

---

[17] *Hermitage, Wat and Some Druids*; Welsh Druids, at that.

'All of which is no help at all. We just carry on and see what we find.'

They had caught up with Athan and John now and the pace had slowed once more. John was moving very cautiously across the ground.

'There are signs of movement here,' he said, pointing to the ground where the dust clearly bore the marks of many feet passing by. 'We proceed with caution.'

'Either that, or we're on a busy path,' Wat observed.

They were amongst trees now, which at least gave them some cover, but Hermitage did wonder if four people was perhaps a large number for proceeding with caution anywhere.

He had spent a lot of his time proceeding with caution trying to avoid the attentions of troublesome monks; and he had been on his own. It hadn't worked then.

'There,' John called quietly, crouching down.

They all crouched as well, although Hermitage couldn't see what they were crouching about.

He peered through the gaps in the trees in the direction of John's pointing and could make out some sort of structure. It looked like a wooden wall; the sort Normans built around their castles.

As he adjusted his position to see more, he could tell that this was no Norman construction. There was no great mound of soil inside with the main fortification on top. This palisade appeared to surround an open area.

It wasn't really like anything he had seen before. No Saxon village set itself up in this manner, and the Welsh had displayed no interest in this sort of thing. If they wanted a tree between them and their enemy, they went and stood behind one.

'Who are they?' he asked.

'I think we'll have to go and ask,' Wat replied.

'Is that wise?'

'Probably not.'

'What do we do then?' Hermitage fretted quietly.

'Do?' John didn't seem to understand the question. 'We go in.'

'In?'

'In there.'

'Ah.' Hermitage understood perfectly what this meant, he just couldn't see how the four of them would manage it without discovery. 'Is there a gate?'

'A gate?'

'Yes, a gate to go in through.'

'We're hardly going to walk in through the gate, are we?'

'Are we not?'

'Monks!' John muttered without giving further explanation.

'Monks,' Wat repeated with more interest.

John turned to Wat and raised an eyebrow.

'Very trustworthy, monks,' Wat said in a horribly scheming manner. 'Well, some of them.' He sniffed at Athan.

John nodded. 'Monks could walk up to a gate without any trouble at all.'

'Exactly. While some people who aren't monks perhaps climb over the back of the wall.'

Hermitage didn't even pause to wonder where Wat was going to get some monks. 'You want us to walk up to the gate?' He hoped he sounded horrified because he was.

'Got it,' Wat confirmed.

'What?' Hermitage added some extra horror.

'You don't have to do anything. Just ask for alms or

something.'

'Ask for alms or something?'

'What do you normally do when you bother people at their door?'

'I'm not in the habit of bothering people at their door,' Hermitage protested.

'I bet he is,' Wat nodded towards Athan, who did not demur from the suggestion. 'Probably got an idea already.'

Athan pursed his lips momentarily. 'They're on monastic land,' he said.

'Are they?' Hermitage was intrigued.

'Probably,' Athan shrugged. 'Most people are. And they've got to pay their dues to the abbot.'

'And you two have been sent to collect.' Wat completed the picture.

Hermitage could only gape at the sheer dishonesty.

'They have probably got Cwen in there,' Wat hissed. 'And you don't have to do anything; just keep them busy at the front while we get in the back. You don't need to actually take any dues from them.'

'Although we could,' Athan said. 'Make it more plausible.'

Wat ignored him. 'And you don't have to say anything either.' This sounded like a very specific instruction. 'Let Athan do the talking. Just stand there and look like a monk.'

'Pretty much what I'm doing now,' Hermitage said with some irritation that this plan seemed to have been accepted.

'Well,' Wat said, 'you're crouching now, but pretty much, yes.'

Hermitage could only shake his head sadly.

'Do it for Cwen,' Wat instructed.

Hermitage gave a shrug of acknowledgement that he would do as he was told.

Wat nodded to John and they made their way off to the right. 'Give us a few moments,' Wat said. 'Move when you hear an owl hoot.'

'An owl?' Hermitage asked. 'It's broad daylight.'

'It's a day-owl,' Wat said. 'That place is full of foreigners, they'll never know.' And with that, he was gone.

Hermitage had a lot of things he would like to discuss at this point, but being with Prior Athan always stifled conversation. He simply tried to look meek and obedient.

All too soon there was the sound of an owl; a very loud owl, probably cross at having been woken in the middle of the day.

Athan stood and simply beckoned that Hermitage should follow.

The prior strode with confidence out of the trees and towards the wall. Hermitage followed, hoping that Athan had enough confidence for both of them.

A gateway into this place was not immediately obvious and Athan led off to the left, following the rough path.

Around one corner of this tall stockade, they did find a gate. Hermitage knew that it would be guarded; after all, what was the point of having all this here if you didn't guard the way in? It still gave him no comfort to see two uniformed guards standing there.

The uniforms were interesting though and he had never seen anything like them before.

Sandals, leggings, robes, cloaks and helmets; and swords, mustn't forget the swords. There was something familiar about them though, something that nagged at the back of his head. As if he had seen something like this after all, but in a book somewhere; and he usually remembered all the books he'd seen.

Of course, these guards spotted two monks sauntering up the track towards them and drew their swords.

Hermitage swallowed.

Athan made a horrible growling noise.

They drew up to the guards and Hermitage hung back, just as he had been told to do.

'Quo vadis?' one of the guards asked.

'Eh?' Athan replied.

"Quo vadis", Hermitage thought, his mind suddenly tumbling over itself.

'Where are you going?' the guard enunciated clearly.

'Oh, right. Here.' Athan said.

'Quid vultis?' the other guard said.

'Speak English,' Athan ordered.

'What do you want?' the man sounded quite irritated.

Hermitage was now bobbing his head from one guard to the other. There was no doubt in his mind, these men were speaking Latin. Yes, it was a rather odd accent, but it was Latin. Why on earth would two ordinary guards, standing outside their stockade, be speaking Latin? Ordinary folk did not speak Latin. They didn't even understand it when it was used by the church - which someone had once told him was precisely the point.

And he knew very well that Athan, despite having been the prior of a pretty substantial monastery, didn't understand a word either.

Oh my. Hermitage leaned forward and tugged at Athan's sleeve. Naturally, he was shrugged off.

'We want our dues,' Athan said.

Hermitage tugged again. Athan really needed to be warned who these people were before he went too far and found himself in deep trouble.

'Get off,' Athan snapped.

'I need a word, Father,' he said.

That got Athan's attention. He turned and scowled at Hermitage. 'What is it?'

Hermitage smiled and bowed at the guards and pulled Athan a couple of steps away.

'These people are speaking Latin,' he whispered urgently.

Athan turned his head to consider the guards and turned up his nose in disgust.

'Which can only mean one thing,' Hermitage prompted the thought, which Athan didn't get.

Hermitage looked the prior in the eyes, something he always tried to avoid. He hoped the words would have the right impact. 'This must be a papal legation.'

Hermitage had never seen Athan turn pale before. Nor cross himself and mutter a short prayer for his own salvation. 'Oh, God,' he muttered, seeming to realise that his fate was sealed.

'Well?' one of the guards prompted.

'Sorry,' Athan said quickly, 'Wrong fort.'

Before any more moves to escape could be made, there was a commotion behind the guards and two more of them appeared. These new arrivals bore gifts.

'Murum scandere,' one of the new guards chortled.

'Climbing the wall,' Hermitage translated helpfully as Athan glared at Wat and John who were almost dangling in the grip of two very large guards indeed.

'We were only dropping in,' Wat complained.

'Take them all,' the first gate guard commanded. 'Let Ferox deal with them.'

The other three all looked to Hermitage. 'Fierce', he translated with a hopeless smile.

Caput XXII: Lord, Save Me First

'What are you going to do?' Nicodemus asked as they were all dragged along through the trees towards some unknown destination.

The prime focus of the question was what they were going to do to Nicodemus. What they were going to do with the others was of far less concern; as usual. What they were going to do about bringing back Danelaw to the land and re-establishing an overarching Scandinavian dynastic authority was so distant from Nicodemus's personal welfare that it had even slipped his mind.

'We are going to despatch the Norman invaders and restore proper rule to this country.'

Nicodemus had to think very hard what the man was talking about for a moment. 'I mean what are you going to do now? With me, I mean us?'

'You are the Norman invaders; what do you think we're going to do?'

'Me?' Nicodemus laid on the surprise as thick as thatch. 'I'm not Norman.'

'Me neither,' More piped up.

'We're not sure what he is,' Nicodemus was quite happy to throw anyone to these wolves if it decreased the risk to the most important person in the vicinity; him. 'But I'm not an invader of any sort,' he pleaded. 'I'd be perfectly happy under the Danelaw.'

'You're not a Dane,' the Dane observed.

'I could be,' Nicodemus offered. 'I'm only a humble servant. I simply do what I'm told.'

'He's King William's own personal investigator,' Marcus

said most unhelpfully. 'And will be witness to your death when you fall beneath the king's mighty foot.'

'Ha!' The Dane was happy to have his conclusions confirmed. 'As I suspected. You are all invaders and will be dealt with.'

'Is that where you're taking us now?' Nicodemus had to ask. 'To be dealt with?'

Their pace through the trees was rapid, almost as if they were being chased. Nicodemus had a fleeting hope that this might be the case. If there was a force on their tail it might catch up and deal with these mad Danes for him.

'Where we are taking you is none of your business.'

'But we'll find out when we get there,' Nicodemus pointed out.

'And it will do you no good. Now come.' The Dane gave him a push of encouragement and they continued on their way.

There was little sign of any activity in this part of the ubiquitous forest. They were following a trail, but it was obviously seldom used. Perhaps only by invading Danes, of which Nicodemus hadn't known there were any until now.

His hopes of bumping into a passing Norman patrol were sinking with each step they took. If they came to a main thoroughfare there might be a chance to shout for help, but the main thoroughfares of the country were so few and far between it could be days before they found one.

He briefly imagined that some folk in a situation like this might make a daring bid for freedom. They might dive off suddenly into the woods and seek to outrun their captors. Or they might leap to the attack at the best moment and defeat the Danes.

It was only a very brief imagining, though. It was quickly

put in its place by his sense of self-preservation, which reminded him that running and fighting were things other people did. He really might have to reconsider Athan's position when he got out of this. The man was proving to be more valuable than he had thought.

Mind you. If he'd had any choice, he would never have left the safety of the tower in the first place.

A glance at Marcus, hobbling along and being supported by Hugo, told him that the ones most likely to be useful in any escape attempt were currently not up to the job.

Justan struck Nicodemus as like him in many ways. Not like him in most, but like enough to willingly take up the Danish cause if they turned out to be the ones with the most swords.

More of Lambehitha was not even worth thinking about. He appeared to be lagging happily at the back as if the Danes were leading him to some great feast.

Nicodemus actually had little doubt that he would get out of this; the problem was that he didn't yet know how, and that was always worrying.

There could be some negotiation; some promises made, later to be broken; some simple pleading; bribery. There were many options, it was simply a case of selecting the right one.

His heart sank quite a long way when they broached a small hill and descended into a valley. This was a well-hidden and private spot and was occupied by a small but busy camp of Danes; a small but busy camp, busy with large Danes.

They were all going about their daily business; food preparation, repairs to the camp, sword-sharpening, arrow-making, that sort of thing. They all stopped to consider the new arrivals and Nicodemus swallowed.

The way the sword-sharpeners and arrow-makers looked at him was not at all comfortable.

'Ah,' Nicodemus tried, 'just like being at home again.'

'Eh?' the Dane asked.

'Like the camps of my childhood.'

'Danish camps?' The question was very threatening.

'Well, no, Saxon ones, but they're the same really.'

The Dane looked horrified at this suggestion. 'Danish camps the same as Saxon? Are you mad?'

Nicodemus didn't like to argue the point, so he kept quiet.

They were now pushed over towards the middle of the area and its dark and worrisome interior.

'I lived in Lincoln for a long time,' Nicodemus bleated. 'Right in the middle of the Danelaw, Lincoln.'

'Pah,' the Dane dismissed this. 'A Saxon who's now the servant of the Norman king should start praying to the Gods.'

If they gave him the names of the Gods in question, he would start straight away.

In the centre of the camp there sat a large and imposing tent. A comfortable fire blazed outside and tree trunks and logs were set around as seats. In any other circumstance, it would have been quite nice to pay a visit.

The Dane led them all over to one long log and made it quite clear that they were to sit. A pointed finger then advised them not to move while the Dane walked off.

Marcus got himself as comfortable as he could and bent to examine the wound in his leg. Hugo stood at his side as if guarding him from some sneak attack.

Justan sat nearest to the fire and stretched out his feet to warm them.

'Where's More?' Nicodemus asked quietly as he realised

that the boatman was not with them.

The others shrugged that they had neither idea nor interest.

'Perhaps he slipped quietly away to organise a rescue?'

Justan gave a weary laugh. 'If he managed to slip quietly away, he's already organised a rescue; his own.'

Nicodemus was not willing to give up hope of More being useful in any way whatsoever. It may be to his credit if he told the Danes that the old man had run off. He would keep the idea in reserve.

He watched as the Dane spoke to another man who then came over to them. As far as telling one Dane from another was concerned, Nicodemus was happy to surrender to any of them.

This one did look more important, somehow. His beard was neater, his weapons bigger and his look more piercing.

'I am Troels,' the man introduced himself.

'Trolls?' Nicodemus asked with worry.

'No, Troels,' Troels corrected quite fiercely. 'It means Thor's arrow.' He cast his gaze around them all. 'Thor as in the God of War; and arrow as in what we shoot Saxons and Normans with.'

'Troels,' Nicodemus repeated obsequiously. 'Got it.'

'And you are going to tell me the disposition of the Norman forces.' He banged his fist into his hand to emphasise this very reasonable request.

'It's a disposition too mighty for your feeble band,' Marcus retorted. Hugo nodded his agreement while Justan looked as if he'd quite like to be somewhere else just at the moment.

'Erm,' Nicodemus had a thought, but was nervous about voicing it. Being threatened with the God of War's arrows was helping him concentrate.

'What is it?' Troels demanded.

'It's probably nothing. It's just that I thought the Normans were Norsemen? You know, Norseman, Norman? All from the same place?'

'Ha, ha!' Troels had a good laugh at that idea. 'The great traitor Rollo? Is that who you mean?'

Nicodemus didn't have a clue, but the "great traitor" did not sound like someone to be associated with.

'That weakling may have sworn fealty to the King of France, but he did not speak for us. And anyway, he was from Norway, not Denmark.'

Nicodemus didn't like to say that people weren't generally concerned about the niceties of exactly where their Viking came from. 'Of course,' he said instead.

'Now, these Normans. Where are they, and how many?'

'Where are they?' Marcus asked with a sneer. 'Everywhere. How many? Thousands. If you think anyone can drive the Normans away, ask King Harold. Oh, no, you can't. He's dead.'

'Thousands?' Troels asked mockingly. 'Thousands of Normans? Pah.'

'There were ten thousand just at Hastings,' Marcus said. 'And that was only the start. William has been crowned. He has distributed the land to his followers and thousands more now count England as their own.' He frowned at the Danes. 'How could you not know this?'

Nicodemus thought that was a very good question. These Danes were well hidden in their valley, but it was only a short distance from London itself. It would take an idiot like More not to notice that the area now had quite a lot of Normans in it.

While there were quite a few people scurrying about the

camp, it certainly wasn't enough to reverse the whole Norman invasion and then deal with the Saxons. Perhaps they were as stupid as More.

Troels waved this problem away. 'We are an advance party sent by King Sweyn, grandson of the great Sweyn Forkbeard. The forces of Denmark are at our back, but we have come secretly.'

'So secretly you didn't notice all the Normans? Still won't do you any good,' Marcus scoffed.

'More goes on than you know, Norman,'[18] Troels sounded alarmingly confident.

One question had occurred to Nicodemus, and although it seemed small, it was troublesome.

'You came at the bidding of your king to assess the Norman strength?'

'That is so.'

Nicodemus held Troel's eye and gave a very subtle nod. To his mind, the content of the nod was perfectly clear. He needed to have a private conversation with the Dane; a conversation that could be to their mutual advantage.

Troels saw the nod but looked at Nicodemus as if he had something in his eye.

Nicodemus increased the intensity of the nod to an almost flagrant level and even went so far as to add a slight tip of the head. Surely, even a Dane could get such an explicit message.

'What?' Troels asked.

'What?'

'What are you twitching for?'

'Me? Twitching? Don't think so.'

Troels moved on. 'Now. These Normans. Tell me what

---

[18] And if you'd like to know more, try *The Domesday Book (Still Not That One)*

you know.'

'Never,' Marcus said.

'Never,' Hugo repeated.

'Normans?' Nicodemus asked innocently. He gave Troels the biggest invitation yet to take him on one side.

With a heavy sigh, the Dane eventually seemed to get it. 'Right. I shall deal with you one at a time. You first.' He grabbed Nicodemus by the collar and hauled him up and away from the fire.

'What are you squirming for?' Troels asked. 'Ready to betray your friends? You look the type.'

'Friends?' Nicodemus asked. 'They're not my friends.'

'The one with the wounded leg said you were their king's investigator, which sounds pretty disgusting to me.'

'I am, but they made me do it. You don't know what it's like being trapped by the Normans. They forced me to become this investigator thing; I don't even know what it is really. Then they made me track some people and we ended up on the river. Where you shot at us. I only want to help.'

'Help yourself, mainly?'

Perhaps the Dane wasn't as ignorant as all that.

'Marcus is right though,' Nicodemus went on. 'There are thousands of Normans. And they've got a big castle in London and have built a lot more around the country. A force like yours would never be able to do them any serious harm.'

Troels looked suitably disappointed. 'The king said that we should only engage if we could be certain of victory.'

'Very unlikely, I'm afraid.'

'And the Saxons have really capitulated?'

'The ones who are still alive? Yes, pretty much. William came up with a highly effective strategy for stopping the

Saxon leaders fomenting dissent; he killed them all.'

'Ha.' Troels sounded as if he wished he'd thought of that.

'The best thing you can do is probably take word back to King Sweyn and let him have a think about what to do next.'

'I shall send word to the king,' Troels was definite about that. 'The bulk of us will remain here. We can harry the enemy and have them fearing for their blood every time they step on the road.'

'You could do that, yes, of course you could,' Nicodemus tried to sound supportive. 'But one substantial Norman patrol and you could be finished.'

'And what do you suggest, Saxon? Not that I'd trust a suggestion from you to float a duck in a pond.'

'Erm, yes, quite.' Nicodemus saw the risk of dealing with the savage man, but he really had no choice. 'What you can do is send me back.'

'Send you back? A fine joke.'

'Then I can pass on information that would help your cause. I mean, our cause.'

'Such as?'

'Where the Normans are going, what their plans are.' Nicodemus lowered his voice and leaned forward slightly. 'Where William himself is going. After all, he's shown the way; kill the leader and the followers will fall.

'You must admit, such information would be useful and you're not going to get it sitting out here in your camp.'

'I wouldn't trust you to tell me the way to Roskilde.'

Nicodemus had no idea where that was but thought that nodding would be best. 'Of course not, but you have hostages.'

'The Normans? The ones you say are not your friends?'

'The two difficult ones are not, but the quiet fellow, Justan is close.'

'Really?' Troels did not sound convinced.

'He's my brother.'

'Your brother?' Troels's cough was clear contempt for this idea.

'Different mother,' he explained. 'We've only just been reconciled.'

'He appears to be a Norman,' Troels pointed out.

'Father got around,' Nicodemus shrugged.

'And now you would leave him with us?'

'He'd be safe with you. You are trustworthy. Unlike the Normans.'

Troels was clearly not convinced. Which was pretty sensible, really.

'What have you got to lose? You've still got the others, they're real Normans. You could try getting information out of them. And you'd have the chance of something from me as well.' Nicodemus tried to look helpless and cooperative, which he did quite frequently.

'I'll tell you what,' Troels said with a horribly sly look. 'You can go back to the Normans with the promise to pass information on.'

'Of course,' Nicodemus tried to hide his relief. He'd known he would get out of this somehow.

'And I will keep the others.'

Nicodemus nodded that this was only reasonable.

'And I will tell them all where you have gone and why.'

'What?' The word burst from Nicodemus.

'That way you'll have an incentive to keep that promise of yours. If the Normans manage to get word back, I imagine your stay will be quite a short one. And if you betray me, I can make sure that such word does get back.'

'But, but..,'

'I should set off now if I were you. Before I change my mind.'

There really was no time to hesitate and so Nicodemus turned and headed off into the trees. As he went, he was already composing his explanation to de Sauveloy that he tricked the Danes into releasing him so that he could bring the news of their camp

'Oh, yes,' a voice caught him almost immediately. 'And where do you think you're going.'

'Oh, what now?' Nicodemus turned with irritation. Off to his left, he saw a group of men dressed for the woods; and for sneaking around in them. He would normally ignore such interruptions, but when they came with swords in hand and bows across backs, he tended to err on the side of caution. 'I surrender,' he said wearily.

Caput XXIII: Ferox The Fierce

Being taken before someone called "fierce" was enough to give Hermitage the shakes. The name being in Latin only seemed to make things worse.

He had heard about the sort of thing that papal legations did to those who stood in their way. He was keen to make it clear as soon as possible that none of them was in anyone's way.

Wat and John were being pushed ahead, which he supposed was understandable, as they'd been the ones caught climbing over the wall.

Hermitage and Athan followed on with their own guards to keep them company.

Despite the basic horror of the situation, Hermitage had a deep longing to know what a papal legation was doing in England. He knew that the pope had supported William's conquest, but he didn't realise they were close. He supposed it was only reasonable that the pope would want to see first-hand how things had gone.

Which made it a bit of a puzzle as to why these people were out here, rather than being given the hospitality of the king.

He knew that he understood little about how the great and the good worked, so had to assume that this sort of thing was normal.

And he and Athan were monks, after all. They were all part of the same community so would surely be treated as Brothers. Mind you, their behaviour had been pretty suspicious so it was only reasonable that they should be questioned.

Being questioned by a papal legation brought more fears to mind. Most worrying of all was the fact that Athan had started quaking at the very idea. Athan didn't quake. He caused quaking in others but had never demonstrated it himself. If Athan was worried, Hermitage should be very, very worried.

Perhaps a degree of ignorance was bliss. And he might find that this papal legation was doing some interesting work in the field of the post-Exodus prophets.

'Get in here,' one the guards shouted as he pushed Wat and John into a fine-looking tent.

Obviously, the guards wouldn't be studying the prophets.

The two monks followed, Hermitage looking around with interest at the very well-ordered interior of the tent. Athan looked around much more nervously as if expecting something to jump out at him.

They were directed to stand at the front of the tent, before a low dais, and wait. Hermitage took the moment to consider the guards once more. Their dress really was most peculiar, and the feeling of recognition was bothering him intensely. The knowledge that he had knowledge, but didn't know what it was, was always irritating.

As this was a papal legation, perhaps he had seen some representation of the soldiers in a relevant text. He quickly ran through the catalogue of books that he kept in his head.

From humble beginnings, he had actually seen more books than he might ever have dreamed of. Most recently there was the library of Colesvain of Lincoln, although that had included some very dubious volumes.[19] Then there was the treasury of books recovered from the Monasterium in the

---

[19] *The Hermes Parchment*, being one of them.

east.[20] He passed over the titles in his mind and couldn't recall any with illustrations of soldiers. Mind you, he tended to skip the books with pictures in them.

The nagging feeling in his head prodded him again. Something he had just thought about had set him off. The Monasterium. Oh my. It wasn't a book at all, it was a statue. That place had been a repository for a number of ancient statues from days long gone by. Days of the Romans. These soldiers were dressed as Romans.

He was so relieved to have got the answer that he didn't immediately bother considering why they were dressed as Romans.

They'd come from Rome, obviously. That was where the pope lived so it was only reasonable that his soldiers should look like this. It was slightly surprising that after all the hundreds of years since the Romans left, they still wore the same clothes, but it was the clear answer.

There was a rustle at the back of the dais, and the guards who were standing with them snapped upright.

A section of the tent was thrown aside and a very well-dressed Roman soldier indeed appeared. This one had a shining breastplate, a resplendent robe of crimson and a helmet that had a thick brush of what looked like horsehair across the top.

Presumably, this was to make the soldier look taller. Hermitage could only think that this particular Roman needed all the help he could get.

In fact, as he considered the shape, the clothes all seemed to be too big. The breastplate rattled and slipped about, the cloak trailed along the floor and the helmet had slipped down so that it covered the face.

---

[20] *The Case of the Clerical Cadaver;* a lot of books and a murder.

'The prisoners, Ferox,' one the guards called, slapping his hand to his chest in salute.

Hermitage chanced a glance at his companions and saw that Wat was almost bent double, trying to look under the helmet of this Ferox.

Seeming to reach a conclusion, he slipped from his guard with a cry that sounded confusingly happy. He bounded up the dais and wrapped his arms around Ferox, lifted the little Roman from the floor and swung him around.

Hermitage could only think that this was not wise. Swinging the soldiers of a papal legation around was probably the most awful sin.

'Oh, my God,' Wat cried. 'You're here. You're safe. Thank God, thank God.'

Hermitage could only hope that Wat knew this soldier quite well.

Wat released his grasp on the soldier who was now a complete mess. Breastplate, robe and helmet were askew and the soldier was staggering a bit to recover his balance.

The guards stepped forward to deal with Wat, but the one on the dais held a hand up to stop them.

Hermitage thought it was quite a small hand as well. And a disturbingly familiar one.

'But what the devil are you doing dressed like that?' Wat gasped.

The soldier now managed to untangle his arms from his robe and pushed the helmet back from his face.

'Cwen?' Hermitage asked. His mind simply could not make sense of this situation. He felt giddy as he looked at what appeared to be a Roman soldier with Cwen inside. Or was it Cwen with a Roman soldier on top?

Why was Cwen dressed as a Roman soldier? Had she

always secretly been a Roman soldier? If so, why hadn't she mentioned it before?

Did the Romans know they had a weaver for a soldier? Was it some local recruitment campaign? Were all weavers really Roman soldiers?

Had the Romans made her dress up like this? In which case, why? Had she perhaps stolen these clothes in a bid to escape them?

That seemed wrong as the soldiers had called her Ferox and seemed to recognise her. He didn't even know they let women be soldiers, particularly papal ones.

Or was it all coincidence that this was a perfectly normal Roman soldier who just happened to look like Cwen? Quite a lot like Cwen. Wearing a uniform that was too big for him. That seemed to be asking a bit much of coincidence.

'Hello Hermitage,' Cwen smiled.

'It is you.'

'It certainly is.'

'Then, why? I mean, how? I mean, why and how? And who, probably?'

'It is a convoluted tale,' she said, coming down from the dais.

'Pah,' Athan growled. 'I might have known.'

Cwen gave him a withering glance. 'I can order you taken away and dealt with, you know.' She nodded to one of the guards who took half a step forward. She raised a hand to stop the man but wagged a cautionary finger at Athan.

'Mistress Cwen,' John sounded as if he had expected something like this all along. 'You definitely didn't go ahead to Derby then.'

'I got a bit distracted.'

John looked about him. 'This is quite a distraction.'

'You can let go now,' Cwen said to Wat who was standing at her side holding her hand. 'The other soldiers will laugh.'

'Are you a papal guard now then?' Hermitage asked. It seemed to be quite a jump in trade.

'Papal guard?' Cwen sounded puzzled and gave Wat a frown as he was now simply standing at her side staring at her with a vacant smile on his face.

'Yes. The papal legation,' Hermitage spread his arms to indicate their surroundings. 'We thought Peter might have taken you.'

'Peter did take me, and this is not a papal legation. Whatever one of those is.'

'A legation from the pope,' Hermitage explained.

'You're alive,' Wat said quietly.

'Er, yes.'

'I thought you were dead in the bush. We found your boots.'

Hermitage thought that this was perhaps not the time to ask if she had killed the large man who had her boots. Now that she was a soldier, it could be that she was allowed.

'I told Peter you'd find me,' Cwen nodded and turned her face to Wat.

He reached forward, cupped her cheeks and kissed her. She didn't resist.

'You're not really supposed to kiss the soldiers,' she reprimanded lightly.

'I'm Wat the Weaver,' Wat smiled. 'I can kiss who I like.'

'Are we going to get an explanation?' John asked. 'Or do we all have to kiss her?'

Cwen nodded that the guards could leave them after which she turned and took a seat on the dais.

'You were right,' she said to her audience. 'Peter did take

me. He's really a Roman.'

'I thought he was Saxon,' Hermitage said.

'So did the Saxons. And the Normans, but really he's Roman.'

'From the pope,' Hermitage nodded.

'No, from the Romans.'

'Any Romans in particular?' Wat asked.

'They say they're from some island called Avalon, or something like that.'

'Oh. Those Romans,' Wat nodded.

'You know about them?'

Wat shook his head. 'No.'

'Very helpful. Anyway, there are Romans living on an island in the west. They've decided that they're going to overthrow the Normans and take back control of the country.'

'Interesting,' John noted.

'Peter's scheme was to get close to William and then deal with him. After which the Romans would march into London and take over. And he did this by first of all pretending to be a Saxon.'

'Very devious,' Wat agreed, sounding as if he couldn't really see the point. 'Had they heard of Le Pedvin?'

'Quite,' Cwen agreed. 'And in any event, there aren't enough Romans left to take over a fish market defended by dead fish.

'Their next plan was to capture me and make me do a huge tapestry.'

'A tapestry?' Hermitage couldn't see what use that would be.

'That's right. This would show the people that the Romans were really in charge and that the Normans, and the Saxons before them, were usurpers.'

'Stupid idea,' Wat commented.

'Certainly is,' Cwen agreed. 'I told them they should be much more direct.'

'I bet you did.'

'They aren't sufficient to mount a full attack, but they could harry the enemy. Cut away at their edges while at the same time build popular support to overthrow the hated invaders.'

'That is me you're talking about', John objected.

'It's your father and his friends, mainly,' Cwen said.

'So they put you in charge of harrying,' Wat concluded.

'I was the only one who had any ideas at all. They've been on their own in the west for too long. Haven't got the first clue.'

'I bet Peter was pleased,' Wat said.

'He's not happy,' Cwen smiled.

'And they named you Ferox,' Hermitage finally relaxed a bit.

'Good, isn't it? It means fierce.'

'Suits you,' Wat said rather dreamily.

'I like it. I think I'll be Cwen Ferox from now on.'

'You're not really going to harry the Normans yourself though, are you?' Wat enquired, coming to his senses with some concern. 'I mean, they do tend to kill people quite a lot. Especially ones dressed up as soldiers.'

'It'll be fine,' Cwen reassured him. 'They'll never know what hit them.'

'I do have to object to this, you know,' John said. 'I really can't have you attacking my people, even if it is only harrying.'

'I know,' Cwen was sympathetic. 'You've been extremely

helpful to us. Actually quite nice, for a Norman. But you are a prisoner now.' She sounded very sorry about this. 'Of the Romans.'

'The Romans! It's ridiculous,' John pressed. 'There are no Romans anymore. Yes, you might have a few here but they are only a few. They can't achieve anything against the Normans. You've seen what William and my father are like. They'll be through this lot in an afternoon.'

'We'll be like the fox in the night,' Cwen said with some mystery.

'People have been trying to get rid of William since he was about seven years old,' John explained. 'And a lot of them tried it in the night as well. They all died. Usually before morning.'

'Cwen,' Wat took hold of her shoulders and was very serious. 'You cannot go into battle against the Normans, not really. It's one thing to talk about it and to hate the Normans, that's fine. But picking up a sword will get you killed. You don't even know how to use one properly.'

'I can learn,' Cwen was serious personified.

'You can't. I've seen people die just learning. And if you are the leader, William will go for you first. In fact, he probably won't even come out of the tower, he'll send Le Pedvin to do you.'

'We have to do it.'

'No, we don't. If you succeed, who's going to be in charge again? The Saxons? They're all dead. You want the Godwinsons back on the throne? Harold and his family were just as bad.

'And what if you do kill William? And Le Pedvin and all the others loyal to him. He's still got sons.'

'Oh God,' John wailed. 'Don't let William Rufus get on the

throne. I wouldn't trust him not to go out hunting and shoot himself by mistake.'

'Did you think I was joking?' Cwen demanded. 'When I kept going on about the hated Normans and what I'd do to them? I'd lay down my life to get them out of our country.'

'You'll lay down your life all right,' Wat agreed. 'And the Normans wouldn't even notice. Anyway,' he softened his voice. 'I don't want you laying down your life. I like it where it is.'

'Hermitage,' Cwen said. 'You talk to him.'

Hermitage didn't know why he was being brought in as an expert on battling the Normans. All he could do was shrug and look around. 'It would seem to be a fairly hopeless cause,' he tried to sound apologetic. 'The Normans defeated thousands of Saxons near Hastings and now they are even stronger. William's own rebellious barons can't even stand up to him. And, as you say, these Roman soldiers do not appear to be versed in the art of war.'

'They're not what?'

'Not very good at fighting.'

'Oh, right.'

Cwen's mouth was tight. 'I am not going to throw away this opportunity. I have got to do something. I would regret it for the rest of my life if I didn't.'

With coincidence still loitering in the vicinity, the tent flap was thrown wide and one of the Roman guards appeared. 'Ferox,' he cried. 'We are under attack!'

'Attack?' Cwen asked, suddenly looking quite worried.

'We think so.' The guard didn't sound too sure.

'You think so? How can you think you're under attack?'

'We've never been attacked before. Erm, what do we do?'

Caput XXIV: Attack Is The Best Form Of Attack

'You have closed the gate, I assume?' Cwen asked as they all ran out of the tent to find out what was going on.

'Shouldn't we have done?' the guard enquired.

'Of course you should. The attackers are going to try and get in, and you have to stop them.'

'Cornelius said it would be something like that.'

'Cornelius?'

'The Centurion.'

Hermitage didn't like to enquire whether Centurions weren't supposed to command a hundred men. He hadn't seen a hundred people in this place, let alone soldiers.

'He's in charge of the soldiers?' he asked instead, wondering how Cwen fitted in.

'Well,' the guard was tentative. 'He's read a lot of books about it.'

'God above,' Athan muttered. 'We're doomed.'

Cwen ignored him 'And where is Cornelius now?' She scanned the area to see what was going on.

'Over there.' the guard pointed to the gate. 'Having a look.'

'Having a look,' Cwen scoffed as she hurried in the right direction.

'I don't like to tell Cwen I told you so,' Wat confided in Hermitage. 'But I think I might have to soon. If it's Normans at the gate, the Roman rebellion might be over much sooner than expected.'

'Normans?' Hermitage hadn't really thought about who might be attacking. Now he did think about it, he concluded that it probably was Normans. Who else?

'All we need to do,' Wat went on, 'is make sure it's a

surrender and not a slaughter.'

'I'm not so sure Cwen will be keen on that option.'

'When she sees a hundred Norman swords pointing in her direction, I think she'll see sense.'

'Really?' Hermitage thought that might only make her more angry.

'What's going on?' Peter appeared off to one side, hurrying towards them.

'You're under attack, we think.' Wat said.

'Oh, God. What?' He looked over towards Cwen as she was leading the way to the wall. 'It's that woman. She's brought this ruin upon us.'

'It was you brought her here in the first place,' Wat pointed out. 'So if it's anyone's fault, it's yours.'

'I didn't know she was going to cause such chaos.'

'You only had to ask,' Wat replied.

They arrived at the wall and Hermitage saw that there were ladders conveniently placed for people to climb up so that they could see over the top, which must be at least ten feet tall.

Cwen and several Romans were already up there while Wat, John, Peter and Athan scurried up vacant ladders to see what they could.

Hermitage was quite happy to stay at the bottom and receive reports from the tops of the ladders. He thought it another mark of the hopelessness of the Romans' situation that there were more ladders than actual soldiers. Why they'd bothered putting so many of the things up would be a question for another time; if there were any other times.

If this was the Normans hammering on the gates, he did not hold out much hope for their survival.

Not that anyone was doing any hammering yet.

'Hermitage,' Wat called down. 'You have got to come and look at this.'

'It's fine, really,' Hermitage considered the nearest ladder and didn't care for the look of it.

'Can't even climb a ladder,' Athan called down. 'Why am I not surprised?'

'No, really, Wat urged. 'It's quite safe. Come on.'

Wat clearly had a different definition of safe, but Hermitage chanced a single foot upon the lowest rung of the ladder. He hoisted himself up and found an easy solution to his concerns. There was a small gap in the wall-posts here, and he could peer through it without climbing at all.

'I can't see anything,' he called up.

Wat looked down and shook his head in disappointment at Hermitage's position. 'Off to the left.'

Hermitage peered off to the left but the gap in the posts was not wide and his range of view was limited. There was one figure in sight though. 'Is that More?' he asked.

'I don't know anyone else who looks like that,' Wat replied. 'Now look to the right.'

Hermitage did so and couldn't quite understand what he was seeing. 'How did he get over there?'

'That's not the same one, Hermitage. There are two. One must be Lambehitha'

Hermitage knew the similarities between the men, but from this distance it really as if More was in two places at once. 'Is he the one attacking?' he asked. 'I mean the two attacking.'

'Climb up the ladder and see, Hermitage,' Wat instructed.

Reluctantly doing as he was told, realising that peering through a small gap in a wall was not really much help, he gingerly put one foot on the next rung up. He gripped each rung above fearsomely, not releasing anything until he was firmly planted.

Once he got his head just above the parapet he stopped climbing and clung for dear life to the ladder, wrapping his arms around the thing, praying that it didn't decide to fall backwards with him on it.

The sight over the wall did look like an attack, or rather an attack in preparation. Both the Mores were there, which comforted him somewhat. He didn't like to think that More really could be in two places at once, although he wouldn't put it past him.

In between the Mores there was a host. And as far as he could make out it was a host of Saxons. Well, that was a relief.

It wasn't a massive host - perhaps thirty or forty people stood before the walls - but that was twenty or thirty more than the forces inside the walls.

'Have they come to join us?' Hermitage asked.

'We'll find out in a moment.'

'What do you want?' Cwen's voice called out over the scene.

One of the figures from the Saxon gathering stepped forward. Hermitage recognised him.

'It's Beorn,' he said. 'From the Saxon hall.'

Wat peered down. 'You're right. Hello Beorn,' he called brightly.

'Silence,' Cwen commanded from her ladder.

'Sorry, I'm sure,' Wat whined slightly.

Beorn looked up and scowled. 'What are you doing in this place?' he demanded.

'Defending it,' Cwen replied. 'If need be.' She considered the crowd before her. 'Why aren't you still hiding in your roof?'

'Him,' Beorn shouted out and pointed a finger to the ladder Peter was occupying. 'And we weren't hiding anyway. We were massing.'

'All right, why aren't you still massing in your roof?'

'Peter betrayed us. Our secret was revealed. We had to move out. We had to go and mass in the walls. And then the Normans started getting suspicious, so we had to leave altogether.'

'And why here?'

'We put our best man on the task of finding Peter.'

More put his hand up. It was hard to tell which was which, but Hermitage was fairly sure that this was their More.

'Your best man?' Cwen sounded surprised. 'Really?'

'He found Peter, didn't he? He listened and waited and made sure he was in the right place at the right time. Then, as soon as he could, he came back to tell us where to find you. In fact, he says you sent him back to wait by the river, which was just the chance he needed.'

More's head bobbed up and down with glee at this tale.

Hermitage found it hard to believe that More had actually been quite clever all along. Surely the impression he gave of not knowing what was going on in front of his nose could only be genuine. Had he really found out that they were pursuing Peter and followed along for his own purposes?

And what was the other More there for? Perhaps the Saxons simply sent out a flock of Mores, hoping that one would get lucky. And theirs had.

Beorn continued. 'And it seems he's found Peter's collaborators as well.'

'His what?' Cwen called.

'Those who work with him,' Hermitage called over, the

urge to etymologise being unbearable. 'From collaborare, you see. Co-labour?'

'Yes, thank you, Hermitage.' Cwen didn't sound very grateful. 'We are not his collaborators. I've replaced him.'

'You?'

'Yes, me.'

'What are you dressed like that for?' Beorn sounded quite mocking.

'I've joined the Roman army. In fact, I'm in charge of it and we're going to attack the Normans. So, if you're really massing yourself to go against them, and not just hiding in the thatch hoping they won't find you, you can join us.'

'The Roman army?' Beorn sounded completely bemused. 'They're all long dead and gone.'

'No, they aren't,' Cwen was defiant. 'There's, erm, lots of them left.'

'I don't believe you. And anyway, we're attacking the Normans, not you.'

'Our strength would be greater if we fought them together.'

Even Hermitage could see that this was true, there actually being more Saxons in this one field than there were in the entire Roman army.

'We're not fighting with you,' Beorn called out. 'We should be fighting against you. What are you pretending to be Roman for anyway? This is a Saxon country.'

'Oh no, it isn't,' a strong male voice called over.

Hermitage looked along the wall and saw a fit young man dressed very similarly to Cwen, except his clothes fitted. He wondered if this might be Cornelius, the Centurion.

'You Saxons can't just come over here and say the country's yours.'

'You shouldn't have left it unattended then, should you?'

Beorn retorted.

'We were here all the time.'

'You should have spoken up, it's too late to start bleating about it now. We'd been running the place quite successfully for years until the Normans came.'

'Success?' Cornelius demanded. 'You call this success? Letting the Normans wander in and walk all over you?'

'People, people,' Cwen called from her ladder. She had even climbed a couple more rungs to make herself heard. 'It doesn't matter what went on in the past, it's today we have to worry about. And the Normans.'

'That's right,' Beorn agreed.

'Quite,' Cornelius concurred.

'So we fight them together,' Cwen urged.

'Never,' Cornelius and Beorn responded in unison.

'First of all, these Saxons have to go back where they came from,' Cornelius demanded.

'Southwark?' Beorn enquired, clearly wondering what use that was going to be.

'No, Saxony.'

'Saxony?' Beorn didn't seem to recognise the name.

'The place the Saxons come from? It's in Germania.'

'You're a fine one to talk,' Beorn retorted. 'Saxony is probably a damn sight closer than Rome. You go back where you came from.'

'We've been here longest.'

'Then you've outstayed your welcome. We were here most recently so we win.'

Hermitage didn't like to point out that the Normans were even more recent arrivals.

'You're both losing against the Normans,' Cwen pleaded. 'Stop fighting one another.'

'We haven't started yet,' Beorn said with clear intent.

'Look,' Cwen said. 'I'm a Saxon, aren't I?' There was no reply, so she took that as acceptance. 'And now I'm Roman as well. You can be two things you know.'

A very worrying title crept into Hermitage's mind, Anglo-Norman. He thought it best not to mention it.

Cornelius appeared to be nodding. 'It is a fine tradition of the Roman Empire that when we conquer a people, we allow them to become citizens.'

'Oh, very generous, I'm sure,' Beorn called sarcastically.

'All you have to do is swear fealty to the emperor.'

'Emperor, pah. There isn't one anymore, you idiot. The Romans have all gone and they left you behind. Probably for good reason. Tell you what, we'll conquer you and then you can swear fealty to our king.'

'The dead one?' Cornelius asked pointedly.

'No,' Beorn insisted. 'King Edgar the Aethling is our true ruler.'

'Let him come forward then,' Cornelius called.

'Ah, well, he's not actually here at the moment.'

'Not here?'

'No, he's, erm, just gone to Scotland for a moment. But he'll be back.'

'Ha,' Cornelius crowed. 'You are nothing but a rabble. If you are to have any chance against the Normans, you need to join us.'

'We need to join one another,' Cwen tried again.

'And then be attacked ourselves?' Cornelius asked.

'You're all mad,' Wat spoke up. 'You've both been going on about defeating the Normans and here's your chance. And what do you do about it? Worry about attacking one another. What if the Normans sailed up the river now, what would you do?'

'We'd defeat them alone,' Beorn called.

'No, you wouldn't.' Wat corrected. 'You'd all be slaughtered while the Romans hid behind their walls. Then they'd be slaughtered. Well, I don't want anything to do with either of you. If this is the best idea you can come up with, I'll leave you to it.'

'Traitor,' Beorn called.

'Traitor? Betraying who? You, the Romans? Edgar the Aethling, King William, who has been crowned, by the way? I'm just getting confused.

'I think we should just leave all those who want to fight to get on with it. The rest of us will clear up afterwards.'

'We can't fight alone,' Cwen added. 'Or separately.'

'Well, we're not fighting together,' Beorn said, which got nodded agreement from Cornelius.

'Leave them to it, Cwen,' Wat called over. 'They all deserve what's coming. We'll go back to Derby and do what we've always done: sell tapestry to anyone who wants it, no matter where they come from or what they call themselves. They all look the same with no clothes on. I should know.'

Because coincidence clearly considered that matters weren't quite confused enough, there was a loud shout from the trees off to the left and what could only be described as a band of screaming warriors flew out of the cover, weapons raised.

'Normans!' Beorn shouted as his men gathered around him to prepare their defence.

The new band seemed to have their attention more behind them than ahead as if they were being chased.

Hermitage wasn't sure he could cope with any more bands of fighting men but did think that the latest arrivals didn't actually look much like Normans.

When yet another group followed the first lot, shouting and waving their own weapons, he gave up trying to understand what was going on.

The very latest group were clearly more Saxons and had chased the first lot out of the woods.

Everyone came to a juddering halt as they all considered the scene they had stumbled across.

The Romans looked down on the field from their fort, while the ones on the ground simply stood considering one another.

'Who the devil are you?' Troels the Dane demanded of the ladder people behind the wall. 'And what are you doing in King Sweyn's country?'

Caput XXV: Battle Is Disjointed

'Oh Lord,' Wat held his head in his hands, which Hermitage considered to be quite a risky manoeuvre on top of a ladder. 'How many more people are going to turn up claiming that this is their land and no one else is entitled to even a bit of it?'

Hermitage looked out over the assembly and had to admit that the situation was confused to say the best.

The Danes were ready for a fight but had obviously been chased out of the woods by yet another band of Saxons. That made two Saxons, one Danes, one Romans. And the Normans down the river; he mustn't forget them.

'Ha ha,' Beorn was crowing for some reason. 'Now we have you.'

'You have no one,' the very large Dane who seemed to be in charge replied.

'We knew you were hiding out here somewhere. It only took our best man half a day to find you and winkle you out.'

This time the other More put his hand up. Both Mores exchanged happy nods, which was perhaps the most disturbing element of the whole scene. To expect a single More to effectively track down and expose enemy forces in their hiding places was surprising. That two could coordinate was simply beyond belief. That they were both referred to as the Saxon's "best man", only confused him further.

Hermitage gazed around to left and right to see if anyone else wanted to come and join in. Could there be Druids coming down the river from Wales? Edgar the Aethling and the Scots from the North? Barbarians from wherever they came from? The whole thing was getting simply ridiculous.

Out of the corner of his eye, he saw some further movement in the direction the Danes had come from. Surely no more?

Four individuals came very reluctantly onto the field of conflict. One of them looked like he already had a wound and was limping badly. It was Marcus the troublesome Norman. He had obviously been troublesome to the wrong person and got hit in the leg for his trouble.

So, the Normans were here after all, even if not in great numbers. And who was with him? Two more Normans, and one further shape who hung back and seemed to be trying to hide, if not go in the other direction altogether.

'Nicodemus,' Wat sighed. 'I might have known he'd be in the middle of a pile of trouble without any of it actually touching him.' He turned to Hermitage. 'Do you think he caused all this?'

'Him?' Athan scoffed. 'Something must have gone horribly wrong to get him out of William's fortress at all.'

'Perhaps the rest of the Normans are following?' Hermitage suggested.

'Well, that should settle things quickly,' Wat said.

The Danes and the Saxons still seemed to be in a bit of a stand-off. Hermitage couldn't see any real reason for this as the former were now virtually surrounded by a much larger number of the latter.

The former did have their weapons in their hands and looks in their faces that said they were prepared to go down fighting.

The latter seemed to be more lacking when it came to the urge to die in battle.

'Come on then,' the Dane called. He even thumped his chest. 'See if any of you have the courage to take on Troels the Dane in single combat.'

No single Saxon leapt at the opportunity.

'That's the way to settle this,' Troels bellowed to all who could hear. 'Single combat. Me against your champion. Who is it?'

No one spoke up.

'That would be Beorn,' Wat offered from the safety of his ladder.

'Oy,' Beorn complained.

'And why are you lot cowering behind your walls?' Troels called up. 'Come down and join the rest.'

'We're nothing to do with them,' Cornelius replied. 'We're not Saxons, you fool.' He sounded quite disgusted at the suggestion. 'We're the rightful rulers of this land.'

'Oh no, you're not.'

'Oh yes, we are. We are the empire of Rome.'

'What, all of it?' Troels considered the size of the fortification and was not impressed.

'The British contingent.'

'You gave up your rights when you left,' Troels informed him.

'That's what I said,' Beorn agreed.

'Shut up,' Troels instructed. 'The Danelaw is to be restored and we are here to see that it happens.'

'Just you?' Beorn mocked their numbers. 'I don't see that working.'

'We will be joined,' Troels assured them. 'Once we have a safe path, King Sweyn will send his forces.'

'Only when it's safe, eh? Doesn't sound like much of a king.'

'More of a king than your Harold, who is dead, by the way. Once Sweyn is here the rest of you can go back where you came from.'

'Danelaw is for Denmark,' Beorn replied. 'And this is not Denmark. It is England.'

'What are you called Beorn for, then?' Troels asked. 'You sound like a Dane to me. In which case you're a traitor.'

'People, people,' Cwen cried out.

Troels turned to frown at the female voice coming from the wall.

'We have a common enemy,' she began. 'The Normans. Never mind who was here when, or whose rule is best, we have all been displaced by William and his men.

'It won't be long before he goes to the north.' She directed this comment at Troels. 'Any remaining chance of Danelaw will be gone when that happens.

'And he will go west,' she turned her head to the Romans. 'Your numbers are small, you have to understand that you stand no chance on your own.

'As for the Saxons? He has already killed the best of us and now tramples us into the ground.'

She held her arms wide to encompass them all. 'What is the answer then?'

None was offered.

'Come on,' she urged. 'This is easy. You can't defeat him on your own, so…?'

Beorn spoke up. 'We defeat the Danes, despatch the Romans and then turn our strength on the Normans.'

'No,' Troels cried out. 'It is the Saxons who will fall. And these paltry Romans who have no right to be here at all.'

'The Romans will defeat you all as we have in the past,' Cornelius retorted. 'Then true rule will be restored.'

Cwen looked over at Wat and Hermitage with despair in her face. She slowly took the helmet off her head, held it out in front of her and dropped it over the wall. 'I give up,' she said.

'Ha,' Troels gloated. 'A surrender to the might of the Danes.'

'She surrendered to the Saxons, you fool,' Beorn said.

'She didn't surrender to anyone,' Cornelius cried. 'I don't even know who she is!'

'I'm not surrendering,' Cwen shouted. 'I'm simply giving up on the lot of you. You're useless; together and apart, completely useless.

'Here we are in the middle of being conquered and the last thing any of you will even consider doing is cooperate. Is the most important thing in this situation that you personally should be in charge?'

The looks on faces said that this was exactly the most important thing.

'And you're prepared to sacrifice the country to the Normans, rather than let anyone else lead, or work with them in any way whatsoever?'

'That won't happen,' Beorn said. 'Although I do begin to see your point.'

'At last,' Cwen sighed.

'Yes,' Beorn nodded his head in thought. 'It could be that our combined forces would have a better chance than us each separately.'

'That's exactly what I've been saying,' Cwen sounded quite cheerful now.

Beorn had reached a conclusion. 'I for one am prepared to make a great sacrifice for the country.' He looked down his nose at Troels and Cornelius in turn.

'That's good,' Cwen encouraged. 'You see,' she criticised the others. 'It only takes one to do what's best.

'Yes,' Beorn agreed. 'The Danes and the Romans can come under my leadership.'

'Never,' Troels snapped. 'I am prepared to accept your forces under the Danish throne.'

'The Romans are the only true leaders,' Cornelius put in. 'In fact, you can all become citizens, which will make the whole thing a lot easier.'

'Oh, for God's sake,' Cwen despaired. 'I think I'll go and get William myself. None of you deserves to even be in charge of one of More's boats.'

The two Mores appeared to wake up at this.

'Look,' Cwen pointed towards Nicodemus. 'There's some Normans over there. Why don't you simply give yourselves up to them and we can get this over with.'

Justan certainly didn't look keen on this option, but Marcus and Hugo stood tall; well, as tall as Marcus could manage.

Nicodemus took a broad step away from the Normans.

'They are our prisoners,' Troels informed the crowd. 'You see, we are the only ones to have successfully defeated any Normans. That's why we should be in charge.'

There's only two of them!' Cwen cried out. 'And it looks like one of them's got a bad leg.'

'That's because we shot him,' Troels said proudly.

'Shot one Norman in the leg, eh?' Cwen asked. 'I'm sure William will quake in his boots.'

Despite his leg, Marcus did hobble into the middle of the field with Hugo at his side. Justan was happy to see how this went and then move accordingly.

Once he was in position, he addressed the crowd.

'I am a Norman as the woman says. My name is Marcus of Cabourg.'

'Oh Lord,' John muttered from the top of his ladder. 'He's going to complain that we're not fighting in the right order.'

'Marcus?' Cornelius enquired. 'That sounds like a Roman name.'

Marcus ignored him. 'I represent King William and his forces and give you three simple choices. One, kill me and Hugo and Justan over there right here and now…,'

'Erm,' Justan wanted to say something.

'Then, when the Norman forces find you, they will slaughter you all. Because they will. You can try to ask any of the Saxon nobles who went to Hastings, but you won't get much of an answer.

'Two; get on with whatever pointless fight you all have between yourselves, after which the might of the Norman army can pick up the pieces and be grateful that it didn't have to kill you itself.'

No one seemed keen on either one or two.

'Three; you can do as the woman says, which would be the courageous and noble action. Band together, combine your forces and attack William's stronghold with your greatest strength.'

Hermitage thought that was a bit of a strange suggestion from a Norman.

'Then we can kill you all in battle, which is much more satisfying, really.'

This still got no coordinated response.

'Oh,' Marcus said. 'There is a fourth. You can all surrender to me here and now. Swear allegiance to William and go about your business. Or go home, I don't care really.'

'This is our home,' Troels announced.

'Ours, actually,' Beorn replied.

'You're both wrong,' Cornelius concluded.

Marcus just looked about him, apparently with as much contempt for these people as Cwen had.

'They're hopeless,' she called down.

'I can see that,' Marcus agreed. 'How did any of them ever manage to run a country in the first place.'

'I don't think you're seeing the best of their various people. These are just the left-overs.'

'Do you mind?' Beorn called.

'Well, you are. All the Saxon nobles have gone.' She turned her attention to Troels. 'The Danes have gone, most of them defeated by Harold if you cast your mind back just a year or two. And now your king stays safe in Denmark while you're sent ahead on your own.'

'Ha,' Cornelius crowed.

'And you're the worst of the lot. Your people went home, how long ago, Hermitage?'

'Oh,' Hermitage was pleased to be of help. 'Erm, about six hundred years, if some of the texts are to be believed.'

'Six hundred years!' Cwen shook her head in disappointment. 'At least the Saxons and the Danes only lost in living memory. In another six hundred years it'll be, the erm..,'

'Sixteen hundred and sixties,' Hermitage answered.

'There you are,' Cwen said. 'The Normans arrived in ten sixty-six. What do you think this place is going to be like in sixteen sixty-six?'

No one could imagine so distant a future.

'Certainly not full of Normans claiming they still run the place, that's for sure.'

Even the Normans had a little chortle at that ridiculous idea.

She waved her arms about to encompass the whole area.

'The entire place could be on fire, for all we know.'

This foretelling had cast a gloom over the place and the various factions seemed to have calmed somewhat.

'So grasp the moment,' Cwen said.

'Carpe diem,' Cornelius muttered.

'Do you mind?' Cwen sounded mightily offended.

'It means seize the day,' Hermitage translated.

'Oh, right, yes, that,' Cwen said. 'Seize the day, combine your forces and attack the Normans. Beorn can lead the Saxons, Troels the Danes, and Cornelius the Romans. Sort out your differences afterwards.'

Finally, they seemed to all see that there was some sense in this.

'Ah,' Marcus spoke up.

'What now?' Cwen asked.

'I forgot to mention that there is a fifth option.'

For a man with three options, Hermitage thought that Marcus was coming up with far too many.

'And that is?'

'Don't surrender to me, surrender to them.'

He turned and gestured back towards the river.

Even from the ground, the assembly could see the tops of sails as a number of vessels approached from downstream.

As the tops of the sails were most definitely Norman in shape and colour, it was a fair assumption that the ships below would be Norman as well. In which case they'd most likely be full of Normans.

Marcus seemed to be weighing up the number of ships and working something out in his head.

'About three hundred, I should say. At a rough estimate.' He turned his attention back to the gathered forces. 'Should be enough for the job.'

Beorn seemed quite cross about this. 'Have you kept us talking here while that lot arrived?'

'You did most of that yourselves. Standing about arguing while the enemy was on its way.'

'We didn't know.'

'You didn't think. You're right,' Marcus called up to Cwen. 'They are all useless. Still.' he rubbed his hands. 'They won't be a trouble to anyone soon.'

The Normans were obviously well used to arriving on ships and getting stuck straight into a battle as shouts and the clangs of metal drifted up from the river.

Troels and Beorn looked at one another and at the number of their men.

'This isn't over,' they said simultaneously as, with a signal to their men, they turned and ran back into the woods.

'They won't get far,' Marcus said. 'We're coming by land as well.'

'A trap,' Wat said with a shake of the head.

'A big complicated one,' Marcus agreed. 'But one that worked very well indeed.'

Caput XXVI: Surrender Is The Better Part Of Valour

Unfortunately, being inside a solid Roman fortress, there wasn't anywhere the others could run. What they could do was climb down from their ladders and at least be on their feet when the Normans arrived.

Cwen did cast a questioning look at Cornelius but got a shrug in reply. 'Our leaders are too old to be running off into the woods. It took us a week to get here, we'll just have to take what's coming.'

'There are so few of you,' John said. 'If I were you, I'd just open the gates and not put up a fight. William is much keener on oaths of fealty these days. Give him one of those and you might be all right.'

Hermitage wondered if William himself would actually come on this mission. More likely he would send Le Pedvin, who liked this sort of thing. Getting on the better side of that man might take more than an oath of fealty.

He almost jumped out of his habit when there was a loud thump on the gate. 'That was quick,' he said nervously. He just hoped that whatever Norman this was, he would consider the service he and Wat and Cwen had done in the past and give them some credit. The alternative was to be murdered with everyone else in the fort. Which would not be good.

Cornelius wandered over to the gate. 'No point in keeping it closed, I suppose.'

'Not really,' John agreed.

They all stood watching as the gate was heaved open to reveal the gathering storm behind it.

As soon as the gap was wide enough to let anyone pass,

Marcus limped through, followed by Hugo. And that was it.

'Just you?' Hermitage had to ask.

'The others will be here soon enough,' Marcus said.

Somehow, Hermitage had hoped that the whole host would be there and get this over with.

A considerably more timid entrance was made by Nicodemus, followed by Justan, both of whom who looked as if they were seeking permission to bother the occupants.

'Ah,' Athan said. 'I was wondering if you were going to go in the other direction.'

Nicodemus frowned at this unhelpful comment.

'What dragged you out of the comfort of the tower? It can't have been a desire to do your job.'

'Prior Athan,' Nicodemus said with supreme condescension. 'You know very well that I am at the king's command. And that of his closest advisers.'

'Advisers, eh?' Athan scowled at this and looked very suspicious.

Wat folded his arms. 'I suppose it was you who led the Normans here.'

'Certainly not,' Nicodemus protested. 'I simply came looking for Peter,' he nodded at Peter. 'Doing my duty as King's Investigator. That's all.'

'You idiot,' Cwen sighed her disappointment at the man. 'You came looking for Peter with how many Normans in your boat? Three was it?'

'We were shot at,' Nicodemus protested.

'Pity they missed,' Cwen said. 'Marcus obviously had people following him, and you never noticed. Or maybe you did. Who cares really? We're all here now and some very cross Normans are going to arrive very soon.'

Nicodemus straightened himself and sniffed at Cwen. 'I

am the King's Investigator,' he said pompously. 'I answer to the king, not you.'

'You can answer him directly, I expect,' Wat said, which caused Nicodemus some obvious discomfort.

The sounds of a large force of men looking for a fight was drawing quite close now. Hermitage was worried what they might do if they didn't find one. He had to accept that Nicodemus was the King's investigator and so carried what authority went with the position. He would be safe enough in the company of the Normans.

Hermitage had never wanted any authority, ever, in his whole life, but Nicodemus seemed to seek it out. And it was Hermitage's fault that the man was in the role now. He could hardly expect any speaking up in their favour when the moment came.

The moment arrived with surprising rapidity. Hermitage thought that the Normans must have run up here from the river; which they probably did, what with it being an attack of sorts.

The first Norman, a warrior if ever Hermitage saw one, burst through the wide-open gate and skidded to a halt in the face of no opposition whatsoever.

'Argh,' the Norman warrior cried in a very warrior-ish manner. He glared at them from within his helmet and waved a dangerous looking sword about before clattering it on his huge shield.

Hermitage marvelled at the strength the man must have simply to have carried that lot up from the river, never mind run with it and be ready to fight when he arrived. He began to realise what a problem the Saxons must have had at that battle near Hastings.

'Come on then,' the Norman almost screamed, which was

quite unnecessary.

'There's no one to fight,' Cornelius said.

'What?' The warrior did not sound happy; not that he'd been particularly cheery when he arrived.

'No one to fight. We're not resisting.' Cornelius looked out of the gate and saw many more Norman warriors running towards them. 'There aren't enough of us. We surrender.'

'You what?'

'They surrender,' Marcus hobbled forward. 'I've already sorted this out. The Saxons and Danes have run off. The land force will get them. This lot are no trouble now.'

'Surrendered?' The warrior didn't seem to understand.

'That's right.'

'What about my men?' The warrior sounded quite confused now.

'What about them?' Cornelius asked.

The warrior shook his head. Hermitage could only think it was in the manner Wat used when someone had offered him a paltry sum for a tapestry. 'I've got three hundred men coming up from the boats. What am I going to tell them?'

'That there's no need to fight?' Wat suggested.

'No need to fight?' The warrior was incredulous. 'You can't get three hundred Norman warriors into the fighting frenzy and then tell them it's all off.'

'Tell them they've won without striking a single blow,' John suggested.

'That's no good, is it,' the warrior complained. He clearly recognised John. 'It's all very well for you nobles, you've got things to do. Three hundred fighters who haven't had a good fight in weeks have been promised one. If I tell them to go back now there'll be hell to pay.'

No one had anything to offer.

'Can't you fight a bit?' The warrior asked. 'Just a few of you?'

'We'd get killed,' Cornelius protested.

'It would calm the men down,' the warrior said.

'Sorry,' Cornelius apologised.

The warrior sighed his contemptuous disappointment for the lack of cooperation he was getting 'Isn't there anyone else?'

'I'm afraid not. The others ran off.'

'There you are,' Cwen said. 'You can chase them. You might catch up before the land forces get them.'

The warrior seemed to consider that this might be an option. 'Which way did they go?'

Everyone pointed in the direction of the departed Danes and Saxons.

The warrior made a quick decision. He turned and faced his horde, which had now arrived at the gate and looked ready to do their worst.

'They've run off, lads,' he cried.

'Cowards,' someone from the back called out.

'Into the woods,' the warrior commanded. 'Let's get 'em.'

To various chilling cries and promises of ridiculously violent retribution, the Norman force swung around and headed off into the woods.

Hermitage breathed a sigh of relief.

It was short-lived as a much smaller and much calmer group of Normans walked up the hill towards the fort.

They were also a much more important group and Hermitage recognised the king, Le Pedvin and Ranulph de Sauveloy in their number. He supposed it must be a real privilege to have them here in person, but it didn't feel like one.

Nicodemus subtly moved himself to the front as the three men and their guards arrived at the fort.

'Pathetic,' the king said as he appraised the construction.

John, Marcus, Hugo and Justan bowed their heads at the king, which he acknowledged with a casually raised hand.

He considered the assembly before him and his eyes rested on Cornelius. 'What are you supposed to be?'

'I am centurion Cornelius Crassus of the first Britannia legion.'

Hermitage's urge for accuracy in all things was telling him to point out that there wasn't a second legion, but he managed to restrain himself.

'Legion of what?' the king asked.

'The Roman Empire.'

The king looked to Le Pedvin and Ranulph. 'Is he serious?' he asked.

'Probably a loon,' Le Pedvin said.

'He's a well-dressed one. How many in this legion?' he asked Cornelius.

'We number, erm, twenty.'

'Not really a legion, then. And you really think you're Romans?'

'We are.'

William looked more bemused than anything. He clearly didn't think twenty people who thought they were Roman was worth coming all this way for. 'And you're in charge, are you?'

'No, no,' Cornelius replied. 'Our senators are in charge.'

'And where are they when you're being attacked?' William demanded.

'They're erm, resting,' Cornelius said.

'Resting?'

'Yes, they usually have a bit of a sleep towards the end of the day. They are very, erm, old.'

William frowned that this was turning out to be completely ridiculous. 'And why's she dressed like that?' he asked of Cwen.

'No idea,' Cornelius replied. 'She just turned up.'

'And tried to urge the various forces to combine against us,' Marcus said unhelpfully before Cwen could open her mouth.

'Did she now?' William mused.

'Without success,' Marcus continued. 'They've been routed and our men are hunting them down.'

'Excellent,' the king noted. 'It'll keep them busy. Now.' He cast his eye around the rest of the group. 'That's the one we want isn't it?' He pointed at Peter and asked the question of Le Pedvin.

'That's him, Majesty. The one who killed Malf.'

'That's right.' The king recalled the event.

'The one who was working as de Sauveloy's clerk,' Le Pedvin specified.

'The one Le Pedvin introduced to the court in the first place,' de Sauveloy added.

'Don't you two start again,' William commanded.

Peter was looking extremely nervous about his situation, which was probably the right approach.

'Death?' William enquired nonchalantly.

Le Pedvin shrugged. 'Or I could take him north with me on the harrying. He'll probably die anyway, just a bit more usefully.'

'As you please,' the king said. 'No one liked Malf anyway.'

Peter clearly didn't know whether to be grateful for his fate or not. At least the death was still some way off, so he tried to smile and bow, which looked more like he was grimacing and going weak at the knees.

'That's the monk and the weaver.' The king nodded at Hermitage and Wat. 'And these two?' He indicated Nicodemus and Athan.

'Your humble King's Investigator, Your Majesty,' Nicodemus stepped forward and bowed the bow of a man who knows how to bow.

'Yes,' the king said quite cautiously. 'You and your prior, is it?'

'Prior Athan, Majesty,' Nicodemus bowed again and gestured that Athan should do the same, which he did, but with much less enthusiasm.

'De Sauveloy?' William invited a comment.

De Sauveloy nodded. 'Yes, this is the King's Investigator,' He confirmed. 'He replaced the monk.' He dipped his head in Hermitage's direction.

Nicodemus basked in the recognition and did some bowing under its weight.

'He's the one who implied that Le Pedvin's son had betrayed us to the Saxons.'

Nicodemus froze.

'When really, John was only trying to find Peter.'

John shrugged that Peter had been found, so that had worked, hadn't it?

De Sauveloy continued. 'This Nicodemus then wanted a small force to go after them.'

Nicodemus now started making the subtle gestures people make when they want someone not to say any more.

'And his plan was to get rid of the others, including his prior, and get John back.'

'Oh, was it?' Athan asked bluntly.

'At which point you went and told Le Pedvin,' William

confirmed.

'Exactly,' de Sauveloy said, giving Le Pedvin a modest nod of the head, which was reciprocated. 'We can't have uppity Saxons thinking they can play us off against one another, can we?'

Hermitage was sure that he heard Nicodemus whimper now.

'You devious little sod,' Athan said.

'That's when I organised Marcus and the others,' Ranulph concluded. 'Le Pedvin got the main force together and here we are.'

'You see,' William was encouraging. 'You two can work together when you want to.'

Both men looked as if they really didn't want to.

'But this is really not the sort of thing we want from the King's Investigator,' William said to Nicodemus, who tried to keep his eyes from landing on anyone remotely Norman. He paused for a moment. 'Death?' he seemed to ask the assembly in general.

Le Pedvin and de Sauveloy appeared to think that was appropriate.

'Can I do it?' Athan asked.

'Your Majesty,' Hermitage stepped forward, knowing that he had to.

'Ah, yes, the monk. Well?'

'Of course, you could execute Nicodemus...,'

'Yes, I could.'

'But I feel partly responsible myself.'

'Shall I kill you too?'

'Oh, erm, no. I mean, it was I who recommended him for an office that he was clearly not suitable for. Can we hold a man responsible for not being able to do a job that he can't do anyway?'

The king looked quite confused about that question.

'Would you execute me for not fighting well in battle when I don't know how to do it?'

'I might,'

'Oh.' That wasn't the answer Hermitage had been hoping for.

'You want me not to kill him?'

'Well, yes. Please.'

'The world's gone mad.' William shook his head.

'I'd prefer it if you didn't kill anyone,' Hermitage said. 'I am a monk, after all. Forgiveness and mercy?' he suggested timidly.

'What do we do with him, then? I don't want him causing any more trouble.'

'Perhaps Le Pedvin has another space on his suicidal mission to the north?' de Sauveloy suggested.

'Why do I have to take all the cast-offs?' Le Pedvin asked.

'Because you're the one most likely to get them killed.'

Le Pedvin happily acknowledged that this was probably true. 'I suppose I could send him in to open negotiations with a rebellious baron or two,' Le Pedvin mused. 'Knowing that if they throw his head back over the wall like normal, it won't matter.'

'I want to throw his head over a wall,' Athan complained quietly.

Nicodemus seemed to think that keeping still and saying nothing was best.

'Your Majesty,' Hermitage continued. 'There is one more thing I'd like to ask…,'

Caput XXVII: Full Circle

William sighed. 'You want me not to kill the woman as well?'

'Oh, er, yes, please.'

William considered Cwen carefully. 'She's dressed like one of these Romans.'

'She is,' Hermitage admitted. 'But she was taken by force and dragged here against her will.'

'And made to put on Roman clothes?' The king did not believe this, and why should he?

'And she is a friend,' Hermitage pleaded. 'And has been vital to all the previous investigations.'

William sighed. 'Very well. But I'm not not killing anyone else after this. Last one, yes?'

'Er, yes, Majesty. But actually, it wasn't that.'

William's look invited an explanation.

Hermitage just hoped that he could give one that made sense.

This most recent experience had been an awful one, it was true, but then most of his experiences where the Normans were involved were awful. There was an added hideousness to this one, which still gnawed at him.

Cwen had been in danger. Well, they knew that she'd sorted it out herself in the end, but that wasn't the point. Hermitage had been helpless to do anything about it. One of his only true friends in the world had needed his help, and he hadn't been able to deliver it.

And why hadn't he been able? Because of his own selfishness, he saw that now. He had put his self-interest ahead of that of others. And there was an argument that this concentration on what he wanted had caused all this trouble in the first place. If only he had taken his responsibilities seriously, they wouldn't have had to go through this truly horrible day.

Looking around, he found it hard to believe that all of this had only taken a single day, but perhaps a collection of horrors made the days longer.

Most of the suffering of this day was down to him and he needed to put it right.

'Your Majesty,' he said, taking his courage. He had the words ready and would just have to let them out. 'I know it was only yesterday…,'

'Well?'

'If you would be so gracious, I would like to be King's Investigator again.'

Wat and Cwen drew breath at this.

'Really?' the king sounded as if he was not going to acquiesce to this.

'When we found that Cwen had been taken, we tried to find her. No one would help because I was just a monk. I said I had once been the King's Investigator, but that didn't help. If I had been able to say that I was the King's Investigator, I would have got a lot more cooperation and we wouldn't have ended up in this awful mess.'

'Hermitage,' Cwen said. 'You don't need to do this.'

'I wanted to pass on the role because I didn't like it. I now see that was a very self-centred motivation which ended up putting my friend in danger.'

'I was fine,' Cwen protested. 'I was always going to be fine.'

'And you do have a vacancy again,' Hermitage pointed out as Nicodemus tried to shrink so that no one would notice he was there.

'I would really rather not deal with murders at all, they are truly appalling, but I did it because it was my duty. I now see that it is better to have someone like me in the role if there has to be one at all. Those who would treat it as an opportunity for personal advancement will never get to the truth.' As he said this, he realised that he was going to have to get to the truth about the body in the bush. And that might not end well at all.

True, no one had asked him about it, but was that the right way to go? Ignoring it because it was inconvenient was the sort of thing Nicodemus would do.

William was looking thoughtful, which Hermitage thought might be either very good or very bad. He would find out soon enough.

'You were investigator to Harold,' William said.

'I was.'

'And then I made you mine. Next, you say you don't want to do it any more and I graciously grant your request.'

Hermitage bowed although he didn't think it had been that gracious.

'And now you say you want it back again?'

'In the circumstances, your Majesty. Unless you have someone better in mind?' Hermitage took a shine to that bright idea.

But William had no one to offer. 'You can't keep changing your mind like this, you know.'

Hermitage thought that was a bit harsh. He'd only changed his mind once. He didn't want to be King's Investigator and never had. Now, he was saying that he would do it.

'If I agree, you have to stick with it this time.' William sounded like he was reprimanding a child.

'Yes, your Majesty.'

'No coming back in a year or two saying you don't like it again.'

'No, your Majesty.'

William appeared to come to his conclusion. 'All right,' he agreed.

Hermitage felt both satisfied and deeply disappointed.

'But count yourself lucky.'

Lucky; he would have to remember that.

'It's only because this idiot has proved to be even more useless than you were.' William nodded towards Nicodemus, who shivered. 'And it just so happens I might have something for you to do.'

So soon? Hermitage almost bleated the words out loud.

'One of the bishops has been complaining that his monks are murdering one another and he can't make them stop. You can go and sort it out. I'll send word that you're on your way.'

'That's, erm, very kind, Majesty.' Hermitage wanted to say that it was a complete disaster. He hadn't expected things to start off again quite this quickly. And murderous monks?

'Right,' William clapped his hands. 'Let's get these two prepared for their journey to the north.' He waved a regal glove at Peter and Nicodemus who regarded one another with loathing.

'And us?' Cornelius asked.

'What about you?'

'What do we do?'

'I don't know what you do. I'm not sure anyone does. And I think that's part of the problem. Whatever it is you do, you should go back and carry on doing it. You're of no interest to me. Dressing up as Romans? Ha!'

Cornelius seemed happy that they'd been excused for their plan to overthrow the Normans, although he wasn't sure how or why. He obviously thought it best not to be seen any more so made a hurried retreat back to the tent.

John gave them all a bow and a smile and went over to join the king and his father. 'I just hope he doesn't want me in the north with him,' he muttered as he went.

Hermitage looked nervously at Prior Athan.

'Don't worry, I'm not staying here,' Athan said. 'I just want to enjoy Nicodemus's plight a bit longer.'

Nicodemus's pale face glanced up at the mention of his name.

'You were only King's Investigator for a day,' Athan sneered. 'And look what you managed to do. I'm better off without you.' He then looked around to see who was left and seemed to notice the fine tent of the Romans. He rubbed his hands in a horrible manner and set off after Cornelius.

'Hermitage.' Cwen now approached and put her hand on his arm. 'You didn't need to do that, really you didn't.'

'We know how much you hate the job,' Wat said, 'so to ask for it back so soon?'

'It really was a problem not being the King's investigator,' Hermitage said. 'No one would do what I asked. I had no authority. I know some people have it naturally, but I have not been blessed.'

'You may never need it again,' Cwen said. 'It's an awful sacrifice to make for something that's now done.'

'There was another reason,' Hermitage said cautiously, making sure that no one was around to hear.

'Oh yes, what's that?' Cwen asked.

Hermitage took a breath before laying the problem before her. 'The body in the bush.'

Cwen just looked at him. 'The body in the bush?' She glanced at Wat. 'Should I know about this?'

'It was wearing your boots. Or trying to.'

'My boots?' Cwen frowned in thought.

'Oh,' Wat said. 'I've got them here. They quite went out of my mind what with all the Danes and the Saxons and the Romans and the king and everything.' He released them from the tie at his waist and handed them over.

Cwen took them and hugged them close. 'Lovely,' she said. 'But what have they got to do with a body in a bush?'

Hermitage lowered his voice. 'The body in the bush was wearing your boots.' Surely Cwen was going to realise what he was talking about and confess all. 'And if the king had found out from any other route, things might have gone badly.'

'Oh, him,' Cwen said rather nonchalantly.

'Big fellow,' Wat explained. 'Very big, in fact. We found him in the bush at the spot the boats left from.'

'Yes, that's the one,' Cwen expressed her relief at this suddenly making sense.

'Yes, him.' Hermitage thought that she shouldn't be quite so happy about recalling a man she'd killed.

Cwen nodded. 'He died.'

Hermitage suddenly felt very cold. 'We know he died.'

'As you say, he was very large and we had been running around in the trees for quite a while. He was an accomplice of Peter's and they had to carry me part of the way. I put up a bit of fight, as you can imagine, and I don't think it did him any good at all.'

'No good at all,' Hermitage shook his head.

'I kicked my boots off so that you would be able to follow the trail, you know, investigate.'

'I do know,' Hermitage said woefully.

'Well, I sort of kicked them at him, really'

'And what happened?' Wat asked.

'He got terribly angry, which was also not good for him. He staggered about a bit, fell backwards into the bush and didn't get up again.'

'Your boots.' Hermitage was now in a bit of a daze.

'Peter and the other one blamed me, but it was his own fault.'

Hermitage drew the appalling conclusion. 'You mean he just died?'

'That's it,' Cwen agreed. 'Peter was quite happy to leave him, which seemed a bit heartless to me. Why, did you think…, Hermitage, you didn't?'

'Erm, didn't what?'

'You didn't think I'd killed him?'

Wat spoke up 'You do say you're going to kill a lot of people. Me quite frequently.'

'Yes, but I've never done it. Oh, Hermitage.'

Hermitage hung his head. 'There wasn't even a murder,' he muttered, unable to take it in somehow.

Cwen brightened. 'Still, it's nice that you thought I might have done it.'

Hermitage scowled at her.

'I could have if it had been necessary.'

'Sounds like we've got some more to deal with now, anyway. Murderous monks, according to the king.'

Hermitage sagged and nodded. He still knew that he had done the right thing; it just wasn't quite as right as he'd hoped it would be.

'Are you going to put those clothes back?' Wat asked Cwen.

'I quite like them,' Cwen said. 'They are a bit big though. Perhaps I can make some of my own. I think I'll see if I can find the helmet though. I could keep that.'

'To look like a Roman soldier?'

'There are worse things to look like.' Cwen cast a disparaging glance at Wat.

'What's wrong with the way I look? My clothes are the finest.'

'Yes, but the trouble is you look like Wat the Weaver.'

Cwen slipped her hand through Wat's arm and led the way towards the gate.

Hermitage followed on behind, trying to make the best of the situation. He was now King's Investigator again and had even asked to be so. And he had a band of murderous monks to look forward to. Still, at least there hadn't actually been a murder at all this time, that was good. Or was it bad?

As he followed the others, an inconvenient thought occurred to him. 'We don't actually know where these murderous monks are,' he pondered. 'If they're real and the story hasn't been confused somehow. We'll have to ask the king where we have to go.'

As he said this he passed through the gate and leapt back with shock as two ghostly apparitions appeared on either side of him.

'Did you order a boat?' one squeaked.

'Because we've got one,' the other said in an almost identical voice.

'We've got two,' the first corrected.

'Oh, yis.'

Hermitage couldn't wait to get to the murderous monks.

Finis

Brother Hermitage continues his unavoidable travails in the inevitably titled: A Mayhem of Murderous Monks

The first chapter of this remarkable volume follows almost immediately....

A Mayhem of
Murderous Monks

By

Howard of Warwick

(The Meandering Chronicles of
Brother Hermitage)

Caput I: Bishop's Move

'The bishop will see you now.' The clerk bowed to Hermitage, Wat and Cwen and indicated with a humble hand that they could now follow him into the chamber.

Brother Hermitage was a monk; he assured himself that this was the case and so there was no need for concern at being sent to attend upon the bishop. As fellow men of God, they would have much in common.

Hermitage was also the King's Investigator and so a person of some import. Not much import, according to King William himself; or Le Pedvin, de Sauveloy or any other Norman noble who might be asked; nor most of the ordinary Normans, come to that.

Nonetheless, he was a monk and he was the King's Investigator, that must count for something.

And he had been sent to the bishop's London residence by the king himself. The bishop clearly had need of him and so would welcome his arrival.

A monk, the King's Investigator and needed; there was absolutely nothing to worry about.

He further reminded himself that he had once met the Archbishop of Canterbury and so an ordinary bishop would be a matter of routine.[21]

None of this had any effect on his quaking knees, his gurgling stomach or the twitch that had developed in the corner of one eye. He had heard all about bishops and had been told in lurid detail what the worst of them was capable of. He didn't know if this one was one of the worst, but he

---

[21] *The Bayeux Embroidery* covers that meeting. (covers, embroidery... get it?)

was about to find out.

Neither Wat nor Cwen seemed to share his concern.

Wat was looking around the place as if weighing it up for a sale. He even reached out to feel the quality of a wall hanging and lifted a jug from a table to test its weight. He appeared very satisfied with the results.

Cwen considered the place with obvious contempt. She turned her nose up at the comfortable padded chairs and the plates of food lying untouched. She lifted the jug after Wat had put it down, smelled the contents and tutted at anyone who would have wine at this time of the morning.

And this was only the outer chamber.

The clerk led them on and pushed open a grand door that led to the bishop's inner sanctum.

Hermitage couldn't help but wonder why this accommodation was grander than the king's. It was larger, better furnished and a lot warmer with a large fire blazing under a central chimney.

He supposed that the king was a man of war and so his surroundings would be appropriate to his calling; spartan, functional, even aggressive and uncomfortable.

But by that argument, the bishop's chamber should be that of a man called by God; a humble and modest servant.

This place looked as if it was the one God himself used when he came down to earth. Perhaps the bishop had to keep it this way in case of a visitation.

Hermitage was almost startled by a movement as the bishop himself stood from behind a table that was big enough to build a hovel on.

'My lord, Geoffrey, Bishop of Coutances,' the clerk bellowed so that the three people who were standing right next to him would know that they hadn't come to the wrong bishop by mistake.

Geoffrey, Bishop of Coutances didn't come out from behind his table to greet his visitors, rather he indicated with an outstretched arm that they were allowed to sit on the chairs arranged before him.

He was a mature man, well built and comfortable in his fine clothes. Hermitage couldn't help but think he had more the look of a warrior about him than of a bishop. But then most of the Normans looked like warriors; mainly because they were. Hermitage was in no doubt that this was a bishop who would pick up a bible to castigate sinners and then a sword to finish them off.

The clerk bowed deeply and left.

Hermitage nervously took his chair.

Wat ran a hand over the carving of his before sitting.

Cwen pulled the thing back with a scrape and sat.

Geoffrey followed suit and made himself comfortable behind his table. 'Brother Hermitage,' he said with quite a kindly voice. Hermitage hadn't expected it to be kindly. 'The King's Investigator, I hear?'

'Erm, that's right, your grace, my lord, erm…,'

'My lord will do fine,' Geoffrey smiled.

Hermitage was sure he heard a cough from Cwen but was too distracted to notice.

'Wat the Weaver and Mistress Cwen,' Geoffrey gave them welcoming nods.

'Cwen the Weaver,' Cwen corrected.

Geoffrey accepted the clarification. 'The king has told me all about you.'

Hermitage couldn't help but think that the words, "all about you", really did mean all about them.

'A remarkable gathering,' Geoffrey commented. 'Wat the

Weaver in a bishop's chamber, eh?'

He did mean "all about them".

'It isn't the first,' Wat said.

'Oh, I can imagine that. If what I have heard is true, the nature of your old tapestries might provoke interest from certain individuals, many of whom, unfortunately, hold positions in the church.' The bishop gave a laugh at this thought.

Laughing bishops gave Hermitage the shakes. And he knew what type of certain individuals had an interest in Wat's frankly disgusting tapestries. He just hoped that this bishop wasn't one of them.

'You are a young trio.' Geoffrey steepled his fingers. 'Have you really dealt with as many murders as is told?'

'I'm, erm, not sure how many you've been told,' Hermitage said. 'But it is quite a few. Unfortunately.'

'Unfortunate indeed, that such sin should be visited upon anyone.'

Hermitage thought it best not to mention the many visits the Normans had arranged since they landed on the beach.

'But fortunate that you have been sent to deal with them.'

'I do my best.'

'A very effective best, if the king is to be believed. And of course, the king is to be believed in everything.'

There was Cwen's cough again.

'I imagine you have a murder?' Wat asked. 'Hence the king asking us to see you?'

'Ah, straight to the point, eh? Yes. I do. Well, not me personally, but one of our establishments. A monastery.'

'A monastery,' Hermitage said. The king had told him that this was all about murderous monks, but he hadn't really believed it.

Despite Geoffrey's confidence, Hermitage's experience was that believing everything the king said was usually quite rash. It always paid to get the facts straight. No one ever contradicted the king and so he must come to believe that what he said was, by definition, true.

A monk may have come and told him about a murder and so he leapt to the conclusion of murderous monks. He then repeated it to someone at which point it became the truth. It wasn't as if he was deliberately lying. He genuinely believed that it was murderous monks. That he could be wrong simply didn't occur to him, or anyone else close by.

It would be up to Hermitage to find the true truth if there was such a thing, rather than the king's truth. The difficult bit would then be telling the king about it.

'Hard to believe, I know,' Geoffrey said with what seemed to be genuine sorrow. 'Murder in a religious house. Unthinkable.'

Bishop Geoffrey of Coutances obviously hadn't managed to get to the monastery in De'Ath's Dingle yet; he'd be able to think of all sorts of things after that visit.[22]

'The king mentioned murderous monks?' Hermitage half hoped that the killer was already known. In which case, why ask for an investigation at all? Perhaps the perpetrator had simply run away and they had to track him. It could be that the bishop had got the wrong idea about investigation.

'I imagine he did,' Geoffrey said. 'The king is a busy man who has little time for detail. A monk is dead, therefore he assumes that a monk did it.'

'But he didn't?' Hermitage's half-hopes were now on the wane to nothing.

---

[22] *The Heretics of De'Ath*: Read it and think of all sorts of things yourself

'Who knows?' Geoffrey replied. 'All I do know is that there has been a death. It is reported to me as murder and as such, I mentioned it to the king. He said he had just the man for the job.'

Hermitage took what little comfort he could from that. William had painted a picture of a chaos of murderous monks running around killing one another in some sort of frenzy.

'One death?' Cwen sounded quite contemptuous. 'Does it really need the King's Investigator?'

At first, Hermitage quite liked the sound of that. He was far too significant to be bothered with one simple death. Then he thought that the alternative was being sent to deal with a lot of them. Perhaps one at a time was best.

'Can't the nearest abbot deal with it?' Cwen asked.

Hermitage shivered slightly at the challenge.

'Unless the abbot did it, of course,' she added as an impudent afterthought.

'It is a complicated situation,' Geoffrey said. He settled himself in his chair. 'Will you take wine?' he asked.

'No thank you, my lord.' Hermitage shook his head.

Cwen gave a curt gesture of refusal.

Wat fetched the jug and a cup before sitting again.

'Brother Egeus,' Geoffrey announced.

Well, the name meant nothing to Hermitage. But then his investigations usually began with him knowing nothing; and frequently ended in a similar manner.

It wasn't a very Christian-sounding name though, having more of the Greek about it. A strange nomenclature for a monk. He cast his mind through some of his texts and could only come with something to do with goats. He'd look it up if he got the chance.

As usual, he told himself to concentrate on the fact that the fellow was dead, not what he was called. Or was he the killer? He really should pay attention.

'Brother Egeus, eh?' He said thoughtfully, hoping that some more information would be offered.

'A pious and learned fellow taken from us too soon,' Geoffrey summarised.

Good, he was the dead one then.

'Is there any knowledge of how he died?' Hermitage asked. He thought that asking who did it would be a bit too blunt.

'No. I have only had word that he is dead and that there is suspicion about the circumstances.'

'Ah,' Wat said through the top of his wine goblet. 'We do suspicions.'

'Erm, excellent.' Geoffrey tried to ignore the distraction.

'It might not be murder, then?' Hermitage asked with a little too much hope in his voice. From a gaggle of murderous monks to a possibly suspicious death, this investigation was making good progress. And he hadn't even left the room yet.

'It is possible, I suppose,' the bishop accepted. 'Although, as I say, he was a young man and a well one. There would be no reason for him to simply die.'

'Horrible accident?' Wat suggested.

'They are few and far between in a monastery,' Geoffrey said quite firmly and with a frown for Wat.

He really hadn't been to De'Ath's Dingle.

'I also have my own doubts about his passing,' Geoffrey went on. 'It is too much of a coincidence,' he continued quickly before Wat could say anything. 'He was doing important work for the church and to be lost in the midst of it is more than fate.'

'Important work?' Hermitage asked. He didn't like to

question a bishop's use of fate as the determinant of human life, instead of the Lord.

The bishop considered the three people before him and seemed to come to a conclusion. 'Brother,' he said to Hermitage as he stood. 'May I have a private word?'

Hermitage wasn't about to refuse a request from a Norman bishop but gave Wat and Cwen an apologetic look as he rose from his chair.

Cwen scowled at him but Wat gave a little wave and poured another cup of wine.

Bishop Geoffrey directed Hermitage back towards the door and they left the room, rejoining the clerk who was sitting at his own table, working through some correspondence, by the look of it.

'Wilfrid, could you leave us for a moment?'

The clerk stood, bowed and left the room as requested.

Hermitage started to feel quite trepidatious. What could the bishop possibly want to say to him that couldn't be repeated? And if it couldn't be repeated, how was he going to tell Wat and Cwen? Whatever this was, it was obviously key to the investigation and if only he knew it, there was a good chance it wouldn't be any help at all.

'This is a delicate matter, Brother,' Geoffrey said.

Oh, dear. Hermitage didn't like delicate matters, they usually broke in his hands.

Geoffrey stepped close and lowered his voice 'Brother Egeus was doing some investigation of his own, one might say.'

The bishop had said it, so Hermitage just took it as true.

'Investigation?' he asked. 'Not another murder?'

'No, no, nothing like that. But we can take the translation of the Latin vestigo, vestigare to cover all tracking, no?'

Hermitage was very happy with that.

'Then Brother Egeus was investigating.'

'Investigating what?'

'Perhaps investigating who, might be more appropriate.'

'Investigating who?' Hermitage complied. A brief scintilla of excitement bothered him as he wondered if this investigation of Egeus's might be into the post-Exodus prophets, his own area of particular interest. That was unlikely. If Egeus had been dabbling in those waters, Hermitage would have felt the ripples.

Geoffrey shook his head with disappointment. 'We do not know who.'

Hermitage had nothing more to offer. He knew that he hated investigation and didn't consider himself remotely qualified or capable, but to be investigating someone and not know who it was seemed careless at best. He thought about saying, "I see", but as he didn't, it wouldn't be much help.

'These are difficult times,' Geoffrey said.

Hermitage thought that stating the obvious wasn't very helpful either.

'And it is important that we know where people stand.'

Hermitage resisted the urge to look at his feet.

'There are those in the country who still resist the king's rule. Rebels, if you will.'

Hermitage had heard that some of William's own nobles weren't that keen on him being in charge. Again, this did not seem the best topic to raise with a Norman bishop. He also wondered why the subject of rebels had come up.

'The king addresses them directly, but there are others who either keep their intentions to themselves or who give secret support to others.'

Hermitage gave a nod as it seemed to be expected. He

managed the nod despite a horrible sinking feeling inside.

'Some of those operate from within the church and its institutions.' Geoffrey said this as if it were unbelievable. Hermitage believed it. 'It is important that we know who these people are. Brother Egeus was finding out.'

Ah, now Hermitage got it. And he didn't like it one bit. This Egeus had been trying to uncover those who opposed William. No wonder he was dead.

He struggled not to let his voice break. 'You think the people he was investigating killed him?'

'It is certainly possible,' Geoffrey admitted.

Now Hermitage's worries swarmed over him like a wave of wasps. A band of murderous monks would be better than a collection of William's opponents; opponents who seemed perfectly content to kill monks who went around investigating them.

'The death of Egeus is a dramatic step,' Geoffrey said.

That wasn't the word Hermitage would use.

'Mayhap he had uncovered something of vital interest and had to be stopped.'

'And you want me to find out who did it?' Hermitage tried hard not to make this sound like it was the last thing he wanted to do; but it was.

'That would be good, but I suspect they will be long gone,' Geoffrey downplayed the problem.

As far as Hermitage was concerned, however long gone they were, it wouldn't be long enough.

'Egeus's work must be recovered though. He was sending regular reports and we have those but they are of little import. In his most recent though, he indicated that he had gathered some very pertinent details, but before he could send them, he was dead.'

Hermitage let his mouth do the talking while his brain tried to hide in a corner. 'Find out who killed Egeus if possible, but in any event, recover his work and the details of William's opponents.'

Geoffrey rested a hand on Hermitage's shoulder. 'I see the king's confidence in you is not misplaced.' He started back to the main chamber. 'How much of this you tell your, erm, companions I leave to your discretion. Needless to say, they must be absolutely trustworthy in this matter.'

'Absolutely,' Hermitage agreed through the fear that was making his teeth chatter. He was now wondering how to tell Wat and Cwen that they were being sent to their deaths.

Discover how things turn out in:
A Mayhem of Murderous Monks

Coming soon, probably too soon.

Printed in Dunstable, United Kingdom